That Water, Those Rocks

WESTERN LITERATURE SERIES

Katharine Haake

That Water, Those Rocks

UNIVERSITY OF NEVADA PRESS / RENO & LAS VEGAS

Western Literature Series

University of Nevada Press, Reno, Nevada 89557 USA

Manufactured in the United States of America

Design by Carrie House

Library of Congress Cataloging-in-Publication Data

Haake, Katharine.

That water, those rocks / Katharine Haake.

p. cm. — (Western literature series)

ISBN 0-87417-530-5 (pbk. : alk. paper)

1. Dams—Design and construction—Fiction. 2.

California, Northern—Fiction. I. Title. II. Series.

PS3558.A145 T48 2003

813'.54—dc21   2002012927

The paper used in this book meets the requirements of
American National Standard for Information Sciences—
Permanence of Paper for Printed Library Materials, ANSI
Z39.48-1984. Binding materials were selected for strength
and durability.

This book has ben reproduced as a digital reprint.

11 10 09 08 07 06 05 04 03

5 4 3 2

Excerpts from this book have appeared as follows:

"The Quality of Listening," in *New Letters* 67, no. 1 (2000).

"A River to Walk," in *Volt* no. 6 (2000)

For my sister, Mary

What does it matter who is speaking?

—MICHEL FOUCAULT

Acknowledgments

For this book, I am grateful to so many others.

My sister, Mary, who, in 1994, took a back road trip with me through northwest California, where we swam in several rivers and encountered several forest fires. Mary chairs the East Bay Sierra Club Water Policy Commission, and her commitment to sustainable water use in California is a constant inspiration to me.

My other sister, Irene, who designed and built her own home in the Sacramento foothills. I remember her pounding nails on her roof when she was pregnant, a small bowling ball of a woman in Lee's overalls. If I could build a house, I would. Wouldn't you?

My parents, who took me to dams when I was growing up, bought the land and built the cabin, and believed in me all my life.

My husband, Jeffrey Tanzer.

My children, Sam and Joey, always.

My engineer uncle, Frank Lord, who worked on the dams.

My aunt, Louise Rubis, who gave me the baskets.

My grandparents, who met and married in Kennett, now under Lake Shasta.

Sharman Apt Russell, a wise woman and dear friend.

Wendy Bishop, for all the years of writing and talk.

My writing group—Annette Leddy, Rod Moore, Mona Houghton, Nancy Krusoe, and Scott Sandler—whose patience, insight, and careful reading guided and supported me through draft after draft, and saved me from my own bad ideas.

Alan Clark. Jay Lepreau.

The geologist William Murphy, who generously reviewed the facts of this book.

"Facts," Murphy explained, "are data that have survived the skepticism of scientists. Metaphysics is for people who are skeptical of facts."

The other geologist, Jeffrey Mount, on whose book, *The Rivers and Streams of California*, I have heavily relied.

Marilyn Jacobs, again.

Art historian Linda Nochlin, for the observation that "Nothing is more interesting, more poignant, or more difficult to seize than the intersection between self and history."

Francois Camoin, who taught me.

My students, who also taught me and who, in such important ways, saw this book through.

Sarah Lane. Noreen Webb.

Excerpts from this work have appeared in *Volt* (2000) and *New Letters* (2000), and I want to thank their editors for publishing my work.

California State University, Northridge, which has generously contributed to this project through a variety of grants and awards.

The editor, Trudy McMurrin.

All the other people at the University of Nevada Press—Ron Latimer, Sandy Crooms, Sara Vélez Mallea, Carrie House, and Chris Campbell, who, with this book as well as my last, have helped see me through. Julie Schorfheide, the generous and ever patient copy editor, who let me work.

You, for reading it, which is another act of faith, as my own mother stopped believing my stories by the time I was ten.

"Don't listen to her," she would say. "Katharine is always making things up."

Well, for what it is worth, let's try this: *let me tell you a story.*

That Water, Those Rocks

≈

≈ ≈

≈

~
~
~

If you take the idea of a story:

If you take the idea of a story and spin it off the tips of your fingers, what will it look like, I wonder—random splashes of color? a mitotic organism? something woven?

I wrote that, then, for no apparent reason, I thought: *my friend Patty used to say I never call her, she's right, I never called her, I should have called her.*

As I think this, I experience the same anxiety and dread that overcomes me when another child snubs or otherwise turns against my younger son, Joey, for Joey, in the paradoxical manner of the cheerful and outgoing among us, is also finely tuned and sensitive and has moved, in middle childhood, full-on into the self-consciousness I had hoped (oh, how I'd hoped) he might be spared. This dread, which surfaced in the long months before the boys were born, starts at the center of my chest and spreads outward, where it clings to the underside of my skin and can linger for so long I must finally probe myself to remember what provoked it. It is not, I think, the snub itself I dread—for Patty, I feel certain, would have loved to hear from me—but the complex human interaction a call to her stirred up, as well as the possibility things might sour.

I know I should have called her, but now it is improbable I ever will again.

What would have happened, I wonder, if I had?

Or perhaps we should wonder, instead: what is the relation between the story you spin off the tips of your fingers, and the rawness of a person's vulnerability, exposed like the nerve of a shattered tooth, in complex human interactions.

And anyway, Sam is the one with the shattered teeth, my older son Sam, now full on into adolescence, but who, when he was younger, used to break his teeth routinely, each of his broad incisors, two in baseball, two in soccer, a graceful and athletic child who played with such abandon and intensity that, from time to time, he'd howl—a terrible sound—and rear up from his game, spitting blood, and then stumble dazed off the field, one apologetic coach or another trailing awkwardly behind, to bring me the glistening shards of his teeth, cupped in his sorrowful hands. Even streaked with blood, they were beautiful teeth, and, yes, I would mourn them as Sam, a small boy, cringed more times than I can bear to remember in the grip of the dentist's green chair, opposing his will to that of the bent-over man who hovered, half coiled, above him, as dangerous as he was well-intended. In other respects, Sam is more contained than his brother, though not less sensitive. I do not think this makes things easier for him, but certainly there is a difference between a face that closes off, and a face that cracks open, with grief.

Years ago, when I first started writing this, I was not so far away from the moment I had held Sam in the night and known myself as someone who had chosen to bring a child—this tiny human being and one small new beginning—into a time and place and world where the Iron Curtain still held things together. If you take the idea of that curtain and the curve of an infant's small back in the crook of your arms, what remains, if not story? I mean that. Their temperaments come with them and all you can do is spin and spin the stories you hope will keep them safe, though you also feel foolish for relying so completely on only language, only words, only really the trace of their memory after you've formed them.

It would not be any different if I had called her, for Patty and I grew up in the unsettling shadow of that curtain (how could a curtain be made out of iron?), which would collapse, despite us, long before either of my sons could calculate any geography beyond the tight circle of their home, their school, their park. I know I am not supposed to say this, but as I spin my stories out one whole complex century spins to its close, and whatever other sense I can make of things for them, they stand too straight and tall and facing forward to pay much attention, either way. It is a kind of courage I could never even have imagined for myself, and it has taught me, with such incalculable exactitude, how to love the strong lines of their backs, even as they turn them away.

~
~
~

Once, years before:
Once, years before, I also loved a painter whose paintings, bright splashes of

color like living organisms, spun off the tips of his fingers, but when we slept together, those very fingers turned blunt-ended and inelegant, no grace about them at all.

"Why do you hold so much back?" he would say.

And this is what would happen: my tongue, inside my mouth, between my teeth, would go all fat and swollen and numb, and a stubborn fist of muteness would clench around my heart.

Bemused, he would say, "You have no will."

He would lay one blunt-ended finger across my lips and whisper, "Shh, no need. Shh."

Then he too would turn away, his back a sturdy wall against my chest as he curled even further away into sleep, and it was then I understood that the muse, without a story of her own, must be silent and lack, as well, a will.

And yet, I swear to you I loved him; though loving him, it would take years before I would discover that the story I'd spin off the tips of my fingers would have nothing mute about it at all. It would be all words, light and airy, like something you breathe. It would be a house with mostly windows open to the light, and some breeze sweetened with a scent you cannot name. It would not have anything in it of the formless inside-the-body dread that is the unspeakable vulnerability of your child, for how could you have known that in the act of sex the child you conceived would split your heart—your life—like that, forever?

The state of grace and love is characterized by exactly this splitting, but my story would be the water around it. Either that, or fire. And I don't know, what should we call the inability to choose? If it is not faith or love, it must be grace.

⌇

⌇

⌇

Only the knot:
 A few more things I can safely say I know now:
 I do not think my story is different from that of other women.
 Nevertheless, it is the knot of my muteness untying itself.
 Even now, I cannot tell you what it is.
 Just water. Just fire.

Just my sister. My lover. My uncles, both real and imagined. Patty, Sam, and Joey, who never asked for this but don't complain.

For it is also true that in other respects I have run plumb out of stories, having told them all already. In this respect, I am all told out.

Only the knot remains.

~

~

~

Because this story:

Because this story is also about the damming up of water, you will read the dams as a metaphor for my knot, but you will be wrong.

Imagine, instead, the hand of a blind woman exploring a contour map of California. Years before, her father and my uncle were among the first civil engineers to remap state distributions of water. They sat on swivel stools before high drafting tables and dreamed out the arcs of their dams on blue tissue paper. What a miracle it was, as they first conceived it, bringing water to the desert, a lush, exotic garden from one end of the state to the other. Back then they were important men, held in high regard, even, in some sense, revered. Eminent politicians broke champagne bottles over the backs of their projects. President Kennedy himself spoke at Whiskeytown Dam, his voice recorded in a monument that slows now when the weather is cold.

These days it is different, and the blind woman's father, well into his dotage, is vexed and rancorous, a bitter man. He reads the paper every day, and keeps himself informed about the long-range plans of such ill-considered groups as the California Coastal Commission, the Sierra Club, or any other misguided environmental agency that might be working to impede the expansion of the garden at every step of the way. You can't even build your house where you want to anymore, and soon they'll be pricing lawns right out of the market. Even in flood years, he knows, there will be talk of water rationing in southern California. Full of foreboding, the blind woman's father envisions a future of icebergs dotting the coast from San Francisco south, cooling the ecosystem, degree by disastrous degree.

My uncle, on the other hand, believes you can't fight history and has his own concerns about the rising saline content in the delta, the poisoned birds along the aqueduct, Mono Lake. A measured man, my uncle sees the larger view and is at least willing to entertain the possibility that one generation's vision of the future might not serve another's, despite what might remain as lasting trace. For example, he is six-of-one, half-a-dozen-of-another about the Shasta Temperature Control Device, recently installed on Shasta Dam in an attempt to lure the salmon back up the Sacramento River, from which they had almost disappeared. A major, 80 million dollar federal endeavor and the largest underwater welding project ever conceived, the STCD is an 8,000-ton, 25-story steel subaqueous building designed to reconfigure the outflow system of the dam so that, during critical runs, water can be drawn up and released from the bottom of the lake, turning the river downstream cold enough for salmon to spawn. Throughout the course of its construction, saturation diving welders lived four weeks at a time so far beneath the surface of the lake—300 feet—that they were forced to breathe a helium-rich oxygen mixture and talk like Donald Duck, high and nasal the whole time. Helium changes the body's reaction to heat. In their underwater quarters, these men lived smack in the middle of a four-degree range between sweltering and freezing, and at 100 pounds of atmospheric pressure per square inch, it took three days to depressurize on the way up before they could go out and get drunk.

"At least they're getting rich," my uncle said.

But, like I say, he is mixed, because as much as he considers the whole affair to have been a government boondoggle of the most grievous proportions, his ninety-plus heart isn't in it. No one really knows if the salmon will turn out to be smarter than we are, sensing by some heretofore unknown sixth animal sense that the supercooled lake bottom waters are a trick, but my uncle has a hunch that, despite whatever grandiosity might be at work, we'll come to watch the salmon spawning someday where they've never spawned before, and that this too will be part of a vision of progress that just won't hold steady or changeless. At his age, my uncle has some equanimity about this. He still loves his dams, of course, but he's always also loved salmon.

When I was I child, I believed it was for this love alone that he lived his life among dams, but now I think that, in addition, his was a primal need for power, for big things poured in concrete, for the sheer perverse pleasure of closing off the gap between two canyon walls just because you can conceive it, just because you can. My uncle is a good and patient man, who nursed two wives through long terminal illnesses and still faithfully serves his church. I want you to know this about him. A sought-after ladies man in his retirement home, my uncle wears a parrot on his shoulder.

Meanwhile, his colleague's blind daughter sits poised with her hand on the humps and the valleys of a state contour map. She knows where every dam is, and it is for the breadth of that knowledge, rather than her blindness, that she is in this story.

Call her Patty.

～

～

～

In the whole scope of horrific events:

Late one summer, before Patty lost her eyesight in a freak construction accident, she visited the site of what would become Claire Engle Lake, the rocky-bottomed reservoir behind Trinity Dam. The river, by that time of year, had slowed to a trickle, but there were still places, here and there, where water pooled deep among rocks, forming green swimming holes, and it was to one of these spots, a local favorite, that Patty's father took her late one afternoon after a hot day of tromping through the dusty stubble of a pine forest mown down for the lake. Patty was thirteen, a long-legged adolescent who had her hopes pinned on one particular bikini. Her father brought a thermos of martinis, and crouched contented on the rocks above the water.

I suppose that in the whole scope of horrific events the world holds in store for its children, this is not that high on the scale, but Patty, sleek in her red maillot, had led a sheltered life, and though she was more or less accustomed to the quiet drunkenness of her father's martini-laced stay-at-home evenings in front of the new console color TV, the kegger she stumbled on that afternoon was so far outside the range of her experience that she couldn't really name or recognize it. From where her father sat higher up on the rocks, he could not see the keg, and in his own inebriation, the local boys, drunk on beer, just looked happy to him. He was happy to see them happy. Magnanimous, he was happy to see his daughter among the happy boys. If he saw the other girl, the tear-streaked, flaxen-haired waif, he made no sign of it. She was maybe nine years old, with a new blue bruise blossoming out from the side of her mouth, and she was naked.

As Patty started down the trail toward the water, she found the hoots and whistles of the boys faintly titillating. The sun beat hot on her back, and she kept slipping on the rocky trail, struggling for balance. Behind her, her father admired the curve of her butt, then let his gaze drift off to the craggy Trinity Alps in the distance, one range red, one range white. He thought about how, after the dam was built, the river would never be diminished like this, but though reduced in total volume, would maintain a constant flow throughout the year and thereby put an end to flood and drought. He thought about the end of flood and drought. Then Patty's father thought about a summer playground—children in inner tubes, mothers sunbathing on newly bulldozed beaches—a small private vision he dreamily went on to embellish with a pair of yellow kayaks shooting Class 3 rapids where, at present, only scummy clots of water lingered, putrid and stinking. This pleased him so enormously he took another chug of gin from his thermos, and almost did not hear his daughter's cry.

If it was Patty who was raped that hot afternoon by the drunk local boys, but it wasn't. Or if something happened then to cause her blindness, but it didn't. No, it was the other girl that day, the nine-year-old flaxen-haired waif. And it wasn't the blood running down the insides of her legs that made Patty cry out, or even the blossoming bruise at the side of her mouth, but just the simple fact of her nakedness, and the paleness of her girl nipples, and the beer she was drinking as fast as she could, though even in that heat she could not stop shivering.

When she saw Patty, she spat, and it was pink, tinged with blood. Then, amazingly, she grinned.

"You know what?" she said. "There's going to be a dam here. Glub, glub," she said. "You're drowned."

Patty held out her towel for the girl, but the girl shook her head. "I got my own, you know."

"Patty?" her father called down from above. "You all right, Patty?"

Then Patty looked up and saw three boys on the rocks behind the girl, leering at her. One of them held his hand out to the girl, who took it and pulled herself up. Her knees were bleeding too, Patty noticed. Patty doesn't really remember if this happened or not, but she thinks one of the other boys had grabbed at his crotch and was shaking his swollen penis at her.

As she turned and ran up the hillside, behind her she heard the girl say, "My name is Miranda. Remember that: *Miranda*."

~

~

~

The last time I saw Patty:

Three years later, at the Oroville Dam construction site, an accident occurred, involving Patty, another drunk, and a piece of heavy equipment that rendered Patty sightless in one eye and with rapidly diminishing vision in the other. As I first imagined it, it was another sweltering day, and Patty was again tagging after her father. They'd been inspecting the various parts of the site— the base of the dam, its unfinished turbines, and now, toward the end of the day, the cusp of its rising crown—when Patty found herself clambering over a pile of debris just as a steel spring or metal shard sprang loose from a nearby machine, and with a devastating ping, sheered off a rock and into the corner of her eye, severing the optic nerve irreparably. This is how I first imagined it and how it would fix itself in my imagination, as shocking and persistent as if it really happened that way, but of course, the optic nerve is lodged deep inside the brain, and damage to one eye will not necessarily compromise the other. However difficult it is to reconcile Patty's loss, which was permanent and grievous, with this apparent paradox, and whether it stemmed from some physical anomaly or, inexplicably, some other kind of failure—a lack of will, perhaps, on Patty's part—within months of the accident, she was completely blind, and now, for the rest of her life, she will be unable to separate her image of that boy's engorged penis, swathed by the electric blue nylon of his swim trunks, from what she knows a normal penis must look like, just prior to the act of love, or after.

The last time I saw Patty, years and years ago, was at a banquet held in honor of the early dam engineers, grizzled men in their seventies and eighties. She was seated at a table near the entry foyer, her hand poised over an old contour map of California, the look on her face between serene and beatific. Later, my uncle was dancing with her, around and around the polished dance floor. Still later, I might have seen her by a window. She might have been weeping, but of course I can't be sure.

∾
∾
∾

Miranda was different:
Miranda was different.

How do I know this? Sometimes it is possible to arrange, like small river stones, certain moments in your life so that they form an iconography of memory or a kind of map. The stones may be warm from the sun, and as you finger them to decide where you might place them, you cannot tell the difference between the warmed skin of rock and your own skin. There is something both intuitive and logical about the patterns that emerge, a kind of grammar even, though of course you do not always recognize it. You just put the rocks where they belong, and later it will be as if everything, everything spins out from there.

Such moments occur in all of our lives, and sometimes we know them at once, and sometimes it may take years to realize that a girl dreaming out a warm and sleepy afternoon high in the mottled shadows of her father's cherry tree will never not be haunted by the sudden anguish of a boy's cries in the distance beneath the railroad trestle that traverses the broad swath of flood-plain spread out north of the curve of the river that runs below the humped hills her house sits on. If you are that girl, as I am, you will perhaps remain stunned that, as the years pass, the sound of those cries through the dappled light and sun-drenched ripe fruit sweetness of that day will grow ever more acutely forlorn, for you will be increasingly uncertain as to whether the cries were the cries of the boy who fell and died, or those of the boy who watched and lived.

Years later, I will catch a glimpse from the sour lobby of a dive motel, circa 1940, on the Northern California coast, almost all the way to Oregon, of Miranda's daughter, Sky, in the back room and it will be, instead, like a stone already set, prescient and sudden. She was just standing there, hunkered down over a pot of spaghetti, pale and thin and angular, and dressed in old jeans and a man's flannel shirt. Really, she could have been anyone—a runaway, a drop-out, a hippie—but she wasn't, she was Sky, and she had a look about her, be-tween tranquil and forlorn. Also, a strange light accrued around her body from the burners she'd turned on for heat, a light which did not really attach itself to her somehow, but seemed instead to emanate from her physical being, extending outward all around, an eerie glow. In her stillness, she was as if etched, and it seemed to me that if she were to move, even just a tiny bit, all that she was struggling to contain would spill over, out into the world. I believe that in that moment, edgy and with the fog just beginning to roll in, I knew everything already, Sky's whole history, even Patty, up to and including Miranda as a girl, that wan and unreadable smile. But what I couldn't do was put it into words. It would take this writing, Sam's shattered teeth, and Joey's emerging self-consciousness for me to know and name the strange affinity between us.

"Sky," I wanted to say, "don't look so sad," but she was not anyone you could really speak to.

In fact, it was a complicated moment, well on into dusk, with the stink of salt and wetland, and the fog, that particular kind of cold, dense and penetrating. I was on a road trip with my sister, who had just gone back to the car for our sweatshirts, and we had been driving since dawn, starting at our father's cabin off the upper Sacramento and ending somehow here, where we had never planned to be, planned instead to spend the night in Hoopa thirty miles inland on the reservation, when, just seven miles short of our destination, what turned us back was fire.

Fire is a thing you grow up with when you grow up in those parts. Even now, as I am writing this, seven fires rage in Northern California and a hundred homes have burned in a small valley just west of where I grew up, a valley I remember as a gentle cup of grass and oak and long-needled digger pine, and everything dry as tinder, now with the roar of flames bearing down. And how do I even know flames roar when they bear down? How close have I ever been, even, to flames roaring down? Flames roar when they bear down, and we know this because, here in California, fire is such an integral part of our imaginations that it is never as if we have not faced it, never not been called to pack our most valued possessions, in a frenzy of choosing, into a single carload, never not stood flailing linked garden hoses from our roofs, ash drifting like snow from above. We are so attached to this image of ourselves that we continue to see ourselves as uncanny partners with our own annihilation.

For surely there is something about the fire that, like a living thing, we love, and maybe what we love is the certain thought that we must not love it, not the shadow of the first plume of smoke against the brilliant blue of an August afternoon, nor the whiteness of the smoky sky, not the violence of yellow grasses lying down before the overheated wind, nor the scorched and blackened stubble moments later, not the first thrill of alarm, nor the worried looks of grown-ups all around us. We know we must not love it, but there is something in those looks that makes us know we are alive in a way we never are when everything around us is not threatened.

On this day, the day we came closer to fire than we ever had before, but not since, my sister and I had driven over from the other side of the mountains on not much more than a whim to explore the back country northwest of our father's cabin, a remote part of California we'd grown up on the edges of and thought we knew as well we would ever know a country, but not well enough, it turned out, to account for the likes of Miranda and her daughter, who when I saw her that first time in the back room of the motel was hunkered down over a pot of spaghetti, the ends of her hair stained with sauce.

My story, the one I'd spin off the tips of my fingers, begins with that whim, and my sister, and our long mountain drive over roads we just discovered on a map yet never once had traveled on, despite having spent our entire childhoods in that part of the country, where we still go every summer—I with my children, my sister, who is single, alone—to visit our parents and the land that defined us.

My husband no longer comes with us, for he finds both the heat and my family oppressive, and is the kind of man who believes that the function of maps is to get you from one place to another. You know the kind of man I mean. We'll just be driving along, when suddenly he'll get flustered and angry. "Help me," he'll say, thrusting a folded map at me. "Aren't you supposed to be Sacajewea?" Then, before I can tell its top from its bottom, he'll grab the map out of my hands, steering one-hand and cursing.

For this reason, I have long mistrusted maps as just another testy simulacrum of our marriage, and so have never told my husband how my sister and I sat down by the creek one summer evening, how we studied California's remotest northwest sector, how we chose the smallest, least developed roads, how what we saw was not the route from one place to another, but just the going there, the web itself of distant roads that once moved gold or copper, and people, through the mountains to the sea.

Today, you can drive hours up there without seeing anyone—maybe a few green-jeaned forest service crews, a handful of loggers or reclusive campers, people intent on disappearing—and this was where we headed that day, my

sister and I, beyond the edge of the edge of the north part of this state to a
stretch of Salmon River where we had never been, never even yet imagined,
for, like many children, we'd grown up accepting the boundaries of our lives,
and strangely incurious about the world.

"Eat your peas," our mother said. "Think," our mother said, "about the
starving children."

And because we'd seen the pictures and knew the starving children to be
gaunt-limbed and bloated-bellied, hollow-eyed, we did as we were told, and
counted up our blessings. But we had seen the other pictures, too—the mush-
room clouds, the haunting shadows etched on glowing concrete—and also
had, in those days, our lingering palpable dread of and anxious preoccupation
with nuclear war. That was the paradox of our precise historical moment—
lucky not to have been born in some distant Third World country, destined to
be blown up by the Bomb. Thus convinced that the world was about to end, I
worried constantly and suffered from a morbid fascination with what it might
actually feel like to be transformed in a flash, to light itself, with all that remained of my body—what I could touch—just an eerie human trace on the
side of a building or sidewalk, my own atoms dispersed into nothing at all.

That is how completely my imagination was rooted in my culture. I ducked
and covered, I ate my peas, but I wonder: did I ever even wonder about the far
side of the mountains that ringed our town on three sides—west, north, and
east?

I knew what we all knew: *The other side of the mountain would be all that
we could see.*

I knew it was up to me to prevent forest fires.

Now, my husband says that women are not interested in facts (quick: *how
many people live in India?*), and though I'm not saying *yes* or *no,* I know that as
a child many things seemed opaque and mystifying to me: geology, the
sources of rivers, places on maps, numbers of things. It gives you such a hunger
for naming things when you grow up, but between limestone and granite, how
much of that is knowledge, how much something closer to desire?

One day, my sister and I just got hungry is all. Ravenous, we got out our
maps, poured over our tour guides, and learned that the Hoopa Valley Reserve
is one of the few reservations in the country to have been located on ancestral
lands. Bowl-shaped and ringed by mountains, its valley flares south from the
confluence of the Klamath and Trinity Rivers and forms what the Hupa Indi-

ans believe to be the center of the earth, where they have lived continuously since the creation of all things.

And so we started out, my sister and I, headed for the center of the earth, where the Hupa Indians have lived since the creation of all things.

Early one morning, we gathered our maps, kissed my children in their sleep, and took off, escaping the family.

We had gas in the car, and my hat, and we were driving fast, first north, then west, on back roads through the Klamath and Trinity Mountains, deep into that remotest sector of the state no one can truly imagine who believes in California as just another coast.

Imagine California, instead, as such an expanse of the most heartbreaking land that it contains, on one end, the massive craters of Death Valley and, on the other, the rugged wilderness where many mountain ranges cluster—the Trinities, the Marbles, the Siskiyous, the Cascades, the Coast. Imagine, instead, a blind woman, her hand poised.

In Death Valley, even now, a slight miscalculation and what happens is your blood, deprived of its essential fluids, slows and thickens in your veins until, with one last fatal flowering, they swell and burst open inside you. This still sometimes happens, just as hikers in the mountains still sometimes wander off and succumb to hypothermia and frostbite. We live, in California, by extremes. The engineers who chart the history of this state with their intricate canals and aqueducts once planned to turn its whole northwestern sector into a mammoth reservoir behind a dam near the mouth of the Klamath River, and that was the country my sister and I drove through that day, what would have been the rocky bottom of the Ah Pah reservoir, another California no one ever talks about. People know it, if they know it at all, as the apocryphal back-country haunt of survivalist drug dealers and their killer dogs.

"You're going where?" our mother said to my sister and me before we started out. "Oh," our mother said, "you know what happened there."

"What happened where?" my sister said.

"Oh, never mind," our mother said, not wanting to alarm us that the bodies of three hikers had turned up only weeks before, some ways out of Happy Camp, that, despite their long decay, had shown signs of violence. In another century, not even Indians lived here, who lived instead—the Wintus and Shastans, Hupas and Pits—in the gentler valleys on the edges of these mountains, beneath the southern flank of Mount Shasta, bordered on the north by

Oregon, on the west by the Pacific, and on the east by the meanest of deserts, spotted with turquoise blue alkaline lakes.

Five rivers lace the rugged country there: the Salmon, the Klamath, the McCloud, the Sacramento, the Mad.

Imagine a contour map of California.

I'm not quite sure how to put this, but it has something to do with where geography meets history and it is a story without words in one version of which I have another uncle who lives high in the Peruvian Andes and who, in such a time of longing, would cup his hands over my eyes and, letting them lie there, coolly, gently, remind me that every intersection of land and people has evolved into heartbreak. And what he will not say because we will both know it in our hearts is that this heartbreak is related to the sound of a river rolling over the stones in its bed, to the very roughness that binds it to this earth. However hard I try, I cannot separate the water from the rock, cannot hear what it would be like in the instant before the elements converge, creating sound. Sound is what enables us to know us, who we are: before sound, would that be a place without grief?

And it is not even grief I would assuage with this story.

Before my sister and I left on that road trip, our mother warned us also about bears, yellow jackets, and to take plenty of water, good hiking shoes, sunscreen, and our down sleeping bags, just in case.

My sister wanted her camera.

We had no clear destination, except Hoopa, and despite our ceaseless chatter, we were headed beyond language that day.

We drove and we drove, and as we drove, our accumulated memories piled up inside the car like the slag heaps along every river we had ever known, the whole long day like one perpetual déjà vu, for though we'd never been exactly here before, it was all strangely familiar, as if we'd known this land before, in different parts and places, and now it kept coming back at us all in a rush.

As children we rode for hours on Sunday afternoons, crammed into the back seat of our father's station wagon, through forests like these on dusty dirt roads.

As a Girl Scout I hiked, whining, among nearby mountains.

As a college student, I backpacked deep into the Trinity Alps, trailing doggedly behind my boyfriend because I knew that at the end of the day, there would be a lake, a fire, his body.

Other indigenous peoples of this continent believe that the center of the earth is wherever a person's foot has been planted, at any given moment, the body through the flesh of the foot, which is connected to the earth it walks upon and makes us who we are, and I'm convinced it must be so because the memory of this landscape—fringe of mountains, rush of water in its channel—is so tangible in my imagination it is as if I carry it inside my body, like another body altogether.

Nothing really happened on that trip. We drove for hours, splitting off on isolated roads we just discovered on our AAA map, capriciously curling ever deeper into that back country, growing giddy with our small adventure. We talked, we laughed, we wept. She was forty, I was two years older—half our lives behind us—and still it was as if everything were new again—strangely familiar, but new—and full of promise.

Some hours into the day, the road abruptly narrowed into a single lane just at a small country store and a sign that read *Experienced Mountain Drivers Only*. A gapped-toothed logger stared at us blandly from inside the store, and while my sister and I, our mother's daughters, are both firm believers that roads should go both ways, with room enough on either side to accommodate even full-sized vans or SUV's, on this day and in this moment there was the lure of the road itself, and we were embarrassed by the logger's gaze, implacable behind the greasy window. It was hot, our shorts were short, and the car was an imported sedan, so between the going in and asking for directions, or at least some information as to what might lay ahead, and the pressing on or turning back, we laughed and we pressed on, forty breathtaking miles suspended on the lip of a Salmon River canyon, tracing hairpin curves in and out of slivered sunlight where, if a car would come from the opposite direction, we'd slam the brakes, inching cautiously back to a pullout or other stretch wide enough to safely negotiate a passage, even as the other car careened around our balk. Each close call left us giddier. It was a smoky day.

These fires, we knew, were far to the north—somewhere up in Oregon—but we could smell them, and sometimes, when the wind shifted and turned the air bitter and acrid, we'd feel, momentarily, the old peculiar thrill of fear, almost as a random thing, as if, if fire were to sweep over the crest of the mountains just then and down, like a wave, with its roar, the steep slope of cliff, what would we do? This is how we hold the thought of fire in our minds when it is summer in the north—as something inconceivable and, paradoxically, inevitable. We hold it this way because even as the haze of smoke deadens the sky, we are torn between loss and desire.

In time the road dipped down to a small Forest Service campground, where we picnicked near a stretch of calm water between rapids, clear and deep and green, and with sun-drenched boulders up the other shore, and no one else around for what seemed miles and miles—just us, that water, those rocks.

After we ate, we swam, drifting from one end of the long pool to the other.

"If I swam like this in rivers when I was twenty, and I'm still doing it at forty," my sister called out, "what's to stop me when I'm sixty?"

My sister, in her blue maillot underneath the glassy surface of that water, washed by sun, looked no different to me than she had twenty years before when we had backpacked into nearby mountains with no further thought of a destination than a waterfall, a pass, a glacial lake, and where we had come to know a kind of serenity and grace our whole adult lives had denied us.

A poet once told me that he, too, had loved those mountains, and hiked and camped in them for years, until one night he was awakened by the thought he could be killed there.

"Bad vibes," he said, "what a shame. I packed up and hiked out, and I never went back."

In that instant, an awful darkness flooded me, and though I smiled what I hoped was something of a wry and subtle smile at the poet, I turned away and steeled my heart against him from then on, thinking that a poet should know better than to spread his bitterness around so carelessly like that.

Later, I would wonder what accounted for my own long absence, and if it was something so simple and absolute as just time going by, not really anything you could name, just school and marriage, never easy, and children, just time. To my uncle in the Andes I would write: *how do you get back?* And, though perhaps I will come to regret this, I would also write to my white-haired lover in the East who wanted me to join him: *no.*

If I swam like this, my sister called out, *what's to stop me when I'm sixty?*

I was sunning myself on a strip of white river sand. Her strokes, toward the rocks on the other side, were strong and sure. Not far from where we were, maybe just a few miles north, lay the site of the only direct hit to the mainland in wwii, an implausible casualty of a little-known Japanese campaign to divert crucial national resources from the war effort by setting fire to our northwestern forests with incendiary bombs distributed in blue hot air balloons. The balloons drifted over the wilderness, carrying their terrible cargos of fire, but the campaign itself was a failure because that was one year it never stopped raining. Now, on the other side of the river, my sister hoisted herself up on the rocks and lay there, blue-suited and glistening.

And this is what happened: my heart broke open with love.

No, this instead: my heart became geography, the sculpted valley where we were, and all its wilderness of sun and rocks and water.

No, this: it came to me that long ago, when I had left my parents' home, intending never to look back, I had lacked every basic skill I would need for negotiating any other part of the world, and that for years I'd blamed my parents, my small town origins, even history, carrying an unattractive grudge around that had made me both anxious and sullen. Then, I don't know, perhaps it was the day itself and the accumulated effect of our forty reckless miles on that one-lane twisting mountain road along the steep-cut canyon that had brought us to this stretch of limpid water on the sun-drenched Salmon River, but I found myself so overcome with well-being and serenity, and so completely alone, that when, far away, we heard dogs barking, a strange sort of panic overcame me—for whose dogs could they possibly be? Then, in another instant, something shifted in me and I recognized the failure as my own.

Miranda, I told you, was different. Miranda came from here and never left. Miranda, hearing dogs, would have tromped off to greet them, playfully wrestling them by their ruffs, while I, for the rest of my life, will dream of balloons high above forests. Colorful, they make popping noises when they land.

~
  ~
~

Thus I would have liked:

Thus, I would have liked to have been able to write that, just as with Sky and me, when Patty first laid eyes on Miranda they recognized each other at once, that Patty could see beyond Miranda's blood-stained thighs and that Miranda, despite what she said—*glub,* she said, *dam*—could hold the girl in the red maillot somewhere above the rage and contempt she held for the whole rest of the world. I would have liked that there should always have been something resonant between them, for how could it not seem that the moment in which each acknowledged the other marked the intersection between one's origins and the other's future. Miranda, who began life in the woods on the edge of the world and had always been at risk of drifting out of it, especially now with the building of Trinity Dam, was a harbinger of where Patty would be headed once the dam at Oroville began construction.

Including Shasta, there are three dams in this story, and if that is too many it is because this is California, and California, for the better part of the middle of the last century, was manic with dams. Every place there was a river, someone saw a dam, and every place someone saw a dam, others saw development and growth. In Sacramento, even now, municipal water use is considered too cheap to meter, and in Los Angeles xeriscaping sometimes still requires special exemption from neighborhood bylaws regulating lawns. Ours is such a heritage of uncontrolled expansion that we cannot even consider the possibility of limits on such natural phenomena as the need of plants or industry for water, or human thirst.

If there are three dams in this story, maybe it's because I grew up in the shadow of Shasta and watched the other two—Trinity and Oroville—being built, and maybe it's because Miranda was raped in the watershed of one and Patty was blinded at another.

Oroville Dam, once the largest earth-filled dam in the world, is still, at 770 feet, the tallest dam in the United States. During its construction, as during the construction of Trinity Dam, my father, a smaller, less expansive man than my uncle with the parrot, used to take us to marvel at the monumental project. We'd eat our little picnics—warm tuna sandwiches, with slivered pickles, and chips—in the dirt, and exclaim at the spectacle of it—earth being moved, like a mountain shifting, or the lake just beginning to fill. Around us, the air throbbed with the power of it.

"Feel that," my father would say. "That's the life-pulse of this state."

In fact, today it is sometimes said that more energy is used in transferring water from Oroville Dam to Southern California than the dam itself generates as hydroelectric power; but this was 1961, and no one thought like that back then.

I remember tiny trucks crawling along the vast gravel sides of Oroville Dam, and later, the lake inching up into the dry folds of its rounded foothills. I remember the terrible noise of it. Patty says it wasn't like that at all at the time of her accident. She says it was very still and quiet, with not even a breeze over the water, and everything shut down and peaceful. And though for years I have known I envisioned it wrong, that whatever must have happened, it could not have been a steel spring impaled in a single eye (which would not have caused such total loss of sight), whenever I try to reconstruct what actually might have happened, it is as blank and dark for me as I imagine Patty's blindness is for her. Thus, I remain steadfastly attached to my original, if ill-conceived, idea of the drunk, the machine, the ominous ping, the girl impaled and blinded. As for Patty, she has always said it was the suddenness of the event that made her blindness acceptable, if not agreeable, to her, that, in her memory, life was always one way, then it was another, just like that, and that in her world, as it was transformed, everything became charged with new meaning.

"My own body," she told me, "was as unfamiliar and compelling as a lover's. I touched myself in places I'd never touched before, smelled smells, heard my own heart pounding."

Meanwhile, her father was in mourning, which he tried to soothe with gin. It was the saddest thing, sadder even than Patty herself, the way night after night he would sit on the back porch looking out over the broad Sacramento, drinking straight from his cocktail shaker, and weeping until his eyes swelled up puffy and red. One time my uncle and I went to visit, and Patty's father was sitting blindfolded on the peeling white porch of the house they had lived in since they moved away from our street. All during the visit he refused to remove the blindfold, and whenever he reached for his shaker, he'd grope about clumsily, more than once almost knocking it over.

"Light," he said in a gravelly voice. "Light, light."

Maybe this was the last time we were all together in what now seems like a dogged attempt to reclaim the other languid nights my uncle and Patty's father used to sit drinking on their first back porch, the one down the street from my house. They could, the two of them, drink for hours on that porch, debating desultorily the pros and cons of the new water projects, or just watching the hypnotic pull of the river below, their wide neckties draped over the backs of the white wicker rockers, the looks on their faces on the verge of serene. But there was always something, some frayed edges to the ties or a tightness at the corner of their eyes, something squeezed in the purse of their mouths, that even the gin, in Patty's father's case, and the whiskey, in my uncle's, did not fully relieve. In those years, it wasn't yet drought and it wasn't the future either, which they still believed in and upheld as forthrightly as their red and green suspenders held up their whole manly way of being. It wasn't the slow turn toward the Sixties, those disparate wars, their aftermath. It wasn't even the grim foreknowledge that the kind of men they were was about to wane.

In fact I'm not sure what it was, but maybe you, like I, would like to believe that this faint uneasiness on their part, their drawn facial muscles and the weird angles of their ties, reflected a dim recognition that somewhere in the mountains people like Miranda, and her mother, and grandfather, were subject—their whole lives—to the whims of these engineers' distant calculations. Maybe we want to believe this, but Patty's father, my uncle, and the rest of the men who dreamed up the various projects to redistribute California water never knew the first thing about people like Miranda and her mother and grandfather, never mind rivers themselves, not the way any other person than an engineer might come to know a river, its languorous swoops and curves and precipitous descents, its endless rush of water over rocks, the lambent pools of moonlight on its rippling surface, or by day, its sparkling eddies, the respite of its coolness, mossy taste, sweet, sweet water. For them it was only and all about power, the transformation of the desert, and a kind of progress we've forgotten even how to imagine except in atavistic images of happy women vacuuming, toasting toast, shaking laundry out of their new electric dryers, their faces gone vague with pleasure.

When my uncle thought up every dam he ever was involved with, my aunt was home polishing the windows. Especially at lunch, biting into his home-made roast beef sandwich, he'd think of her and smile, his own smile reminiscent of hers as she folded warm laundry. Even when I once walked clean through their sliding glass door, he'd smiled about it afterward, he was so proud of his efficient, tidy wife. It was in the name of this efficiency, this tidiness that he dreamed up his dams, and Patty's father, even more than my uncle, was determined to establish a certain quality of brightness in every California home.

"Light, light, light," he used say, long before his daughter lost her sight. And now, again, he was muttering, "Light."

My uncle reached over to remove Patty's father's blindfold, but Patty's father twisted away, and there was something truly terrifying about the sound he made deep in his throat. He'd been wearing it all day, he said, and meant to wear it long enough to understand his daughter. Patty herself was staring obliquely somewhere beyond her father's left shoulder, half a smile playing at the corners of her mouth, not at all bitter and only mildly ironic.

"Daddy," she said, "don't." She was sixteen years old, with the most beautiful breasts. Her hair, brushed back from her face, was thick and gleaming, and I don't think I'd ever seen her more certain of anything. All of us knew what her father meant, we were all trying to imagine what could not really be imagined, but every time I closed my eyes it was as if the whole world just disappeared, and this frightened me more than I wanted to admit.

That night I took Patty's hand to let her know that I was there, and she just shrugged. She did not look sad or forlorn at all. My uncle poured himself more whiskey, then offered some to me, and though I choked on it, I managed to gulp a whole shot before Patty stood up and, reaching her hand into the empty space before her, asked me to take her for a walk.

᪐

᪐

᪐

When we were only girls:
Years before, when we were only girls and Patty still had her eyesight and I still had my certainty that we would always be together, there had been a time when, despite the threat of war, or even, perhaps, because of it, the world and its dams still seemed rich with possibility and full of promise. I know that this sounds like nostalgia, that it all sounds like nostalgia, but nostalgia is a hard, intractable thing; and though I know that I should also know enough to ask *was there ever such a time as that?* instead I make myself believe in it, and I believe that you do too because we need it, because nothing has turned out the way we thought, and because life itself compels us to reconstruct a prior moment, before everything swung out of balance and against which we can measure where we're headed.

And so, in those days, every day, I wore thin-soled canvas sneakers, and every night I polished them with a watery white paste rolled out of a bottle with a rounded felt tip. Soon the surface of the shoes, thick with caked-on polish, cracked and flaked apart, leaving bits of white powder on our sculpted brown carpet and in the grass on the way to the car, and though I remained, for the most part, unaware of my shedding, I was leaving traces of myself behind me wherever I went. Patty wore them too, canvas sneakers polished to an almost phosphorescent white, and in the years to follow we were not to know such confidence and optimism again.

Also, I remember light, not the kind that Patty's father meant, but the kind that marked each season, each its own, each as haunting and acute as memory can endure. All fall, clouds would blow in and blow over, turbulent and dark, bringing with them mild ecstasies and a certain restlessness that sent us out into the wind, against our mother's admonitions, and then the steady rains of winter dimmed and softened everything, curling us up on our hearths with our books, until, all at once, spring turned the world shockingly translucent, wet and throbbing with a sunlight that, by summer, had seared everything into a flattened stillness, and we went out again. That was how it was in California, before global warming and El Nino, always the same, an invariable sequence of wind, precipitation, and eight-month summer drought that, like the friendship between Patty and me, was as reassuring as it was predictable. On the weekends, all day and night, we'd be together. We'd make French toast and spill egg all over the kitchen.

Now, here in L.A., another world and time away, I must suppress the urge to call Joey off his skateboard, gather him up in my lap, and imagine him younger. It's not that I mourn these passing years, which are in truth what make me passionate about my sons' growing up, the way they turn more deeply into who they are each year, more resolute in both their temperaments and habits, but what I want, cuddling Joey, is to remember not just his body, still sweaty but smaller and not so muscular, but something beyond that, beyond even the vulnerability of his emerging self-consciousness, made more acute by the widening world he moves through, something, I suspect, about what it is to be new, though not really that at all either, maybe just something more from my own childhood than the passing of seasons and sparkling white shoes. Because though it is true that before the weather changed in California you could anticipate the seasons, it is also true that I made up the shoes, and that now, when the boys spill egg in the kitchen, I am beside myself with irritation.

Once, like my sons, I must have been small, maybe very small, for my mother used to worry about the wind. If it were strong, she said, or suddenly gusty, I should grab hold of a lamppost or car door, anything heavy or attached to the ground. She said that it was possible for me to blow away, and though I knew from the *Wizard of Oz* that she was right, bad weather excited me so much that I turned myself toward it instead, spreading my arms as wide as I could and thinking, hard: *now, now, yes.* I used to play this game with Patty, who, bigger than me, didn't quite believe in the possibility of being lifted clean away like that. We were seven or eight, maybe closer to nine, because it seems now things were starting to matter, if you spread your arms, if your shoes were bright white.

These days, as I watch my own children move into that time of childhood when they navigate the world as if everyone is looking at them, I am struck by how Sam, like me, averts his eyes, turning inward not so much with a cringe as with the steadfast conviction that the self is sovereign only in hiding, while Joey, demonstrative and loud, invites the public gaze as some kind of protective shroud or talisman. But Patty was of that other class of being, who, without self-consciousness at all, receives this public gaze as unfragmenting and benign, and so is able to experience the world as a fluid thing, coextensive with the self and conducive to satisfying feelings of well-being and wholeness. What I mean is, Patty wasn't a dreamer, and despite egg-all-over-the-kitchen Sunday mornings, French toast, and arms spread wide and hopeful to windy afternoons, we were friends as much because we had lived all our lives down the street from one another and shared familial ties to engineers as because we liked each other or had anything in common.

Patty lived there, down the street, until a year or so before the events of this story started spinning themselves out, catching Patty up in them the way a river catches up detritus from a storm. The house, a whitewashed adobe with turquoise blue trim and a flat, terra cotta roof, was dark and cool inside, like water, and my memories of it are, in some ways, stronger than those of my own house, for Patty had a big, corner room in the back, with windows that looked straight down on the river. Almost, it seemed as if we were suspended in that room, high above the earth, almost as if hovering above it, and the constant, swirling riffles of the water below would sometimes give me a vertigo that, as a girl, I found intensely pleasurable. Patty and I moved at whim from one house to the other, eating lunch in one, dinner in the other, and sleeping more nights together than apart. On the sidewalk between the two houses were twenty-seven cracks, but during the whole time I knew her when she could still see, Patty never seemed to worry if she stepped on them or not.

~
~
~

Math:

Of the three dams in this story, only two belong to the same water system. Trinity and Shasta, both New Deal projects, regulate runoff from the mountains of far northern California, but Oroville Dam (where if Patty had just stayed home that one day her whole life would be different, and she'd be, say, an astronomer by now, searching for stars from the Australian outback and trying to get pregnant with mail order sperm) is the imposing centerpiece of the State Water Project and manages watershed from the western Sierra Nevada, where nearly all the rivers and most major streams have long since been dammed for water, or mining, or power. My mother's father used to tell me that land was where the money was, for he, like so many others, labored his whole life under the flawed, but persistent, assumption that California's water is somehow inexhaustible.

Today we are of two minds about it: despite the stingy instructions we give to our gardeners and the complex equations of our water bills, we persist in believing that where there's a will, there's a way. Even so, we are vague about water in general, convinced it is related to the way we have configured our world and its history, without knowing, exactly, how. We subscribe, for example, to the notion that it tastes bad farther south because San Diego gets its water from the mighty Colorado, the outer limits of which we are told we are reaching (which, in fact, is true), but that it tastes good in L.A. because it comes to us here from our own Sierra Nevadas. Aware that we live in a desert, we have faith, nonetheless, in our inconstant snowpack. We believe in desalinization and icebergs, suspect it might be time to tap the water table of the east Mojave, and see ourselves as a resourceful and visionary people, with limitless capacities and unbounded hope. Though we read in the paper that the dry bed at Owens Lake raises enough alkali dust to cause the worst small-particulate air pollution in the nation, that the water quality in our streams and wells is declining, that juncos and robins and band-tailed pigeons, frogs, toads and salamanders, salmon and trout are at risk, we are nonetheless bemused that our new top-of-the line Maytag washers boast infinite water level settings. And in our minds all this is confused with the choking nostalgia we feel for a time—and my uncle confirms this—that never existed in the first place.

Who knows why any man does what he does? My uncle and my father were born to different fathers, both of whom died suddenly and young, and then the Great Depression, their waning circumstances, the scaling back of hope and optimism. In the houses of their relatives where they were taken in, my uncle shared a room with his mother and his own little brother (my father) until, six years later, my uncle left for college. During this time, he gave a hard, uncompromising look at the world, added up its pros and cons, and came down on the side of numbers.

When Sam was young I used to marvel at the way he acquired numbers like a second language. Small for his age, with a solemn, sometimes disquieting gaze, he was a natural at math, moving up and down the number line with ease, marking off the mysterious decimals, performing complex operations in his head, as if the equal sign were not an obstacle but logic. At three, he fell hopelessly in love with the concept of infinity, and entertained us all with his sage speculations. At four, he winked slyly at my father, who had tried to trick him with the problem 9 take away 10.

"I'm sorry, Grandpa," Sam said, and maybe he was, "but you gave me one below zero."

While other children drew simple pictures of themselves, their moms, or dads, or family pets, Sam plotted out elaborate geometries, designed, perhaps, to represent an inner world, meticulous and true. *By George,* I longed to tell him, *I recognize that triangle,* for I'd had no skill at drawing as a child and drew mainly shapes myself, which I privately believed resembled moons and mountains. But Sam's shapes were something else, I knew, and I could only guess at what, for Sam, as I have said, has always been contained.

One night in the difficult weeks after his brother was born, he lay with me in bed and confided that his closest friend at preschool no longer played with him. "It makes me so sad," he said, "as sad as I can possibly get, and the sadness goes on and on, and it won't ever stop."

I believe that was the last time he ever put his feelings into words, and for years I have thought about that sadness whenever his inscrutable face has closed up around one complicated problem or another. More than anything I wanted to break him loose from his stubborn attachment to the equal sign, but I was just his mother and this other, I had always known, was more like his destiny; but what I didn't know, or perhaps what I'd forgotten, was that time will unravel almost any knot, and that for Sam, in time, math would turn into music, as expressive and complex as any language, and deeply private.

My uncle went away to school and came back an engineer. When I was a girl, he wore his slide rule from a belt loop on his hip and made numbers dance off the ink-stained tips of his fingers.

"Like magic," I breathed.

"No," he said. "Math."

In another time in California, all the men, like my uncle, wore slide rules and shared the same vision. It was a dream they had of water that, managed properly, would transform our semi-arid valleys from near deserts into lush and fertile gardens. In such a California, the future California—the future, my uncle assured me, itself—no one would go hungry, and artichokes and strawberries would ripen all year long. Based on the logic of pure mathematics, my uncle predicted teeming metropolises, vast modern cities stretched out from one end of this long, thriving state to the other.

"Paradise, on earth," he used to tell me. "Oh baby, you bet."

Thus, I grew up a disciple of progress, reared on the concept of resource redistribution and other certain principles of power. Once a year we toured Shasta Dam, in private with my uncle. It would be summer, and we'd drive out along the winding road, rising up through scrubby chaparral and rounded foothills, rising, but never escaping the heat of the valley, all of us irritable and anxious to get there, where it would finally be cool. I loved my uncle for this, for taking us inside the dam on the hottest days, for sharing its interior secrets with us, for having the power to do so. But every year, when at last we'd round the bend in the road to the vista point, I would feel as unprepared as I had always been for the spectacle of it—the massive concrete arch (once the third-largest span of its kind in the world) that reaches up, up, up from the narrow river canyon, and behind it, the body of water so expansive it has carved nearly 400 miles of shoreline into the surrounding hills, and beyond even that, the single white cone of Mount Shasta, rising alone more than 10,000 feet from the flat floor of its wide mountain valley. And always, the shock of seeing it again, unchanged and ever imposing, would hit me, a visceral thing, and I'd make my father stop so I could look and look, and then I wouldn't want to leave, because secretly I found looking at the dam somehow more exciting than being inside it. Inside, there were miles and miles of dark, wet tunnels, ceaselessly humming, a separate world suspended in a dreary, changeless season unlike anything on earth.

My uncle was so proud of it all.

"Flood control!" he'd exclaim. "Hydroelectricity, jobs, sport, irrigation! Just think how many times this water will be used before they drink it in L.A."

My uncle considered this a miracle of progress, and I suppose that my father did too because he would nod, and my mother would murmur, "Very impressive," and my sister would shiver, complaining she was cold, while, clear-eyed and deliberate, I would count the cases of canned goods stacked along the tunnel walls, stockpiled against nuclear war in sufficient quantities, I knew even then, to support certain dam personnel and other important government officials, including my uncle, but not us.

Years later, I would find myself with my own young family at the base of a ninety-foot waterfall on the Olympic Peninsula. I'd have carried Joey, then nearly three and big for his age, all the way up the steep, two-mile trail, and now he was happily throwing rocks—the way they did—into the churning pool, but Sam was mesmerized by the falls themselves and could not be lured into their customary sport. Instead, raised as he'd been on the rubric of drought, he stared for a long time at the voluminous cascade of water, pierced by afternoon light from above, the glistening rock face and awesome height and depth of it, as he struggled, I suppose, to get his thoughts around its beauty and its consequence. Then he sighed and stepped back beside me, slipping one hand into mine.

"Mom," he announced a moment later, "they recycle that water, don't they? Mom?"

Some of the rooms inside Shasta Dam seemed always be to blazing with their own electric power, but darkness pressed in all around, and there was a pulsing and terrible roar—what my mother called "the sound of money"— which came, I knew, from the massive turbines and their furious spinning, and seemed powerful enough to suck you in and crush you, in an instant or a heartbeat, if you were careless, if you didn't hold tight to the railings, if you strayed beyond the yellow lines on the observation deck. I held tight, and tried not to think, either, about the force of all that water pressing up against the dam, which, no matter how much concrete my uncle said was in it, I imagined, as a child, to be subject to such freak chance occurrences as cracking or splitting apart.

I thought about that, the water crashing in around us. I thought about such things as pressure per square inch and nuclear attack, the bomb going off mid-air above us, a fatal flower, and then the wall of water flooding everything downstream, including where we lived, the whole house, and all the world as I'd ever known it. I knew that this was possible because, behind where we stood, entombed by concrete, the town where my grandparents met and married lay dead and entombed by the lake.

Once, when Joey was little, we went for a hike on Mount Palomar, taking the Weir Trail. That far south, even the mountains are dry and hot, and we were hoping that the water at the weir would be deep enough to play in. Joey had his friend, Wyler Weir, with him, and Wyler had picked the trail, which turned out to be more arduous than the boys had hoped, but with such unexpected bonuses as a three-foot rattlesnake, coiled in the dirt, and a meadow so densely packed with ladybugs that the grass itself looked to be on fire. But when Wyler took off among them, shrieking and flapping his arms to make them fly away, Joey turned and waited for me, his expression uncharacteristically grave. We walked along together for a little bit without saying anything. Then he, too, slipped his hand into mine.

"Mom," he said, after another small pause, "why do people build dams?"

Between my sons' two questions lies the whole history of this state, and though I long to have some decent answer to offer—if not to them, then at least to Patty, Sky, even my sister—I have never yet figured out how to mediate the distance between me, inside my uncle's dam, listening for the crash and roar of things, in that instant, flying apart, and the uneasy truce I have managed to make with the life that has turned out to be mine.

At the time Patty moved:

At the time Patty moved away from the house above the river down the street where I had spent so many hours that I had come to view it somehow as my own, I had no way of knowing her father's drinking had finally escalated to the point of intervention. Nor could I have foreseen that this would be the final straw for Patty's mother. Her father, I learned some years later, was checked into a clinic, while her mother simply—it is difficult to know this for a fact, but something clearly happened—checked out.

They had moved across town to a smaller wood-frame house, shaded by cottonwoods and fig trees, where Patty's mother waited out her shame, if shame was what it was, or maybe rage, with a studied rigor. Once or twice I went to visit them, but the house felt hollow to me, and when her mother knelt to check in on our play, the pressure of her sheer hose made great white blotches on her knees I understood to signify contagion. She fed us freshly baked cookies with frothy milk, and as soon as Patty's father was released from the clinic, she packed a small suitcase and left.

Hearing this, you must feel for Patty, who was in a certain sense forsaken. Her life, once a steady mirror of mine, had gone all topsy-turvy, with her parents in the balance, and even now I don't fully understand why her mother didn't take her when she went away, why she left her, instead, alone with a father who had returned from the clinic morose and self-contained. That was one time I really should have called her, as we went to different schools now and hardly ever saw each other. But since the day the bent old couple had moved in down the street—them, and their dogs that barked at kids—I had felt stunned by the unrelenting quality of my new loneliness, and anyway, in our house, the heavy, black rotary phone, hidden away in the hall, was a harbinger of mainly bad things: my grandmother falling and breaking her hip, my father staying late at work, my other grandmother, when she had died. If it rang, which wasn't often, the loud, clear sound of it was always startling, and we'd turn, almost imperceptibly, as my ever-vigilant mother would stop whatever she was doing, pause—and there would be this little frown between her eyebrows, a steely purse of lips, as she wiped both her hands on a cloth, or her hips—and move with steady, deliberate purpose to answer the phone.

What I mean is, in another sort of family I might have called Patty, chatted easily for hours, maintained the kind of friendship that meant, who knows, we could have been together that day at Oroville, playing down by the edge of the gathering water, or off among the oak trees, nowhere near the accident at all, or else we might have stayed home and gone to the movies. It could have happened that way, so that Patty, if only I had called her, would never have been blinded, and nothing would have turned out as it did. But I didn't, because the way we lived at our house, with an almost palpable dread of the world, we warded off our natural suspicions by folding clothes in neat, tight folds, maintaining regular hours, and never calling anyone except in an emergency. But sometimes, I'd overhear things—my mother and father whispering, my uncle passing on some news about Patty's father—and what I heard would only serve to bolster my conviction that, out in the world, dreaded things were bound to happen.

I missed Patty terribly, as if the very thing that had made me whole and right as a person had been suddenly and meanly wrested from me, but this did not prevent my taking a perverse kind of solace from my secret idea that Patty, at her new school, must be more miserable than me. I knew, from listening to my uncle, that Patty's father's job would be at risk if he didn't shape up soon, that there were money problems, that her mother was on the verge of what they called a "nervous breakdown." I imagined Patty pale and blotchy-faced from crying. I was convinced that her tennis shoes were soiled. And in more charitable moments, I fantasized about being reunited in high school, where, once again, I anticipated we would become inseparable. I did all this while pretending to read in the stuffed easy chair at the back of our living room, as if, by seeming to occupy myself there, I might somehow soothe the loss of Patty's constant companionship and presence; but though there was no way I could have known it then, this would be a wound that would never heal, festering and permanent as a scar.

Before the dams were built:

Before the dams were built in California, first they moved railroads and highways and bridges and, for a time, the rivers themselves. They leveled grades and blasted tunnels. They mowed down entire forests. They emptied out towns and dismantled their buildings, even as, elsewhere, they established new communities where workers could live. In the case of Shasta, construction included some roads, the entire town of Toyon, and a nine-and-a-half-mile-long conveyor belt, built to carry gravel, like just another river, all the way from Kutras Tract, in Redding, straight up the river canyon to the dam. Once completed, this conveyor belt operated twenty-four hours a day for years, delivering rock at a rate of 1,100 tons—the equivalent of a 44-car train—per hour. If you think about the men who worked on such projects—roads, or

bridges, or dams, or miles-long rivers of gravel—you may, like the men themselves, imagine the projects as markers along a whole continuum of progress.
But sometimes at dusk, when the long hard hold of a hot afternoon eases its
grip on the day and the shadows smudge together and the sky turns gray, it is
possible to imagine the men as merely men who once, long ago, faced the same
darkness and lurched in their bone-numbed fatigue through cold suppers toward sleep.

By the time I was a girl, Kutras Tract, once the hub of dam construction
work in town, had been reduced to a swampy little complex of apartments on
the river, a mangy putting green, and a rat-infested miniature golf course. The
apartments had a vague Tahitian theme, and I was maybe five or six when they
started being built in the reedy flatlands hollowed out on the riverbed by the
long-defunct gravel pit. That was in the fall, and I remember it because, just as
my father would take me to dam sites, he took me down to Kutras, where I was
expected to *oooh* and *ahh* my amazement—some of the apartments were built
on stilts in the water itself, hovering there like ungainly birds—and where a
ragged wind seemed always to blow off the river and chafe my bare knees.
Around that same time, the stately palm trees that lined the major crossroad
where we lived began, one by one, to disappear.

Then there was a terrible storm, the kind of storm we used to have all the
time in California, with howling wind, horizontal rain, and a sky as dark all
day as winter dusk. In my memory of those years, such storms were common
enough, but this one lasted for days, bleak and oppressive, and ominously
punctuated, on the outside, with the periodic rumbling of thunder and, on the
inside, with frequent testy outbursts from one or another of us. Normally, I
welcomed rain as a good excuse to stay inside and read, but this storm had
been going on so long we were all edgy and desperate for it to end. Then, I
don't know, suddenly my sister went completely quiet, the kind of quiet where
you stop everything to notice, and at first I couldn't find her, but when I did it
was worse, because she was kneeling at the back picture window, both hands
splayed on the glass itself, which was fogging up all around them.

Now this is where my memory gets mixed up with the palm trees, because
we also had a tree in our back yard, a huge, old walnut tree, from which, before
he went away, my uncle Ralph had helped us hang a swing, and which, in the
storm, had been wrenched a little from the earth. Looking out at it then, we
were alarmed to see it bent down at a precarious angle, its wet limbs waving
wildly about, and suddenly we were afraid we'd lose it. All that dreary after-

noon and late into the night, my sister knelt at our back window, tears streaming down her face, as our mother fretted behind. This is something about rivers and trees, and my mother and sister. Ralph was already gone, and the little swing was just a crooked wood plank on two fraying ropes, but a swing nonetheless, wide and strong enough for us to swoop on. And every autumn we'd collect the green husks of those walnuts, littered all over our yard, and store them in brown grocery bags until they'd finally ripen, and then we'd crack them in great piles before a roaring fire with the little metal mallet my mother used for cracking crabs and only recently confessed had been her father's, used for bones. I believe that my sister and I both loved that tree, just as we'd later both love the rivers we swam in, but that it was for her my parents intervened, despite my father's stern conviction that the tree should be destroyed, that it was dangerous—old and already weakened where its white bark curled over an earlier lateral rift. I'm not sure how it happened, but one day not long after the storm my other uncle appeared to help my father build a brace that would support the tree until it could grow strong again, and after that my mother and my sister beamed for days.

When the palm trees on the cross street started disappearing, no one did a single thing to stop them. I thought they were diseased. Knowing, as I did, that Redding was as far north as palms could grow, I thought, perhaps, it was just too cold that year. There'd been that storm, of course, and almost daily frost, even one or two flurries of snow. I didn't weep at any window, but yet I mourned the loss of those trees, which I had also loved, and then one day they reappeared at Kutras Tract.

Every child must struggle to adjust the world's seeming logic to her own private principles of order, and when those palms, which had grown straight and tall for perhaps a hundred years or more, were transplanted to the Tahitian Garden Luxury Apartments, they were bent askew and leaned at anxious angles in a weirdly tropical enclave on the banks of the Sacramento River, and it didn't make sense. I used to lie awake wondering how—and why—exactly they had moved those trees: what equipment had torn them from the earth, how were they transported through our city's streets, and at what hour? But what I never wondered was how—or why—they built the dam.

Most of those palm trees did not survive their transplanting to Kutras Tract, and today only a ragged handful remain, but thirty years earlier, other engineers had successfully moved more than 12 million tons of sand and gravel on the conveyor belt from Kutras Tract, in Redding, to the dam site in the mountains, nearly ten miles distant. Enough cement was transported—7.6 million barrels or 25,300 carloads—to fill a single train 215 miles long. Nights now, as we slide toward sleep, I imagine scooping handfuls of gravel from any one of the beds of the rivers that feed into Lake Shasta. The weight of one handful is leaden, leaden. I dream of palm trees toppling all around me.

∽

∽

∽

The thing with Patty's father:

The thing with Patty's father, AA notwithstanding, is that he kept on drinking after rehab, but never fell apart again, not in any way that you would notice, a controlled if heavy drinker who lived to vigorous old age, well into his nineties, with a liver the marvel of his doctors and the envy of his friends. Things resumed, nonetheless, without Patty's mother, somewhat as they'd been before, and once again the two engineers spent frequent evenings together, and sometimes my uncle would take me along, and then, as the grown-ups drank, Patty and I would watch TV and confide deep girlhood secrets over our favorite commercials—Jolly Green Giant, and the one where Mr. Clean swooshed out of his bottle to rescue that poor housewife from her work. Patty and I loved that one, the way he plopped her on the counter and danced around the dinette table with a mop until the entire kitchen sparkled with light, light, light. This was before Patty was blind. We were in love with the housewife's amazement and her subsequent ecstatic swoon into Mr. Clean's arms, a swoon that was somehow both sexual and chaste. It was during my anticipation of this very swoon that Patty told me one night about the patent leather shoes her father had promised to buy her for the first boy/girl party I had ever heard of. They were going to be slip-ons, with pointy toes and neat grosgrain bows.

We were twelve. I knew the boy who was giving the party, had known him for years—longer and better than Patty—and though at the time I had little use for boys, whom I found vaguely repulsive, I still checked the mail every day between then and the party and dreamed of the empire-waist dress my mother had seen in the store and said would be lovely for Christmas. I thought about this dress so intensely—its bodice, ruffled with delicate lace, its skirt, a loose drape of sheer robin's egg blue—that I never quite believed my invitation hadn't come. And I know I must have pestered my mother, because on the day of the party, though the holiday season was still weeks away, she offered to take me to buy it.

If you are a woman and if you ever had a mother, you will recognize this moment at once, for the dress was nothing as I had imagined, was instead a staid tailored affair, without a stitch of lace and not a dreamy blue at all, but a dark and practical navy, prominently featured in the child's special occasion section of Redding's family-owned department store, and as I stood there looking at it, despair rising hard in my chest to match the crushing disappointment of the day, I knew with a stunning finality that lace was for my sister, and that this other, dreary dress exemplified my mother's cardinal rule not to call attention to yourself, which I now also knew applied to me alone, and what I felt was between rage and panic. Desperately afraid I would begin to cry or throw a tantrum, I dragged my mother over to the pre-teen section, where the only empire-waist dress was a bonded polyester, with a dark beige bodice, stiff chocolate-brown skirt, and one flat row of cotton crochet lace that ran from the Peter Pan collar to the misshapen waist, from which two tiny darts rose in a rigid cone. It was an ugly dress, the fabric clammy and unpleasant on my skin, and I insisted that my mother buy it for me, and then I went home and cried myself to sleep.

When I woke up, Patty's father and my uncle were holding forth in the front room.

"It wasn't the whiskey," I heard her father say, "but the Bomb, you know, that did me in."

Then I drifted off again, dreaming of Patty in a blue dress dancing through tunnels that kept collapsing behind her.

Years later, when Patty was blind and I was at home for spring break, I went to visit her.

"You should go see Patty," my mother said. "She's putting on weight and looks pasty."

Patty, in fact, looked terrific to me, serene, and with a fullness to her that seemed incredibly sexy. Because she was blind I could stare without embarrassment at her breasts, which were round and lifted as she breathed. The scooped neck of her t-shirt showed off both their whiteness and some cleavage. Except for her breathing, Patty sat perfectly still. This stirred something in me, and I felt overwhelmed, I think, by the ease with which she inhabited her own body.

What I said was, "Your friendship meant so much to me when we were kids. I don't think I could have endured childhood without it."

Patty looked puzzled, her face going vague. Then she shrugged. "For me, it's all kind of a blur, back then. I guess we were friends. I don't really remember."

When she said that, I remembered with a jolt how thrilled I'd been to hear that she'd been blinded. It's not something I liked to think about, but I'd gotten such a buzz that night, imagining Patty in darkness forever. I knew I should be horrified and grieving. Instead, I kept closing my eyes and stumbling clumsily around my room. I remember that there was a sultriness to the air that night that made me feel, somehow, more alive than usual. I remember becoming aroused. I remember thinking it could have been me.

These days, uneasily cusped:

These days, uneasily cusped in the round middle part of my life, I have taken to thinking once again about rivers, while nights I have dreams of my sister in which we are interchangeable.

Above my desk I keep a photograph, now nearly five years old, of her sunning herself on a boulder on the far other side of the Salmon River. Tiny, she is reflected, also tiny, in the water below, the placid stretch of green river between rapids where we swam.

In one dream there is, again, a vast series of concrete chambers, like the tunnels of our dams, through which many people wander, and I lay my sleeping bag beside the sleeping bag of a man I suspect I desire. As in dreams, the situation is chaotic. There has been some disappointment with my children about bowling, and when I return to the sleeping bag I left to lie beside the man I want, he has zipped it together with others to accommodate new stray people and there isn't any room for me. In this instant, my rage and disappointment are so intense that I split off from myself to become my sister, which I understand because much later we go looking for her and find her shivering on a bus bench just outside the chamber. She is blue with cold, an icy surface to her translucent skin, and when she sees me I am myself flooded with relief— for who, in my life, ever came after me?—and begins to tell me a complicated story about riding the bus until, cold and afraid, she ran out of money. Returning to the chamber we are again one person, though I do not now remember where we sleep.

In other dreams, the houses where I'm living keep unfolding, and floodwaters threaten to rise.

I try to imagine:

These days I try to imagine what my life would be like if I had a river to walk to after dinner. It would be at dusk, when the very air itself turns soft and translucent and things in the world become suddenly opaque. Or maybe summer, just as the light shifts into its dying, acute angle.

I do not have a river to walk to after dinner, but I have the memory of rivers, which begins, almost always, with the quiet brush of water beneath the first conscious awareness of hearing, and because I understand that hearing is the last sense to go before death, I think about how it must be that we give ourselves over, in the act of memory, to something short only of grace, a haunted geography you can't ever touch but yet are keenly drawn to, and yes, as well to wonder if it isn't a little bit like death, this letting go, this giving over, this attentive listening to what begins in what precedes the quiet brush of water, the shadow sound of memory, almost palpable inside my own body, but more like language than a heartbeat or a pulse. Then the feel of air, cooler by the water, like a kiss that anoints all my skin.

In the absence of a river to walk to, I am trying very hard to be interested in the streets that I drive through, which are smelly with exhaust and cluttered with businesses whose names suggest proprietors from all over the world: dry cleaners, kosher meat stores, locksmiths, printers, drug stores, some Starbucks and Blockbusters, gyms with plate glass windows before which people work out adjacent to places of worship, and on one hilltop corner a refurbished luxury hotel rumored to reserve an entire floor for plastic surgery convalescents. When I first moved here, it all seemed such a visual assault that I'd force myself to concentrate on driving, just the car ahead, just the steering wheel in my hands, where the pedals were at my feet. It was as if I were wearing blinders. Also, my children were small.

Now, I try instead to imagine the swirl of these various establishments as the banks of a river, passing by me, as if I were adrift.

In my memory of rivers the visual image almost always comes last and begins with a quiet eddy near the shore I watch through a drape of cottonwood leaves, then a rapid, then a cut through a canyon, though every river is its own geography, and this, in turn, tells a different story.

~

~

~

The stubborn knot:

Before they contained the waters of the upper Sacramento, McCloud, and Pit Rivers behind Shasta Dam, first they sent surveyors up their channels. A surveyor is a different kind of man than the engineer who dreams the arc of the dam off the tips of his fingers on blue tissue paper. I suspect that Mike (Miranda's mother's father), who came all the way from Texas to do cement work on the dam (it was a job), would have made a good surveyor if he'd had the education and any breaks at all, for he had certain gift for triangulation, between him and his daughter and the world.

Along the channel of the upper Sacramento, rugged outcroppings of rocks form cliff-sized embankments, and the occasional beaches are strewn with small stones, rounded and smoothed by water. These same stones, along with scattered boulders, line the riverbed, and the river itself is a classic mixed river, in which long stretches of shallow riffs and deeper, calm waters are interrupted, here and there, by turbulent rapids. The water, fed by both snowmelt and natural springs, is frigid, made even colder now by the new Box Canyon Dam, and though I suspect you would like a story about a young surveyor, say, who, tromping up the riverbank, slips and breaks an ankle beside the icy water, where he finds himself trapped for three days during which he suffers from exposure and has visions of bears who approach him through the water and move on, what I know about instead is the shock of the water against my hot and dusty skin and the way my head constricts, diving in, and the hard rush of current against my vigorous breaststroke as I struggle toward the black rock that rises from the middle of the river, baking in the sun. I know, too, that between rock, water, and sun, there is an elemental grace that sustains me.

Mike made friends with one of the surveyors, who was later killed in a fall down the face of the dam, toward the river. One cold November morning, he slipped. And though I know this is a sad thing, one that even after more than half a century should make us reflect on the grief of the loss of a man who was somebody's son, instead I think about my own sons, their temperaments and habits. I believe that Sam would make a steady engineer and Joey a fearless surveyor. Along the riverbank thickets of blackberries, dense clumps of skunk cabbage, cedars, pine, oak, and some cottonwoods grow. I imagine Joey crashing through them while Sam hunches over a polished oak desk in an elegant office somewhere downriver, working out complicated equations.

Several other things I know: the story I have to tell grows out of this river, and the men whose idea it was to dam it have another story altogether that defines them. Also, Patty and Miranda are caught in the clash of these conflicting narratives, and the purpose of this story, the one I'm telling now, has never been to gratify our desire to resolve the paradox one way or another, but rather to untangle both sides of this stubborn knot to see if there isn't some other way of holding together the contradictory impulses between what lets us go and what contains us.

~
~
~

Shasta Dam:

Engineered to regulate floods, generate hydroelectric power, store surplus winter runoff, irrigate the Sacramento Valley, supply water for municipal and industrial use, and provide recreation, Shasta Dam remains today the monumental centerpiece of the Central Valley Project. A graceful, curved, gravity-type structure, it stands 602 feet high, three-quarters of a mile long, 30 feet thick at the crest and 540 at the base, and drains an area of 665 square miles to create a reservoir with a maximum depth of 512 feet and a total storage capacity of 4,552,000 acre-feet of water.

When California floods, so many rivers—the San Joaquin, the Feather, the Truckee, the American, the Russian—and countless streams and creeks cause grievous suffering, but farther north Shasta Dam routinely contains the drainage from three separate river systems, as if inexhaustible.

The house where I grew up above the Sacramento was on the hill side of the river, not far below the dam. From time to time, when the rains would come with such ferocity that the river would turn turbulent and brown and spread far into its floodplain on the other side, I'd watch from the back picture windows of our house and imagine something terrible—so much water that the floodplain would be overwhelmed by it and it would rise and rise up the hills on either side, like all the water in the world, first to our backyard, then to the steps of our porch, then finally submerging the house itself and threatening my family and me as we huddled on our roof to wait out the maelstrom, rain beating down on all of us. Maybe I imagined this because I could then imagine my father's broad hand on my hunched-over back, its warmth spreading through my drenched skin.

But of course this never happened, not the flood, and not my father's hand on my back, because the dam was our protection and what my uncle and Patty's father called progress.

～
　～
～

Residence time:

Today we know that when a river floods, just as when a fire flashes through a forest, a restorative process is at work on which everything—life itself—is balanced. The land of any floodplain lies waiting to be washed clean and replenished when water rises up and over it, rich with sediment and the water itself, which, as it slows over the face of that fallow plain, seeps down into the earth, down, and down, where natural systems have evolved to store it for long periods known as residence time. All water is mixed—some old, some new, some left over from last night's unexpected rain, some from a prior millennia or time—and of what we drink, for example, or spread on our lawns, or swim in, or wash our clothes with, on average, 10 percent will have fallen in the last year, another 20 percent in the last decade, and another 20 percent in the last century, and the rest of that water, a full 50 percent, will have fallen some time in the last 20 million years—old, old water.

But a river is both its water and its sediment, with the passage of the sediment through the watershed as crucial to the planet that sustains us as is the water itself. Sediment transport is largely determined by an equation determined by both the energy of the river and what it is carrying, and if you watch a river, any river, you see so little of what is really there, beneath the surface of the water, its sediment and bed load, part suspended in the water column, part dragged along the bottom, not, as you might imagine it, in any continuous tumble and roll, but in erratic starts and tops, short bursts of transport interspersed with long, long periods of inaction. A log being dragged along the bottom of a creek may hang itself up on a rock, or between two walls of a ravine, and maybe, before long, the steady friction of water will dislodge it, or maybe your sons will; or maybe, instead, your sons will use it for a dam, and it will be there many years, slowly decaying, shedding parts of itself, its vital nutrients, with each spring runoff, until finally it just breaks apart and disperses; or maybe a flood or heavy runoff will catch it violently up again. And in this way, the earth shifts and changes beneath us.

But as the water slows, so, too, does the sediment passing over the land, with erosion in the upper watershed a critical mechanism for fertilization in the lower valleys that works to create a complex biomass and turn lowland forests into the richest ecological systems in the world. The great Central Valley of California, for example, used to flood annually, water spreading out across it up and down the state, where it would lie for a long time, and slowly, slowly sink into the earth leaving its load behind, until, over the course of 150 million years, 40,000 vertical feet of sediment had accumulated. Now, in the course of little more than a century, we have put an end to landscape-shaping floods.

This was the dream of the engineers, the visionary men like my uncle, who, despite the delicate balance in which all things come down, finally, to the very slowness with which water moves through its system, have been working, instead, to move it more quickly. In the last hundred years alone (.0002 percent of our river history, Sam says), more than 1,000 dams and 6,000 miles of smooth river levees have been built in California, closing off all but one of the rivers and most major streams in a steady disconnection of water from its floodplains that we have celebrated wrongly as a miracle of progress and a triumph of our engineering models. We, who depend on old water, are turning it new.

Except for dams.

For men, like my uncle, and their dreamy fingers, thought only of water—water is life—and did not consider the problem of sediment.

It's just another paradox, they say.

For while a dam, any dam, hugely increases the residence time of its water, it also traps sediment high at the head of its reservoir, just where the river comes in, making it biologically unavailable downstream and slowly starving the water.

And of course, it is also the case that if you remove the heart from the body—everyone knows this—both die.

Downstream, in our leached-out and ever-depleted world, we consider what we know now about what will be required to repair the ecosystem, and though it is a simple project, really—just take down the dams, just poke a few holes in the levees—we are not prepared to deal with the consequence or opposition. In our minds, it is a fecund image, water spreading out and sitting on the land, where, warming, it begins to grow such resplendent organisms as plankton, zooplankton, phytoplankton, regenerating biomass and providing, first, insects with food, then fish, then birds, and so on up the food chain. We can imagine this because we have seen it happen and know that just one breach on a Cosumnes River levee in Northern California yielded forty-foot cottonwoods in a span of fifteen years. We think about a span of fifteen years, we think about our gardens, we think about the farmers, and what we do: we entertain the possibility of enlarging Shasta Dam.

Sam could do the numbers. He could do them in his head. He would turn away ever so slightly, perhaps to hide a smile or his satisfaction, and announce: raising Shasta Dam 6 feet, as some have proposed, would collect just enough extra water to replace the water recent legislation has required as a giveback from the Sacramento Basin to the Trinity River watershed, from which it has been coming and where salmon also are endangered; raising it, instead, 200 feet, as others have proposed, would create a huge dam to rival the Ah Pah. We think about that dam and we don't know what to think. We think about moving our towns and our railroads, our bridges and freeways all over again.

I think about my mother-in-law, who took one look at Shasta and said, "But where did they put all the dirt."

We think about the hole she imagined, and it gets mixed up somehow with the holes our fathers dug in our backyards. And then we think about the prime trout-fishing stretches along the McCloud River, what remains of the sacred lands of indigenous peoples, the places where we learned to swim. We think about all that, but in our hearts we are still torn because we also know that such a dam would provide enough additional fresh water to periodically flush out the delta with manmade floods.

We keep hoping we can have it both ways. For of course not even we can consider the possibility that the dam should never have been built, that California and its salmon should have remained as they were when my grandparents settled in the foothills, that this would be a different kind of progress. We know Utah and Wyoming. We are not fools.

~
 ~
~

If you teach creative writing:

If you teach creative writing long enough, you will hear such family stories, those of immigrants from all over the world, both rich and poor, and the girl from Nebraska who grew up between cornfields (*who cares anymore about cornfields?* she says), and the Jews, and the Native Americans, and the woman whose Mexican father ran off with her Filipino mother and left her to raise three young siblings alone, all doctors and lawyers now. You teach creative writing long enough, you will know that your own power to make anything up is so eclipsed by what has really happened as to render the whole charade of invention both hapless and futile. More and more you grow committed to the ritual of storytelling as a means of leaving marks in the world. You cup your hand to your young son's chin and know that in another month or day it will no longer be the same chin, for it will jut at a new angle, or fold more firmly into its own new growing sense of self. And what do you do? You write: *you cup your hand to your young son's chin,* and you imagine that in this way some things will be sustained.

Imagine an unexpected petroglyph on a far desert wall. Maybe you are hiking miles and miles off any trail you know. Maybe you've just driven to the end of some rough dirt road, and then taken off, by foot, on nothing much more than a whim. Maybe you're floating a river. It, your petroglyph, is faded nearly past recognition, a bare smudge of red or black against the ocher stone, and yet it stops you in your tracks, this ancient record of someone else's passing.

It is the record of our passing that makes our stories form their uneven words and sentences in our heads and mouths, in the curves of our tongues. A dam is the curve of your tongue. You lap water with it. The water curls itself around your whole body. This is the unending curl of your longing, which is not quite desire. Desire is story itself.

I have written many times about my mother's mother, raised in a Catholic boarding school as the sole surviving child of a widowed tailor whose last advice to her was to become a doctor so as not to be beholden to a man, any man. I know and have richly imagined her story, how she took the train from Baltimore, going west, for adventure, how she planned to study medicine at Cal, how, climbing the stairs to the office, she was startled by a bell that signaled the end of an instruction period. My grandmother, who lost her mother to the flu when she was very young and had been sent for proper rearing to the nuns, had grown up, as a consequence, largely unacquainted with such common, everyday sights as her own body naked or young men rushing down a stairwell toward freedom. Now, she dropped her handkerchief, and when no one gave it back, took off across the bay for Stanford, where she became, instead, a nurse, and where her life, as it played out in the aftermath of this decision, was marked by certain social successes and the self-inflicted death of her first son that haunts us still half a century later.

Also, I imagine Kennett, the copper mining town submerged beneath the lake behind the dam, where all four of my grandparents—two doctors, two nurses—met and married, and worked side-by-side, and kept house together, and bore their first children and disappointments.

These stories I have told before and will tell again, each time different, each the same, each layered by my previous failure to in any way fix the mark of their passing. And though I know it does not change things if I claim that they are true, and though I also understand that this is language, which never fixed or held anything stable, I don't really care anymore. You cup your son's chin in your hand, and what you come away with is just nothing, just air, just the already fading memory of the jut of the jaw, like the memory of the undersound of rivers. It will always be just air, despite what you just touched, just as he was always once an infant at your breast.

If you teach creative writing long enough, you will teach your students two things about stories: there are some you tell over and over and over, and some you never can tell, and both are the ones sustain that you.

⁓
⁓
⁓

In the history of any family:

In the history of any family, you have your master narratives, the stories that, through repetition, shape and give meaning to what happened. Like the photographer's fixative, they stabilize the fluid and ever-shifting boundaries of events, all that potential chaos, and allow the mother to say to the daughter *don't lie, your nose is growing*. What is possible to tell then, within the terms set by the family, is strictly circumscribed, and if you try to renegotiate these terms, what you will suffer will range from them looking at you in a certain way to them not looking at you at all. It is a calculated risk. As the daughter, you gaze deep into the mother's eyes. In your head you form the thought *mama I would never mean to hurt you*. You turn your words and the risk over and over, and then you do, as she taught you, what you have to do.

At times the proportions seem all off. What seems important to others in your family is incidental, insignificant to you, a passing comment, a deeply embedded clause in the extensive and complex grammar of an entire life.

When I discovered, for example, that my mother had once attended a meeting of the Communist Party, I found the idea so utterly romantic that I wanted to tell everyone we knew, close friends and random acquaintances alike, I wanted everyone to know—and not forget—that we had a secret and radical past. I imagined myself brandishing red flags at candlelight Vietnam vigils. I swear I was ready to sign up myself. No doubt I further imagined that my mother, on this evening, fell hopelessly in love with a black-haired wild-spoken boy who kept her up all night drinking coffee and discussing world events but never touched her, not even her hand or a loose strand of hair or her shoulder as he helped with her coat. Naturally, my reaction distressed my mother, for in her own imagination what she had once explained—both to herself and others—as a petty indiscretion or natural adolescent curiosity, had been magnified over the years to something if not traitorous, then shameful.

Despite a congenital heart murmur, my father had fought in the war. My mother, who outranked him, served her duty in a psych ward down South. When it was over, the young man I imagined lost his job and his entire family over what he said to my mother that night drinking coffee, and my mother, twenty years later, was still stunned by how close she'd come to ruin.

"Don't," she shushed me. "It was a silly meeting and I didn't even stay. Please don't say anything. It's in the past."

For the longest time I did keep her secret. Then, I don't know, I would mention it, in passing, at a party or over some drinks *yeah my mom was almost a Red, she went to meetings*, like it really was nothing, neither one way nor the other, just a moment when her private life crossed history without leaving any mark. In my own way, I think I was bragging about it, even as I tried to diminish her for the fear—the actual, visceral fear—she had harbored over the years. I'd laugh, and be proud and ashamed all at once.

Now that I have my own family, I want to call my mother on the telephone and tell her, rational or not, I don't blame her anymore. This is between a mother and her children. You look at them and you think about the grave risk you have put them in just by bringing them into this world. Beyond that, the possibility that anything bad should ever truly happen to them makes you animal-like, blank-minded, all raw dread and fury. In the awful wake of their complete dependence we all attempt to reconstruct our past.

Other family stories:

Other family stories, usually older ones, achieve, through repetition, the status of legend. These are the stories no one ever questions, as there is something so pleasurable and reassuring in the telling of them that it is a little like the familiar cadence of a well-loved childhood tune: *I've been working on the railroad/when the earthquake ended, one grandmother said to the other, my that was exciting, I wish that would happen over again.*

Try this, for example: my mother's father once almost bought Carmel Point for $2,000, but decided instead on the calmer interior of the Monterey Bay, near the slough and power plant at Moss Landing. In time, he'd retire to this land—protected wetlands now—settling down in one of two houses he had built, the both of them connected by a single glass-roofed patio and sheltered from the wind on the lee side of humped eucalyptus-covered dunes. My aunt would live in the other house, where, many years later, I would find a garbage bag of California Indian baskets and begin to piece together some parts of the family story that did not make it into our master narrative. As for my grandfather, aside from the matter of his poor investment judgment, it would not be until now that I would stop to wonder why exactly he would choose to move so far out of the world—maybe out of the wind, yes, but also without even a view of the water, the sunset.

At a recent family gathering we read aloud from his memoirs. It was late, after a substantial meal that included a bottle or two of good wine, and each of us chose from among our favorite stories. In retrospect, I have remained as interested in our selection process—*how did we each decide which story was our favorite?*—as I have always been in the stories themselves, which are so well known to me that they are like the very tissue of my body, inextricable from who I am, and yet I can only remember what the women read. My husband was sleeping. And my father? No doubt he picked a mechanical section on early cars, the Hupmobile that my grandfather loved, but honestly I do not know. I have no memory of his voice that night. Perhaps he, too, dozed off early.

But as clearly as if they were reading now, in this room with me as I write this, I can hear the voices of my mother, my sister, who began with the story of an early camping trip my grandfather had taken to Big Sur. Now, the better part of a century later, I think *what did California look like then, name the animals, plant smells, the rocks.* But my grandfather, a boy at the time of this adventure, says only, in passing, that it was more rugged than he had expected and that, had his mother known how treacherous the terrain was going to be, she wouldn't have allowed them to go.

If you have never been to the central coast of California, never stood on a rock ledge high above the pounding surf, never reached behind you to touch the very edge of this unstable continent, you will not be able, truly, to imagine, my grandfather, thirteen or fourteen years old, lumbering along this precipice in a clumsy two-axle wagon, but I have. And I can imagine it well, for the better part of a century later, this is what my sister would say to me on the occasion of my first son's birth: "*Motorcycles,*" she said. She said it softly. Then she kissed me. "*Sky diving, rock climbing, hang gliding.*"

As my grandfather was lumbering in his wagon, he had, for companions, a friend and a ten-year-old brother, boys alone at the edge of the world. They camped their first night out along the mouth of the Carmel River—sweet, sweet river and trees. In the late afternoon, they walked barefoot down the river to the beach, where they pried a dozen or so abalones from the rocks and boiled them, like clams, in a big pot to produce what my grandfather describes as an "inedible white substance, very rubbery, and tougher than the hardtack that formed the bulk of [their] diet that week."

Much of the rest of this entry dwells on their ravenous hunger.

My mother selected a story that night she claimed had always been his favorite, a story he enjoyed telling, she said, when he was red-faced from port, or
just one more time over Thanksgiving dinner, or tucking her into her bed.
This was a medical story that described, in some detail, her father's efforts to
save the life of a young boy whose lingering fever did not respond to conven-
tional treatments. Each day my grandfather visited the house, for the family
could not afford hospital bills, and the boy's bright eyes pleaded helplessly with
him; but nothing my grandfather tried did any good, and the patient began to
lose ground. It was 1926. My grandfather became alarmed that the boy, of
whom he had grown fond, would die, and he stayed up all one night ponder-
ing the problem before deciding, in the morning, to do a blood transfusion,
from the mother to the boy—the first of its kind on the Monterey Peninsula,
and a risky procedure in any event.

Reading from his memoirs that night, my mother's eyes filled with tears
and she had to stop briefly. "My father loved this story," she explained. "He always said it was so hard, as a doctor, to know the difference between God's
work and one's own, but that this one time, he was certain he alone had saved a
life."

My sister and I exchanged glances, for we have long understood how lucky
he was not to have killed them both. My grandfather reasoned that the boy
would benefit from the mother's antibodies, and I don't know. Each of the
three transfusions he performed with crude equipment "borrowed" from the
hospital supply room was flawed in some frightful manner—the syringes
clogged up, the boy collapsed from an air bubble, the mother became hysteri-
cal and had to be sedated—but in a matter of days, the boy's fever dropped,
and he went on to make a complete recovery, growing to manhood and raising
his own robust family.

Based on the success of this procedure, my grandfather later injected 20 cc's
of maternal blood directly through the anterior fontanelle and into the longi-
tudinal sinus of the brain of a failing eighteen-month-old infant, raised on
sweetened milk. A fat, happy baby, but with little ability to fight off resistance,
this child, too, recovered completely.

My sister chose another story, about the night in Kennett my grandfather
disappeared into the back room with some brandy, cocainized his toes, and
cut them off—three whole middle toes at once, because there wasn't any point

in taking just the corns, which would grow back more painful than ever—clean as a whistle. Then he started hollering.

"Nurse," he bellowed, "I seem to have forgotten my cauterizer."

And the nurse, who would, in time, become his wife and my mother's mother, just stood in the doorway and laughed.

As for me, I read about the Indians. I read to where he wrote about their weeping. I read to where he wrote that they were weeping because they did not know who would bury the last Indian. When I finished there was silence, and I knew I'd chosen badly. This was not a master narrative. They looked at me that way, and we read on.

~
~
~

Before you are a parent, and after:

In my family, the most powerful story is the one we never tell, the unspoken master narrative that continues after more than half a century to shape our lives, the one that if we spoke it would tear apart our lives, exposing nerves like the ones in Sam's broken teeth, and who could say how that would change things, even now. I was always such a good girl, all up until I turned bad—turned against the war, turned to smoking cigarettes, turned to writing, turned to predicting the end of nature when I was young enough to be able to conceive it.

"Don't buy oil," I warned my father. "Oil's running out," not knowing then, as we all do now, it is as likely to burn us up first, a slow roast.

Today Sam tells me we have eighty years of fossil fuel left. The young can think like that. They can look into the future, which, when they find it empty, may dispirit them, but they will persevere. I see this all over again in the lives of my students, who, coming up short on their share of history, nonetheless plan their lives and press onward.

This is the difference between before you are a parent and after. When I was young I counted myself lucky enough just to be alive, and in the long years that followed the Cuban Missile Crisis, developed a nighttime ritual where I'd go out to our back yard and stare deep into the black sky, pierced by many distant stars, from which I believed any minute missiles might rain down. We had a fallout shelter, but both of my parents were public employees with civil defense deployments. I knew the routine—the *long/short long/short* sirens, the duck and cover, the bus ride home. But what I couldn't get my mind around was what my sister and I were supposed to do alone in our cellar, waiting the war out. So I forced myself to brave my fear of darkness and hobos (who might, at any minute, wander up from the railroad tracks below), and went out every night into the world to practice a little magic thinking—*perhaps,* I always told myself, *for the very last time that night*—on the awesome wonder of it all, as well as my own haunting awareness that I had been born to the exact historical moment in which I might bear witness to the world before we blew it up: *poof, were we gone yet, was it over?* I counted the years until the Chinese got the bomb. I thought if I could make it until high school, maybe college, maybe even graduation, I'd have lived a full and satisfying life.

Then, suddenly, a quarter century was gone, and holding my newborn first son in my arms, I knew as I had never known before the inconsolable sorrow of the end of everything.

I don't know what I believe anymore. I am just as terrified of war as I have ever been, but you hear, too, about the ozone layer disappearing, and coming plagues, and terrorism, and populations doubling twice over, and you watch your children sleeping, and you think what you would do to keep them safe. It is one thing to dread your own mortality, and something altogether different to know you might be helpless before your children's suffering. So what you do, you steel yourself against it and look with a clear eye for the first time to the future, and you think *this is not just someone else's doing anymore,* and you kiss your children in their sleep, and you tell yourself that whatever else you know, the one true thing you know now is that the single surest way to tempt fate against you is to turn your eyes away and cower from it.

After they left Kennett:

After they left Kennett, my mother's family moved to Monterey, to a house on Franklin Street, not far from the central district, a white wood-frame Victorian house with porches on three sides, two stories, and a vegetable garden out back. This is the house where my mother was raised, the last child in the family, a girl with a wild streak, and though she used to point it out to me when, in town for a visit, we'd drive by on our way to the wharf or the tidepools, I never paid much attention, for, since 1962 and my startling realization that our days on earth were numbered, I was having trouble, also, conceiving of the past.

Then, years later, I would go there again with my own young family, staying so close to Franklin Street that, once I had confirmed the address with my mother, Sam and I would walk there after dinner. We just strolled up the street and there we were. It was, as I remembered evenings often being in Monterey, cool and damp with fog, clumps of gray mist that gathered in low tree branches, and quiet, like a dream, but with every now and then the bellow of a foghorn and, as always at that hour, the mourning doves: *whoo, whoo, whoo.*

I had always imagined the house would be bigger, as my grandfather had been a large man, with capacious appetites and a lap that used to dwarf me when I snuggled into it. But this house Sam and I had discovered, this peeling white-frame house, was at best midsized, and the porches on which my grandmother had doled out her Depression-era lunches, were not, as I had conceived them, expansive and gracious, but tiny landings on which any more than two people would feel crowded—where did the jobless men eat? And inside the house, was it crowded there too? Were they all over each other in small dark rooms?

After a while Sam and I stopped prowling around and settled down on the front steps for a chat. I put my arm around his slender shoulders and he nuzzled up against me, a bittersweet moment. His hair, I remember, smelled salty, and his small body felt warm against my own, as I sifted through my stock of well-worn stories and decided on the famous lunches in the Great Depression.

"Right here on this porch," I finally said, "they gave out lunch to homeless people every single day. Your grandmother—she was just about your age—helped her mother, the way you help me. There were sandwiches and lemonade, and sometimes, big baskets of overripe fruit."

I paused and thought about the men eating apples on that porch, hunkered down on the steps, spitting seeds. However many times I had heard or told this story—lunch served promptly each day at noon—I had never really considered the actual men—were some of them women?—before. My grandmother made them wash up with the garden house, take off their hats. She gave them a chance to say grace.

Then I told Sam about how his grandmother had once thrown a knife across the table at her sister, chased her neighbor with a pitchfork, stolen bootleg whiskey from the basement. I said she was a wild thing, a little bit like him, a girlish rebel, and as I told him this, as he giggled, as we thought about his grandmother chasing the girl next door with a pitchfork, I thought for the first time about all that anger. I thought *why was my mother so unhappy as a girl?* I thought about the story no one ever tells. And then I thought *when did they first know that my uncle was sick?*

About my mother's brother:

This is what I know about my mother's brother, who would have been the eldest of my uncles, a tall one with dark eyes, heavy brow, and a tendency, which I see now emerging in Sam, to slouch: that he was the first one born in Kennett, a sometimes brilliant boy and gentle brooder, that he shared a close—some say unnaturally close—bond with my mother, and that he killed himself one summer afternoon while the others were away at the movie matinee. He used his mother's nacre-butted handgun in an upstairs bedroom, and he shot himself in the head.

Also this: in all the time that I was growing up, his name was never spoken in our house.

How do I know what I know about this?

Along the back of her dresser in Redding, in a row of wood boxes my father made in high school, my mother keeps a gold bracelet, heavy with charms she's collected all her life to commemorate cherished memories. As a girl, I loved to play with it, examining its miniature treasures and dreaming of my mother as MVP in hockey, or a decorated sergeant, or a Berkeley coed, until one day when I was maybe nine or ten, I found a hidden signet ring that wasn't on the bracelet.

"Mama," I cried, slipping it onto my finger and holding my hand out to admire it. "It's beautiful, Mama," I cried. "Put this one on your bracelet, oh please."

My mother, who was folding clothes on the bed, looked suddenly startled, and there was something quite unpleasant in her voice, though all she said, a bit sharply, was to put it back where I had found it. But of course, as a child, I was curious and wouldn't let it go.

So this is one more fact I know about my uncle: once, when my father was a boy and visiting in Monterey, something happened between him and my uncle, no one really knows, but a bitterness persisted to this day.

"Your father," my mother said, "you know how sensitive he's always been. They'd lost their money. They were living with some distant relatives, sharing only one room." Now she looked sad, but she kept on folding clothes, a little grimly. "Oh, I don't know what happened," she said. "I thought he idolized my brother—everybody did—but they went out for ice cream one day, or maybe the movies, and when they came back, your father was upset." *What did my uncle say or do?* The ring was much too large and kept slipping from its own weight against my other fingers. My mother flapped a t-shirt out and finished it quickly with three deft folds. "Oh what does it matter?" she said. "Your father's feelings were hurt, and he's never gotten over it is all." An instant later, she had me in her arms and I don't think she was crying but her voice was high and tight. "I loved your uncle very much," she said. "He'd have never hurt an animal. I can't believe he meant to hurt your father."

Years later, in the attic I found a packet of letters my uncle had written to my mother from—what, school?—surely not the hospital, possibly camp. I remember that they were poorly spelled, and that this surprised me because my mother had always insisted, above all, on his brilliance. I also remember a cartoon he'd drawn for her: Panel 1, a happy round-tummied girl soaring on a plank swing high above a tree; Panel 2, the same round girl, all akimbo on the ground, looking surprised and unhappy as two halves of broken swing flap about her. Underneath, the caption, in my uncle's hand, reads: *little bitty swing, great big you.*

Where, then, between his humor, his affection, and his intellect did the fury of his illness first make itself apparent? Did another boy emerge that afternoon and say, or do, something truly terrible to my father? To my mother, was he unpredictably loving, then cruel, and who can remember now, half a century later? Who really could not bear the sight of his signet ring, or the cool distant sound of his name in our house?

For years, I never really wondered about any of this, accepting my mother's explanations—that he was too finely tuned, that history itself had unstrung him—as adequate. His parents had, in fact, exhibited the poor judgment of sending him off to Germany between the two wars for a "rest cure," and I understand that there were terrible scenes after he got back, some on the back porch, among the transients. To me, the story my own mother told—still tells—about her older brother made a certain, if romantic, kind of sense. It was the '60s after all, and we were keen on seeing madness as a rational response to a world gone wrong around us.

Today, all that remains of this uncle's memory is a handful of photos and a bright yellow, duck-shaped saki decanter he brought back from Germany as a gift for my mother. For years, I kept it on display and thought, perhaps, I'd use it, though I've long since lost its porcelain cups and tiny stopper, and all trace of that kind of nostalgia.

For of course I have no way of knowing what it must have been like for the five of them in that white frame house, not so large as I'd once imagined, as my uncle began his inexorable slide into madness—*what must he have said, or done, to my father?*—mixed with the few lucid times my mother recalls, the times to which he could not hold, despite his own mother's rage to order, his father's clinical determination, his little sister's confusion and love.

In retrospect, I think, also, about my own father, and how we managed all those years to get our mouths around the sadness of his life—that he had lost his father, that he shared his boyhood bedroom with his mother and his brother, that he was sensitive and had his feelings hurt. These are stories we know how to tell, for they explain certain things about the way he is, console us in his distance, and prove our mother's love and compassion for him.

You think I have no decent human feeling, that there is nothing I won't say, no story I won't tell, no person I love too much to narrate. But I grew up with a mother, a sister, and a father—three women to one man—and his were the stories we told among ourselves. If it takes me twenty years to wonder why, to ask where we can locate ourselves in this writing, to realize that wherever that is, or which of the precious few stories we still have as our own I might choose, it will inevitably tell us something about loss, is that so terribly wrong?

Of course Mom was always Mom, the one who chased her neighbor with a pitchfork, was MVP in hockey, and hid her brother's signet ring in a clump of cotton batting. This is the extent of what we know about her. I think about that now. I turn her silence over and wonder, as I never have before, what it must have been like the first time they committed her brilliant older brother to a mental institution. In his absence, in that house, how did they move and speak? Were they somber and ashamed, or did they maintain, instead, some bright and shiny pretense of happy normalcy? Did they believe he'd get well?

Once they took my mother for a visit. "I was shocked," she told me. "His hair was long, over his shoulders, and his eyes were so vacant, just empty. I hardly recognized him. He looked crazy."

It is true, too, about the lunches.

"They'd come to the house begging for money," my grandmother told me, "but if you gave it to them, they just used it to get drunk. So we fed them instead. Everyone knew to do that."

On the porch in Monterey that night, Sam nodded. "Just like with the homeless people in L.A."

At the time, my mother must have been, like him, eight, or maybe nine, serving cheese sandwiches to men like the man who lives on the freeway exit I take to school. He is a large man, beginning to bald, with what remains of his hair matted and long. The top of his head, his whole face, back, and chest—for he almost never wears shirts—is baked to a tough, adobe red. Sometimes in shoes, sometimes barefoot, he shuffles up and down the side of the exit ramp, ranting to himself and occasionally peering into cars. Even in my own car, with the windows rolled up, and as familiar as I have become with his wild eyes, aimless wandering, and undecipherable raving, this man frightens me. Years ago, when he first appeared, I used to think *someone help this man*. Now I think *get him out of my sight*.

And I think about my mother, at the age of nine or ten, pouring lemonade for men just like him. Then I think: or does he more closely resemble her beloved older brother?

Upstairs, from a tiny bedroom window, after he'd come home from his final hospital stay, my uncle used to watch his little sister playing hostess to men with their hats in their laps. As I have imagined it, sometimes he'd come down to eat with them. I imagine the high gray sky, the shuffling of men's feet in boots. I imagine my uncle as, taking my mother on his lap like a hat and holding her there, he buries his face in her hair and mumbles on about such eternal topics as art, or poetry, or the hot wet loins of a woman, the coming end of the world.

You can make a fiction of your uncle's suicide. You can turn his suffering into an embedded clause in someone else's story. You can ravage everything about his memory that you can think of. You can do all this as many times as you can bear your own duplicity, and then one day you cannot do it anymore.

I had planned to make the gun go off just as my mother brought food out to the men who were waiting, as they did every day, on what I now know is a tiny porch at the back of the Franklin Street house. I'd thought I'd go for drama this time, something wrenching. But I haven't tried to write this one particular story since my own first son was born, and I don't know. Perhaps I once believed that story might release us from what had happened in my family many years before, but I have since learned that there are ways of speaking, just as there are of being silent, that continue to inscribe us in the power of our myths.

Shh. *Who is speaking?* This isn't fiction anymore, this is true. One summer night my son and I sat on the steps of the house where my uncle shot himself more than fifty years before when my mother herself was just a girl, not yet fully formed. It happens that quickly and that absolutely. You hold your new-born son in your arms, and then a few years later you hold his small hand in your own and squeeze it, as your mother taught you as her mother taught her, three times to signify *I love you,* and when he squeezes back three times you think for the first time about your mother's mother who lost her firstborn son to a illness for which she could not help but blame herself. Knowing this, you know too that she never stopped talking about it, not until she died, that her last words were about him *blood on the mirror after all these years* the terrible loss of her only son, who was once a cooing newborn in her arms. Bereft of even words in this moment, you listen to a mourning dove *whoo, whoo, whoo* from the eaves. You glance toward it, toward the tiny upstairs windows, and you do not even try to tell your son why you are crying.

⌇
⌇
⌇

Of my two grandmothers:

Of my two grandmothers the one whose story I have never told, nor even yet imagined, is that of my father's mother, the eldest of eight children born to an Irish prospector and his mail-order bride, who died before my grandmother was ten. The miner was a drunk, but I lied about the mail-order part, since all I really know is that she came from somewhere and died young. Did she have a first name, this woman who gave birth to my father's mother and her siblings before disappearing forever from this earth?

My sister and I once looked for her grave in the quaint gold country town northeast of Sacramento, where she died. The cemetery, old by Western standards, lies on the crest of a hill, with thick-trunked pines and arching valley oaks. It was cold, with a bitter, steel-edged sky and some scattered flakes of snow drifting about. Above one Vietnam-era grave, a mobile of model airplanes spun from the split branch of a digger pine. Nearby, a high school cheerleader raised her pom-poms high in the photo where she beamed from beneath plexiglass set in her tombstone, the tears of weeping angels carved in the stone around her. Ishi, the last wild Indian, wandered out of those same hills, and I wonder how many tens of thousands of his people also lie nearby as namelessly as my own great-grandmother. For though we searched a long time among the last century's graves, none bore her name, and it is impossible ever to know now if the miner was too drunk or just too poor to leave any mark of her passing.

My father's mother raised a gaggle of small siblings until the next one could take over; then she, too, went off to nursing school so as not to be beholden— ever—to a man. There, she and my mother's mother would soon become close friends and roommates, riding out the earthquake in their dormitory window, their long skirts billowing around them as the city, below, swayed, bucked, and collapsed.

"My that was exciting," one said when it was over. "I wish that would happen over again."

But then the city started burning, a raging inferno that lasted for days, and as my grandmothers were called, first to evacuate the hospital, and then to tend patients in Golden Gate Park, they saw enough of human suffering to last them their whole lives.

Kennett was a job, with its small typhus outbreak and daily mining accidents—rock fragments in eyes, twisted shoulders, crushed bones—and always, it would seem later, sick and dying Indians, especially children. But that would be later. At first, there was some small adventure involved, and also, my one grandmother—my father's mother—had begun, I suspect, to long for the mountains of home. And so the two young nurses, in time, moved farther north, to the copper-mining town where they would meet the men they married and live for many years, all four of them together in the hospital housing annex.

Look, I am considerably older now than they were when they met. I have my own history of love and disappointment. I know what I know. And perhaps it is true, after all, that opposites, like magnetic poles, attract, for in the case of my grandparents, the two well-bred Easterners (my father's father was recently arrived, in a black hat, from New York) chose the other two, the raw-edged Californians. Even so, it never quite works out right in my head, not the way it is supposed to, not the way we tell it. For in the end, what remains are photographs, yellowing and fixed, and though I know my father's father as a thin-boned man, with delicate feet, I continue to be struck by the fact that, in those photographs, it is always, instead, my mother's father and my father's mother tromping off together for a hunt, Western-style bandannas loosely knotted at their necks, rifles slung across their shoulders, keen-eyed, even now, across the better part of a cruel and complex century.

My uncle was born during a terrible snowstorm. Underneath the white drapes of the hospital room, my father's mother's fingers turned blue from the cold, and when she heard the infant's cry, she tucked his steaming body to her breast where he sucked, a tiny brand of heat.

This was the engineer uncle, the one with blunt fingers and blue tissue paper and, these days, a parrot who sits on his shoulder. My father would not even be conceived for at least another decade. Between them I imagine a third, not an engineer but a surveyor, someone who tromped up riverbeds and lived off the ragged edges of his brother's dreams.

~
~
~

If he were to have a name:

If he were to have a name, this imaginary uncle, it would be Ralph, and Ralph would have a big head, bearded and shaggy, though I also remember him, paradoxically, as a small and muscular man, deep into middle age who, to my mother's everlasting disapproval, insisted on wearing heavy work boots even at formal holiday dinners. In his green Can't-Bust-'Ems and red flannel shirt, he insisted to the day he joined the Peace Corps that the bear in the river was real.

"If the break had been clean," he would say, "I'd have splinted my own leg and walked out. But you make it sound like I sat in that water for three days, as good as dead."

He was drinking Scotch. My mother, hands greasy with turkey fat and onion, called from the kitchen, "Ralph, that's just nonsense, stop."

It would be years before I knew the facts of hypothermia—how it can first confuse, and then kill you—alarming information I picked up on an ill-fated college backpacking trip, when it snowed and we didn't have tents. These days, what with our all high-tech fabrics and book knowledge, we don't have to worry so much about that sort of thing, but back then, as the snow kept on falling—tiny, icy crystals—through the night, we started out cold, then scared, then, at four in the morning, we packed up and began the hike down, shivering and numb-toed and afraid. Because we knew the first sign of mortal danger was mental disorienation, we kept asking each other who the president was and how many years before the new millennium. Then, at dawn, after we'd achieved some lower, warmer elevation and could see our faces, and they were pink, I told about my uncle, how he'd fallen in the riverbed surveying for the dam and shattered all the small bones in his ankle, how he'd waited there for three days (and it was November, and raining), and how, at the end, the bear came.

It was a golden bear, that bear, maybe the last of its kind, with sleek, thick fur and a dark, rough tongue. The gold-tipped ends of the bears' pelts made them gleam in certain lights, as if the fur took in the light itself and let it off again, bright and shimmering, but the day the bear came to my uncle was gray and rainy, with dusk dropping hard, like a fish, and though the bear was gleaming, this could not have been caused by any natural light. At first the shining bear was uninterested in my uncle, for it had come to the river to feed and was batting at the water with his monstrous paw.

Behind him, under his embankment, Ralph was delirious by now, and in his pain and fever, convinced that the water backing up behind the dam would soon submerge him. Now this is the part that no one except me believes, just as I believe in my uncle, who has since become a venerated elder in a tiny village high in the Peruvian Andes. From time to time, he sends me letters with small drawings of his village. They are dirty and the paper is cheap, and just beyond the thatch-roofed huts, in the looming mountains, sometimes you can make out the eyes or the haunches of bears.

The part no one else believes: because my delirious uncle believes he is going to drown, and because he is entranced by the bear's golden pelt, and because when the bear cups a fish to his mouth the fish reflects the shimmering colors of the rainbow, my delirious uncle calls out to the bear, and the bear, at the sound of his voice, turns his black eyes on him. In this instant, the surveyor and the predator share some kind of animal recognition, and though the surveyor knows that in the flooding of this riverbed the bear will lose its fishing grounds, the bear is alerted by the smell of the surveyor's blood.

In one version of this story, the bear kneels at my uncle, who climbs astride him and is carried to safety. In another, the bear licks at my uncle's shattered leg, which, under the lap of the bear's rough tongue, knits itself whole and strong. Then my uncle walks out on his own.

Either way, he quits work on the dam that same day, and so will never be the poor surveyor who falls off its face some years later, because my uncle, by that time, is long gone, and I will know him only as a small large-headed man who appears from time to time at family dinners, wearing work books and Can't-Bust-'Ems, drinking Scotch, telling stories. I remember the soft flannel of his shirt as I snuggled up against it, the wood-smoky smell of it, and the gleam of his beard in the firelight.

Here is one of his sketches from the Andes. I think it is so beautiful. Don't you?

⌒
⌒
⌒

Floods:

In the aftermath of California's recent floods, there is speculation about strengthening the levees. And as we lose our easy entitlements to other peoples' water, there will again be speculation about higher water prices and more dams. We will feel besieged by people who claim water we have long used as our own, but we will persevere, nonetheless, with our vision of our own unfettered destiny.

My uncle predicted this: thriving metropolises, without any end. My uncle, whose dreams of dams, in time, would spread across three states and many rivers, is convinced that it is natural, maybe even necessary, that water should follow the whims of the men who control it. Two inches of my father's creek belongs to Los Angeles, which only has to come and get it. We are a thirsty population, prone to drought, but also periodic flooding. For of course, between what will sustain us and what we must contain, despite all we have done to control them, the streams and rivers of this country will continue to chart their own courses.

Patty's father and my uncle believed in their dam so fervently they never would have wondered what possessed them. There is so much concrete in it that it won't completely cure for 100 years.

What did possess them, I wonder?

Today, a Fresno developer is planning a luxury home estates, complete with horse trails and a world-class golf course, not on the bluffs above the San Joaquin, not on its ancient floodplain, but smack in the middle of the riverbed itself, dry now for fifty years since Friant Dam was built. During California's recent floods, we kept our watchful eye on Friant Dam, which held as the river—above and below—swelled into a raging torrent. It was raining.

"If we're not going to allow houses down here," the developer said, "should we get rid of the fox dens, too? I guess people are so stupid ... we can't allow them to exercise their free rein, but we'll allow animals of a lesser intelligence to exercise theirs."

"I don't need anyone's protection," he said.

His supporter, attorney Jim McKelvey, explains that a river free from houses, roads, sewers, and electrical power lines is an "aberration," raising the concern that if the riverbed remains undeveloped, "housing and urban development will ... be required to leapfrog over (the) area, thereby disrupting the otherwise orderly expansion of urban facilities" (L.A. *Times,* Monday, January 13, 1997, A16).

~

~

~

If I had a river:

If I had a river I walked to after dinner, it would not be the L.A. River in its concrete swaddling. I remember rivers flooding when I was a girl. Some years it won't stop raining, even here.

Last night when I dreamed, it was not of my sister, nor even of an imaginary uncle midway between my father and my uncle, but rather of a third son, midway between the two I have. He was dark-haired and intense, and in my shame at having overlooked him, I lost track of Joey instead.

As a general rule, dreams in writing are uninteresting and ought to be avoided, but Patty and Miranda and Sky are dreams as well, and I wonder what it is that has brought us all together here? Is telling a story anything at all like building a dam, or are they so completely different as not to be contained by the same imagination?

In a recent letter to the L.A. *Times*, Pat Brown's grandson commended both our water projects and our wild rivers, as if the two could hold together, like a wish.

As a girl, swimming off a raft in the green, warm water of Lake Shasta, blue gills nibbled at my toes, and if this is a dream or not, it is nonetheless a vivid memory. Much later, in adolescence, I dreamed of drifting naked down a river through all the seasons of a single year—spring, summer, fall, and finally winter, when I arrived at the delta and flew off into the fog. Last night I dreamed of another river, glistening and full, down which I planned to swim home, but there were guests involved, harried women with babies, and remembering my own days of early motherhood, I knew, with deep regret, that I would have to stay and help the other women.

The last time I saw my real uncle, parrot on his shoulder, he was loquacious and told me many stories about the days when the dam was being built. There was, he said, such optimism then, with the Great Depression waning and war on the rise.

"We had our beliefs," he said, "and history would prove them. But you people lost yours so young."

My uncle looked sad when he said this, though whether he meant it as an accusation or forgiveness, I couldn't tell. Then he cocked his own head toward his parrot, clucking it under its beak until it squawked and ruffled its feathers.

That was when my uncle told me about Miranda's father, Mike, and the friendship he formed with the surveyor who fell. On this account, my uncle was judgmental. They were both drinking, he said, and Mike was just lucky he didn't fall too. I was relieved to have my uncle corroborate stories I felt sure I had invented, but how can I be certain he wasn't lying too?

What I want is the river, and the bear, and the lake behind the dam, and the salmon, and the glistening rock, and my imaginary son or uncle or self, as well as just to know where I might find my great-grandmother's grave, where I believe it all begins, this complex interstices of narratives. The mining town where she gave birth to all her children and then died is smack in the heart of gold country, and as far as the history of this state is concerned, water is the aftermath of gold.

But Western graveyards are haphazard sites, with markers that go back just a hundred years or so, and those of cheap stone, already crumbling, the disordered record of a hugely chastened people, brought down on their way through by the rawness of grief. Just west of Redding, for example, a pioneer baby's grave is today commemorated by a brown historical marker, a tiny iron cross, and clumps of plastic flowers on the ground. Or pick a mission any, any mission, in California. Somewhere between the massive tombstones of the priests and Spanish noblemen, Indians are buried: four thousand Chumash at Santa Barbara, several thousand Gabrielenos at Solvang. Ishi, the last wild Indian, emerged northeast of Chico, where, when he was a boy, bounty hunters had routinely slaughtered whole family groups gathered at their supper fires for a few dollars per scalp: how many thousands are buried in those hills?

On my father's land, just up the back hill from his cabin, there's a tiny private cemetery, maybe twenty graves in all, marked out by flat river stones and dating to the late 1800s. Not long ago, when they were out clearing brush, my parents found a new grave at the high end of the plot, festooned with pink ribbons in bows, and though I know that it disturbs them, for they are private people who plan someday to rest there themselves, I also know that the woman now buried on their property had lived all her life on that creek.

Perhaps, then, my lack of a river truly is connected with the absence of my father's mother's mother's grave, which is connected to Kennett, erased by the water and the will of its very own sons. What I mean is, when you know all this, you know, too, that Patty must be blinded and Miranda raped and Sky—what will happen to Sky?—not because millions of tons of concrete were poured into Shasta Dam, but because the vision of the future they portended did not allow for you to lie down by the side of a river, any river, and let it lap you, for in this vision of the future rivers are commodities and water a salable resource, not life.

At least I know now that the line between nostalgia and progress is mixed, that it must always—and never can truly—be straddled, and that the danger and necessity of doing so is both palpable and real.

At least I know that it is not the same to tell a story as to build a dam.

What I am afraid of is that neither will sustain us, and that in the lack of either, the jut of my son's ten-year-old jaw, the curve of my sister's body on the rock across the river, my uncle's Peruvian sketches, all will disappear. I said that a dam is the curve of your tongue, lapping water, but maybe what your tongue laps is just the impermanence of words, that do nothing but dissolve there, dissipate. Maybe desire is not the story, but the dissipation of the words, what you can't hold any longer than the very instant of their coming into being. Maybe I'm like Pat Brown's grandson, admiring both the taming of the wild rivers and their wildness, except I know you can't have both.

One night, after she was blinded, I took Patty to swim in the river, looking for my uncle's bear. Though it was very dangerous, she arched her back and dived.

∽

∽

∽

Do I overuse the dream device?

Do I overuse the dream device?

I suppose if I thought of it as a device I would have to say *yes,* that I do. I had a writing teacher once—he's pretty famous now—who said if you have to write dreams, don't write more than three in a lifetime of writing. A good girl, an obedient student, I did what he said. I saved up for fifteen years, never writing one, in case I might need my dreams when I was older. In time, I went on to teach countless others *don't write dreams.* Dreams are too easy, I told them, in fiction—things always end up adding up the way they don't in real dreams, and anyway, I told them, it's like that year on *Dallas* when none of it counted, *poof,* like that, your hero wakes up.

Wake up, Sky.

Wake up, Patty.

You see how wrong, how very wrong I was?

And yet, the true thing is, these women dream. They hear things in their sleep, as if from another language altogether. Miranda does too: *shh, listen.*

A dream of my own:

As for me, who am I? *I am the one who came first.*

I remember the day my sister was born, all head and hair. Not yet three, I took one look at her and understood that the only words I had for what was happening to me were whiny and unpleasant: "No, no. Mine. *My* mommy! *Mine!*"

The Navajo culture considers the child among the most precious of all earthly gifts, and whenever a baby is born, she must be carefully watched over until her first laugh. This laugh—the *First Laugh*—marks the birth of the child as a social being, and whoever brought it forth must then provide a lavish celebration in honor of the child.

You may think this is all about language, but long before that it was all about love.

Between my mother and my sister it always was a single breath, half a purring syllable, the twinned racing beat of a single heart, one laugh. Why is it that some babies are born with this same single heart of their mothers, while others come double-hearted from the start?

In retrospect, how can I hold this against them? I've held two babies of my own in my own arms. I have struggled to nurse one while the other fought for my lap, though maybe it is different since they're boys. Maybe boys have their own kinds of hearts. Certainly I'd do anything, sacrifice anything—life itself—for either one of those cherished separate hearts, and I suspect that this was also true of my mother.

But when I was little, when I was growing up, how could I know this, and how, not knowing this, could my own heart not break—doubling over again and again—at what appeared to me to be the closed and perfect union between my mother and my sister. This, I knew, without any other word for it, was love, just as surely as I knew that, in this love, there was no room for me.

What I'm trying to say is that, after my sister was born, I found myself clutching at language and failing absolutely to get my mouth around a single useful word, not a single one that might have let me into the tight circle of their affection. All of the inside of me was the raw gape of longing to place myself within the crook of their embrace or, years later, to share in their kitchen chatter—helping, setting, chopping, stirring, gazing, doe-eyed longing *don't you love me why don't you love me mommy, mommy. Mommy.*

Thirty years later I look back at this speechless child who was me standing silently among their spinning syllables as they spilled all around me, and the same thing happens—tears well up, and I am struck, again, by the enduring quality of my own mutism. What I did was pick another language; it was that simple. I started making things up as I went along, not so much to get attention as to make a space, any space, where I might fold myself and hide. In this way, words turned on my tongue into something both ephemeral and absolute, and the stories themselves, nothing at all like lies, just beginnings and middles and ends, tidy structures complete with suspense and a clear moral purpose. And though of course I did not know this then, you only get so many chances to write yourself into this world, up to and including that infinitesimal space between your mother and your sister, and if you've very lucky, you will somehow realize, before it is too late, that this waning opportunity has always been just language, every word of it.

A dream is language too.

Tell me: *are we dreaming now?*

Thus, by the time I was ten my family had already stopped believing anything I said. *No, no,* they would say, *it wasn't like that. Don't stare, stop exaggerating, keep your oar out. Uh-oh,* they would say, *your nose is growing.*

Look, this is nothing against my family at all. They were good and earnest people, kind people, who supported education and believed, in those days, in taxing the rich. It was just that, like my writing teacher, they thought they knew the difference between what had really happened, and the way I told it later, as a story.

What about you?

Here, for example, is something that really did happen to me: how I lost my virginity (at the time I still considered virginity a condition to be lost) when I was seventeen one August night in the Trinity Alps, on a bed of granite, beside a moonlit lake. The rock, gently curved and with a hollow for my back (which nonetheless emerged badly scraped from the experience, large red welts that later scabbed down the length of my spine), sloped all the way to the water. We were sweaty from our climb, and he had brought a canteen of whiskey. Along the way we'd met a field biologist, camped out for the summer to conduct his research on hummingbirds that nested there, he told us, among boulders.

"If you listen," he had said, "you can hear them thrumming."

So we sat on that rock a long time, listening for their thrumming and watching the sun set, the trees blacken, then fade, into the sky, and then, as the moon rose, blacken again. We were drinking, but not that much. We were talking, but also not that much. Even after dark, the rock remained warm from the sun; water lapped it below. Three days out, his face was rough with stubble, and I felt strong and light. In the morning we would be going back, a thought we must both have shared when he finally touched me. *Hadn't I always wanted this?* Around us—the tips of the waves where they caught the moonlight, the clusters of mica in the granite, the stars above—the whole world glittered.

After he reached climax, I stood up and dived into the water, which was icy. I swam as hard as I could and for a long time.

In those days, I collected postcards, and among the predictable novelty shots of giant jackrabbits and man-sized trout, I also had a handful of World War I Red Cross issue cards, public service announcements—news, however disturbing—from the front. These are mostly photographs of wartime injuries: shrapnel wounds, missing limbs, frozen feet. In one, a man, whose cheek had been blown away by mortar fire, looks clean and well-tended beside a jar of daffodils on a sunlit nightstand. In another, a nurse with sad eyes displays, as if for science, two amputated frozen feet pinned to a white expanse of sheet. Just to see her eyes—never mind the feet—would make you weep. She probably came from Akron, that nurse. She had brothers, parents, troubles. When she died some fifty years later her last word was *gangrene*. It was garbled, of course, and barely audible, but if you listened carefully you could hear her repeating it over and over: *gangrene, gangrene, gangrene.*

Can you tell the difference between when I am lying and when I am telling the truth? This is not a game. Inclined as you are to believe in the sexual encounter by the lake, it is entirely conceivable that the Red Cross nurse remained grief-stricken throughout her life. When skin freezes, it turns black and sloughs off; there is a terrible stench. The postcard itself is yellowed. In it, the nurse, looking crisp but heartbroken, stares out above the feet. But here is the thing, without what someone once wrote on the back there is no way of telling why she is so sad: they are just two blackened, rotting, swollen stumps, unidentifiable as any human part.

It is almost thirty years since I bought these postcards from a graying antique dealer in a dimly lit boutique where she told me that her second cousin on her mother's side had been a nurse, long ago, in the first Great War, but that now the cousin was dead. Because we both knew times were different, I continued flipping through the box of old postcards I'd been looking at—Washington, D.C., circa 1945; Salt Lake City, with a little canvas bag of hardened salt attached; Yellowstone—when suddenly I found myself staring at the mutilated face of a man whose suffering had been documented more than fifty years before. I looked up and, across the room, the shopkeeper shook her head slightly and smiled.

"You can have those," she said, "the whole lot, for a dollar. I think they're disgusting, don't you?"

When I got home I discovered that each postcard was labeled on the back, though in pencil, which was fading, and in a script that was difficult to read. They said such things as *mortar fire, shrapnel wound, left cheek,* and *frozen feet.* Now I knew what I was looking at and some things settled into place, but some things didn't.

Is there any way of knowing? Without the words I could not understand the image, but how did naming what I saw really change things? Out of all of this, in this you must believe me: I am, I swear to you, lying, I swear I am telling the truth.

Ah, but there's a moment, I don't know, the first time, for example, a man with no love interest in you at all attempts to seduce you, and you think *what the hell.* You are so unbearably young. You look into the eyes of your seducer. You think: *I do not recognize this man, he is a stranger.* You think: *this is not my story, whose story is this?*

From then on, all men are strangers to you, even your sons, and when you try to tell them your story, they (the men, though even your sons want you to put swords in the stories you tell them, when you tell them, *once there were two little boys* they chime in, together, *who had two magic swords*) look bored or confused, as if they do not understand. They say things like, "I don't want to hear about your past."

"It is not my past," you protest. "It is just a story, just like yours."

"Where is the proof?" they say. "Show me your proof."

But in your ears—just like Sky's, just like Miranda's, just like mine—*proof* sounds like *poof,* and you say it for them: "Poof," you say. "Poof!"

In time you learn, once again, in order to avoid an argument just not to say anything at all. You begin to understand there are no words for your stories, nothing to hold them together anymore. You have lost your beginnings, your middles, your ends; you have lost your clear moral purpose. It happened over time and without your really knowing. First you could not speak, then words themselves failed you. You kept flipping the postcard over and over. You'd read the words aloud—*frozen feet*—you'd stare at the gruesome photo. What held the words, which you knew to be accurate and perfectly objective, together with these two ruined parts of human anatomy, with that poor man's suffering, with the empathic sadness of this nurse. It wasn't just story that was splitting: you couldn't think straight anymore.

I'll tell you what holds it all together: desire, it's that simple, sheer desire. Think of things flying completely apart. This is your fundamental desire: that that should never happen, that armies should never face off across the night, that your sons will always nestle sweetly in their sleep.

But by the time you understand this, desire itself has already betrayed you. Thus, you have begun to stutter and are unable to finish your sentences. With grocery clerks, physicians, and lovers alike you are tongue-tied and ineloquent. In your most passionate moments, you are dumb. Your lover comes to you with a Neruda poem that begins, *I like for you to be still: it is as though you were absent,* and you believe it is lovely. Lightheaded all the time and tormented by your recollections of a previous self, you tell yourself that it is just a memory, but are filled nonetheless with unintelligible whisperings, unutterable mutterings, savage and forbidden sounds that catch like glass in your throat, until finally you begin to understand that this, what you are suffering, is the terrible synapse between their story, which you already know, and yours, which has deprived you, you also now know, of your only apparent means of telling it. Speechless, you remember that the pathway of the nerve only works in one direction.

Now in this moment, when you are at your most vulnerable and catching you unaware, your seducer for the first time, as if pretending to love you, takes you in his arms and, stroking you, stroking you, insists in his deep, his sonorous, his compelling voice *I know you better than you know yourself, tell mine it is yours, and I will always love you, trust me,* but despite his gentle touch, he has miscalculated badly and is not looking at you, is looking instead a bit dazed and forlorn, for perhaps he knows already it is over, perhaps even he understands that no matter what he says you will recognize yourself in this moment as utterly bereft, for, in such a moment, the unknowable at last is known—*oh, it is known*—to you and it is, after all, that you have no story after all to tell.

Shh: like a dream doesn't count is a lie can't be written isn't real not at all the way things are.

Then for the longest time you sit struck dumb and with your hands up-turned on your knees, like a woman awaiting a transfusion. This goes on for several years at least. You sit, terrified of proceeding, but yet paralyzed as well by the knowledge that you cannot turn back. You wait, sublime with your patience, because there is after all nothing for it, you wait and you wait, and as you wait you find yourself sifting through the debris, numb at first, just sorting methodically through it until, once again catching you unaware but this time ever so gradually, the knot of your muteness begins to loosen, and it, the debris, starts to separate and settle, leaving you finally with everything you needed to begin with—another language altogether, more clumsy, less seemingly natural, but also more terribly vital, and yes you must believe me, the rest of it is dreams.

Here then is a dream of my own.

～
　～
～

Miranda was born:

Miranda was born in Trinity County around about the time the Rosenbergs were killed. Her mother, vastly pregnant, sat glued to the radio, listening to stories about how Julius and Ethel exchanged letters every day, about their boys who were soon to be orphaned. Miranda's mother, known as Rose but whose real name has always been a mystery, was not without ambivalence about them, for it was rumored that the letters did not contain even the slightest shred of remorse but only solicitude for their own family: *was Julius eating? how was Ethel's bad tooth? were either of them sleeping at all?* Still, the detailed plans they drew up for their sons moved Rose, herself a mother-to-be, to tears. Because the thing was, Rose knew about the A-bomb. She'd read every newspaper and magazine article that made it all the way out to Trinity County, and she was only seventeen, and pregnant, and now she couldn't get out of her mind such images as the eardrums of babies bursting open, or the shadows of men etched in city sidewalks, or skin peeling off of whole bodies. These were the things Rose imagined as she listened to the radio, and it made her own skin go unnatural and clammy.

"Glub," Miranda said some years later to Patty, "there's going to be a dam here. Glub."

Miranda was bleeding, she was nine years old.

Before that, before we had nuclear war and its effects on our imaginations, we had a different world, a planned and ordered universe, which to my mind was typified by the government town at Toyon, built in one tremendous burst of efficiency and optimism, and home to as many as 1,000 dam workers at a time, one of whom was Rose's father, Mike. As a girl, I found Toyon fascinating, for it emptied out as quickly as it had once filled and remained a modern ghost town, laid out in a neat grid out around a central square, anchored by a commissary, schoolhouse, and nondenominational house of worship—rows and rows of white clapboard houses with green government trim, and around them, around the little town itself, a scrubby woods of digger pine, chaparral, and oak.

And this was where Mike first appeared, one day without warning, all the way from Texas, sporting the stubble of a three-day-old beard and with his six-year-old daughter in tow. It was like that in those first heady days, men like Mike pouring in from all over, down on their luck like the rest of the world, who had heard of the boomtown and work. And sometimes they came with their families, and sometimes they came on they own, but Mike came with Rose, just the one little girl, who was quiet and well-mannered from the start.

Mike signed on in cement.

A childless couple in Toyon rented them a room at the back of their government bungalow, white with green trim.

Years passed, during which mountains of concrete were poured into forms, five feet, by five feet, by five feet. Mike grew thick and stooped at the shoulders. He was known as hard working, a taciturn man.

Even so, my uncle was always critical of him, and not just for his drinking (Mike drank beer, and he drank it in public), but also for what my uncle had surmised were his left-leaning politics. Mike was the man who made friends with the hapless surveyor who, in his cups one night, fell off the dam.

"It could have been him," my uncle used to say, "who was all in the world that little girl had."

But Ralph never thought it was the drunkenness that did him in, for the way Ralph tells it, Mike was on his way to meet a man—maybe the very man who fell—when he saw something, an argument or scuffle, from the far other side of the dam.

"What the hell," Ralph said, "they were both Reds."

I want to believe this, just like I want to believe in my mother's secret radical past. I want to believe in Mike, his temperament and sympathies, the rippling brawn of his forearms, his wide stance over molds for concrete, even his gingham curtains once he moved Rose to Trinity County. I want to believe he was against management and for the people, maybe even the land, but Mike, in truth, is mainly an enigma, and who can really say. There is, for example, the missing space of Rose's mother, who is just a blank, making Rose the first in the line: first Rose, then Miranda, then Sky.

These are the raw, changeless facts that I know about Mike: he grew up in Texas, the son of a ranch hand; the Depression hit him hard, like it hit most; at some point he fathered Rose, and then he lost her mother. And how is it possible, anyway, to lose a person—did Rose's mother die, or just disappear? Thus, the blank space remains what it is, though I believe that there were also years of wandering, years during which he must have resisted the lure of the trains only because of his motherless daughter, and then the boom promise of Shasta, which led him to Toyon, where something must have happened because one day, as suddenly as he'd arrived, he gave up his dam worker's deferment and signed on for the war, and then when it was over, took his daughter off to the back reaches of Trinity County because there no work on the dam anymore, and also because—I swear this is true—he himself was finished with the whole rest of the world.

The way we imagine them now, the cut-loose men like Mike who, but for his daughter, would have spent his life reclining beneath open skies on the flat backs of trains, we think of them as rebels who refused absolutely in their hearts to be beaten down by conditions that rendered other, commoner men sullen and dejected. We compare them with the men who are homeless today, and find them free-spirited and benign. We believe that between the happy hobo and our own stern fathers lies the difference between our destiny and dreams.

But whatever could have happened between Mike and the bosses, or Mike and the u.s. government or army, or Mike and the rest of the world, to make him give up on everything like that? Rose remembers arguments with the woman who rented them rooms in her house, and who looked after Rose during the time Mike was stationed in the Pacific theater, picking leeches off his legs and desperately willing the war to end. Sometimes the woman would rock Rose against her chest that smelled of cinnamon and sweat and was dusty with flour, just rock her, and rock her, but Rose knew that what was rotting in her father some thousands of miles away from her could not be assuaged by any human touch or kindness.

This, at any rate, was Ralph's view of things before he hurt his ankle and quit the dam.

"Oh hell," Ralph said. "You put enough men together, you work them hard enough, there's bound to be dissatisfaction somewhere." Then he put his hand on Rose's slender shoulder, and felt, in that moment, as inept as he ever would. "Your dad," he said, "you know, he just wants things to be fair. But they're not. Things are never fair."

Rose, who was still a girl, looked up at Ralph's huge head, trying hard to study it, to fix it in her memory, because Rose, like Miranda after, could sometimes see or hear the dark insides of things and knew before Ralph did that he would leave and that, in his absence, the bitter thing inside her father would just get worse. Rose's pigtails were pulling the hair back at her temples so hard she had a headache. Studying Ralph, Rose wanted more than anything that it was Mike, instead, who had been the lone surveyor tromping up the riverbed that fell, and broke his ankle, and was rescued by the bear.

To build a dam:

To build a dam, any dam, one must have both need and desire, but there must have been something about that time in particular, when the country was on the mend and anything seemed possible, that made the two coalesce into a force powerful enough to transform the whole geography and future of this state in a testament to the imagination that has bequeathed us the landscape of Patty's contour map, clotted with its dams and etched through with its canals. There was even that other dam that was never built.

Even just sketched on blue tissue paper, that dam was a dam to behold.

That dam—the Ah Pah—was to have constituted a new order of dam.

That dam, designed to put an end to the influence of drought and turn us into a happy, carefree people, was to have been the final legacy of visionary men—geologists, engineers, and planners—who came together in a time when the confluence of need and desire knew no limit, and decided on the Klamath, up north where no one lived.

Or only just a few, they allowed among themselves, *mostly Indians, and a few little towns.* In their hearts they contained the mild ecstasy of calculating men who see, at the end of a long tunnel, the arc of their dreams coming true.

The Klamath River, which begins in a modest little lake in Oregon, has swelled to monstrous proportions by the time it reaches the Pacific, engorged by countless springs, several rivers, and more than 100 inches of coastal rain per year. The dam itself, designed to close the Klamath River's final gorge at a height of 850 feet (taller than the Pan Am building in New York), would have captured water just at the cusp where it empties, unused, into the Pacific Ocean, and backed it 70 miles upriver to form a reservoir with more than 15 million acre-feet of gross storage and under which would have lain seven towns, one Indian reservation, the better part of three rivers (including forty miles of the Trinity and the entire Salmon), almost all of the remaining steelhead and salmon spawning grounds, and most of the northwestern sector of the state. And then the water would have been rerouted back over mountains it had just traversed through a 60-mile tunnel, blasted out of rock.

And that was the country we drove through, my sister and I, on the way to the fire that diverted us to Sky. It would have been all water, where we were.

All water where we were. The whole northwestern sector of our state.

If what I suffer from is nostalgia, it is as much for the power to imagine such a thing as it is for the tidy universe of Toyon.

If Joey were to ask again, *why do people build dams,* what should I tell him, do you think? Joey was my second son, born, I believe, to humble me, to teach me that whatever I might think I know about the world, I am wrong, a lightning-quick boy who came charged from the start and, despite his tender heart, never would allow me even the illusion that he could be protected, for with Joey, from the outset, it was too late for that. You know the kind of boy I mean. If I let go of his hand at the store, he'd be up the down escalator before I could stop him. Simple excursions to the neighborhood park were a nightmare, with him always running away to flaunt his independence on playground equipment too big or dangerous for his age group. *Be still,* I would whisper to myself, thinking *oh please be safe,* and sometimes he would make as if to turn and I would think *now yes you will be still and I will hold you safe,* but it would be only slightly, and then, like that, he would be off again, and I'd just stand there watching him, torn between dread and marvel.

There must have been a time when I believed I might hold him with my stories. I believed I could say *let me tell you a story,* and even Joey would settle down and listen. His brother always listened, a still, attentive form beside me, and if I stumbled or forgot where I was, even before he could read himself, he'd repeat, word by word, what I had just read, for Sam had developed, at a very early age, a pure reflexive habit of memorizing books, long or short, it didn't matter, narrative as fixed and immutable as it was compelling. But Joey, squirmy and impatient, was an interrupter, driven by the need to claim every sentence, turn it over to his own private principle and purpose, and make it, entirely, his. I would say *let me tell you* and he'd say *the bear went,* and this was the way it always was between him and me, a determined struggle of both narrative and will. I used to worry that this intractability of his was, in truth, a dreadful flaw, some stubborn assertion of the self as impervious to the mind of another as it was to the lure of a story or word, but now I think he was just desperate to be part of the story itself, which was never large enough to contain him, no more than the Ah Pah ever would have been to contain the vision of the men who had conceived it.

~
~
~

If the baby is a girl, she will name her Miranda and place tiny gold studs in the eggshells of her ears:

Rose listened to the radio as Miranda made a languorous loop inside her belly, settling in a little more snugly, and smiled to hear that the children of the Rosenbergs were doing fine. Rose was of at least two minds about it: when the eardrums of children are burst open in an atomic blast, blood pours in glistening streams down the sides of their faces, while on the inside, their whole world goes silent. Rose had such compassion for that silence, as absolute and mystifying as a dream. But Rose also had to consider her father.

What was the bitter thing inside her father?

Rose's father had scars all over his legs from the leeches, but yet, in later years, he never talked about the war, which he had chosen just as surely as he'd chosen to move as far out of the world as he could when he got back. The way Rose looked at it, something must have happened to make him run away and hide like that, and this was why she was so interested in the Rosenbergs that summer she was pregnant with Miranda, for Rose believed, as I do, that her father was a Red. And certainly it's possible. My mother, who should know, tells me that there were still plenty of lefties around, and there were those late-night arguments with the woman who rented them rooms. So I'm not saying yes or no, but Rose's father did have that brawn about him, and Ralph's attention, and then in later years he just went quiet, like a man deprived of a vision.

Either that, or he's merely a contrivance to explain how it happened that Miranda, born the year the Rosenbergs were killed and raised far away from the rest of the world, was nine years old and bleeding where another dam was coming, and Patty saw her and then, years later, I saw Sky. That is the essential convergence of events in this narrative, and if for it to happen Rose's father has to build his cabin in the backwoods of Trinity County, and then take Rose there from Toyon, I am not about to intervene over questions of seemliness or probability.

When I first imagined Miranda, she was just a swollen-eyed nine-year-old girl. What was going to happen had already happened. She was naked, scruffy, and bleeding. Maybe her eye was beginning to bruise. Maybe she had other bruises, too. Her name, inside my mouth, was smooth, like a skin, the same as Sky's, years later, when I first saw her in the back room of the manager's apartment of that dive motel on the far northern coast of this state. She came to me as a sudden image, which I recognized at once, set, like the placement of a small stone, or a boy's falling cry from a trestle high above a river. This part is not about writing at all. It is about Miranda, whom I would have to come to know and understand beyond the stream of blood down the inside of her thigh, and her bruising, and the curious word she used—*glub*, she said, *glub*—in order to do the right thing by Sky.

But Rose, the first in the line, has always been a mystery to me, and I don't think it's accidental that her life was punctuated by a series of losses—first her mother, whom she never knew; then her father, who abandoned her for three years to fight a distant war; then the whole community of Toyon and the all-embracing purpose of their project. One day she was wrapped in the bustle and direction of a town dedicated to a vision of the future defined by both progress and abundance; the next, her father was gone. Three years later, he came back a strangely altered man, and dragged her off to the mountains to start their lives over again. Over and over in her head, she would replay the scenes from before her father went away, when he was still fully engaged in the life of the dam. Rose was still so young at the time that she could never be sure of any of it. There were stories about tunnel cave-ins, snapped cables, workers buried in concrete, and one about a man who fell down the face of the dam. There were brawls, and weekend drunkenness, and Rose also thinks she remembers meetings, in the aftermath of which the woman who rented them rooms would be taciturn and guarded, and sometimes she'd ask Rose's father to leave. Sometimes, even then, Rose believes that there were days and days when her father did not shave or speak to her.

Out of all her memories, Rose is certain only of the night my uncle Ralph came back, a dead man resurrected, from the failed surveying expedition on which he had fallen in the riverbed and been rescued by the bear.

Now, since her pregnancy, Rose has lived alone in a second cabin near her father's that he built for her as soon as he knew of her condition. It wasn't out of either spite or anger that he built it, but from a certain care and knowledge of his own male nature, and he skinned the logs himself, and dug the clay to chink them, and then he cut four windows facing each direction of the compass for Rose to hang blue gingham curtains on. Now, since her pregnancy, Rose sits behind those windows, looking out through half-open curtains, and what she knows, she knows that if the government could kill the Rosenbergs over pieces of a Jell-O box, surely her father should have been more careful. This was so confusing to her. Between one vision of A-bombs drifting overhead in the baskets of hot air balloons, and another of her father strapped into the electric chair, Rose does not know how to choose. In Rose's mind, these two visions occupy the same space, such that all things, and at all times, seem simultaneously to fly apart and collapse inward, bound together in a tidy economy of terror and love. It is no doubt a result of this very economy that Rose became pregnant in the first place, though of course this was not anything she thought about beforehand. Tucked away by herself in the back reaches of Trinity County, dependent on her father's pension and their small gold mining efforts, Rose is seventeen, going on forty, and nothing has turned out the way she planned.

~
~
~

When we were girls:

Once, when we were girls, Patty and I sneaked into Toyon from a picnic at a nearby park, where all the engineers were feasting on fried chicken and potato salad. We were not supposed to go there, and we knew it, not just from the admonitions of our parents and the posted "No Trespassing" signs, but because it was the "government," and the government, in those days, was somehow off limits, with its important-sounding titles, and official green buildings, and the black and yellow fallout shelter signs all over town. After the coming war had started, then we would go down into the cellars of our towns and cities, and we were prepared to rebuild when it was over, but until that time, the only government official you could really talk to was the ranger in the Smokey Bear hat.

But Toyon beckoned to us from an even earlier time, and there was something so provocative about the way it nestled hidden among the dusty hills, at once unexpected and familiar, that whenever we'd drive by on our Sunday afternoon excursions to the dam and it appeared as if out of nowhere—its buildings boarded up and deserted, with KEEP OUT and NO TRESPASSING warnings posted all over—I'd be struck, again and again, by its paradoxical tidiness, a dream of order from another era, behind which I was convinced a different reality lay. I don't know what we really thought, but at school we'd seen the movies on post-atomic blast survival tactics and were well aware that contagion could lurk on even the most sparkling surface and that behind almost any door we might find a manikin-corpse still engaged in some mundane task of daily life—a checked-aproned mother twisting water from a tea-bag, a little boy tying his shoes.

I'd like to claim that it was my idea, that I was the one who, tired of three-legged races and Mother-May-I, slipped out behind the food tables and dragged Patty off to the back side of Toyon, where we quickly found a window hanging open and broken. But of course, it wasn't me, it was Patty, who twelve years old and dressed in tiny cut-off jeans that rode all the way up to her crotch, got fed up with the wienie roast and took off, assuming I'd follow.

I followed. I always followed Patty. That was the way it was between us.

The open window was like an omen or an invitation, and we clambered over the sill, beside ourselves with excitement.

Then we were inside, and what there was, there wasn't anything, just an eerie stillness and close heat. Patty and I looked at each other, not sure what to do. I don't really believe we expected any manikins, shaking out laundry or, feet propped up on old ottomans, reading the remains of crumbling newspapers, but there was still something desperately exciting about what we were doing, as if it were not just forbidden, but actually dangerous.

Patty brushed her shorts off. "This is where the workers lived," she said. "It was so cheap it was practically free."

I must have known what would be coming.

We were standing in the middle of what would have been a living room or parlor, painted a paler green than the trim outside, and with a pile of beer bottles in one dusty corner. Looking out the window, we could see a round humped hill, seared brown with dried grass and a fringe of gray trees. It must have been July, because the air in the room was as hot as an oven, and when I turned back to Patty, she was taking off her blouse, as if to cool herself. I wandered into the next room, half the size of the first one, and yellow, but otherwise the same, with another pile of bottles in another corner. Behind me I knew Patty was touching her breasts, which were round and white, with pink button nipples. She stood in the middle of that empty room in Toyon and dared me to do the same.

In the kitchen, the porcelain sink was cracked and rust-stained, and the fixtures had all been removed, but a bent curtain rod was still anchored to the wall above the one four-paned window. I tried to imagine a stove, the smell of vinegar and meat, a table and chairs, people eating, talking, a family.

"If you had a family," Patty called out, "you got one with two bedrooms. If you didn't you had to share."

There was something in her voice now, taut and thrilling. I tried the front door, but it was bolted from the outside. The only room left was the bathroom, hardly more than a small shower stall and a cracked toilet knocked off its setting. Here there was a sour smell, the walls dark with mold. I was afraid to go back and find Patty completely naked, so I stood there for long time, staring at the place above the sink where there had been a mirror once, and after a while, I saw a girl looking back at me from the dirt-streaked plasterboard. She must have been close to my own age, but with sharper features, and there was a furtiveness about her I would not see again for more than a quarter of a century. She had a small mouth, with even white teeth, and ashy blond hair pulled tight into two long pigtails.

Patty did this sometimes.

I studied the girl in the place where the mirror used to be, and it seemed to me she was speaking.

Patty liked for me to watch, or at least to be close, so I could hear her.

I couldn't make out the girl's words.

Suddenly, I heard the voices of Patty's father and my uncle calling after us from somewhere far away. I didn't think we had been gone that long. Patty made some sounds. I put my hands on the edge of the sink and leaned forward, my forehead pressing against the forehead of the girl in the place where the mirror used to be, and when, a few moments later, I pulled myself away, I was crying but without knowing why.

∽
∽
∽

The way it is with fathers:

You know the way it is with fathers. They have their private dreams, ones you would never imagine, not in a million years.

Long after the other great projects were finished and California found itself on the verge of pulling back and reassessing, my father built a dam. It was not a very big dam, and it never really worked, but it took hold of him, the way dreams do, just as it took the rest of us by surprise. For my father, this was an entirely private dream, and enduring, and it went for many years, starting, maybe, with the slide rule that dangled on his brother's hip, the elegance of numbers it portended, or maybe later, when we'd gone with him to *ooh* and *ahh* over Trinity and Oroville, but we were only girls then: what did we know about longing?

Once, after my uncle had moved on to Flaming Gorge Dam in Utah, he took us to explore its narrow reservoir in a little motorboat, speeding miles up the flooded desert canyon until, somewhere toward the head of the lake, a piece of wood jammed the motor, stalling us dead. It was after midnight before we'd drifted back to where we could see the dam again, white and luminous between sandstone hills, and I grew terrified that we'd be sucked into its detritus-filled whirlpools and drowned. By the end of his career, my uncle had a private office on the gorge side of Hoover Dam. You could stand at his wide, picture window, like flying, and look all the way down, down to the river below.

The land my father built his cabin on off the upper Sacramento was not the first land he purchased to build on. The first land—an acre of floodplain off Coffee Creek in the Trinity Alps—was washed away by the Christmas floods of 1964, and later, when we drove up to survey the damage, all that remained of this particular dream was a litter of felled pines and a few scattered cabins, lodged lopsided amid the debris, holiday wreaths askew on wide open front doors. In one, we could see presents strewn about, an upside-down Christmas tree lodged in one corner. I was just a girl, stunned by the disorder of this new strange world, where it was still raining, but inside the car it was even stranger, and I kept my face glued to the cold window glass, steaming it up with my breath, so I would not have to look at my father crying. My father was driving and crying, not making any sound, but there were tears streaming down his red face.

These days, in my family, though we mostly dread fire (which we also love) because of what it could take from us in a single, cleansing breath, we know, too, about the damage that a flood can cause, know it viscerally, as only a family that has lost its first, best dreams to it can, and so we do not speak to my father about natural land management procedures or watershed redistribution. In a different world, I would like to tell him that the land we lost was only moved, turned to sediment and washed downstream, where, in this other world, it should have fertilized our crops and made us rich and healthy. I would like to tell my father this, but I know that by 1964, the sediment of his most persistent dreams would never have made it past Trinity Dam, and that his rage and disappointment were so deep, anyway, as to render all subsequent environmental logic spurious.

Years later, when my father would again buy land, it would traverse a deep ravine, not susceptible to flooding, with level areas higher up to build on. I was a teenager then, and my father's first act of property ownership was to plant one thousand pine seedlings.

Between either need or desire, what did possess him, I wonder?

One day my father hired a man with a backhoe to dig such a monstrous pit on his land that it would seem, forever after, a gaping wound, proving all over again that, as with my sister's walnut tree, when called upon to do so, my father can be moved to take impressive action.

"By George," I thought the first time I saw it, "now that's some hole."

But it was a sad, sad sight, with the ragged contours of a midsized pond and a depth of maybe twenty feet at the base of its simple, earthen dam. In the deepest part of the pit, a stovepipe glory hole, for overflow, had already been installed.

After a while, I wandered down into its maw, for even then I somehow understood that what drove my father to dig it, to leave his mark, however perverse, on the earth, could not really be so different from what would later drive my writing, but just as in writing we are never able to anticipate the outcome of a sentence, any sentence, my father could never anticipate the outcome of his dam.

This is what my parents did: first they ran linked garden hoses from upstream on the creek to where they hoped the force of gravity would fill their little lake. This is what happened instead: water poured in and seeped out in a constant and steady exchange.

Then my father had a drink and thought about his options and his dam.

Bentonite, an especially impermeable clay mined only from one place on earth and widely marketed as a sealant, offered a natural solution, and for the first two summers, my parents scattered it throughout their hole, though sparingly, because it is expensive. At the end of each summer, the floor of their lake had turned into a dark and sticky mud, and sometimes, a small puddle collected.

So my father had another drink and decided to line his hole with plastic.

Then he drank again, and while we argued with him, changed his mind to concrete, a three-year, labor-intensive process, during which my mother would mix the concrete in an old wheelbarrow beneath the outside faucet at the cabin, and then wobble it down a steep path to my father, who would be kneeling in the pit, waiting to scoop out the concrete, and spread it, and smooth it, both of them sweating in the blazing sun, until, over the course of those three long summers, the entire lake bottom was covered. We swam that final August in water diverted from the creek into the lake, and returned the following spring to discover hardy pine seedlings sprouted through my father's concrete in a complex web of cracks. Finally, in one last staggering burst of angry resolution, my father laid water-impermeable asphalt, which worked, although it caused a minor oil slick, an iridescent sheen on the surface of the clear, cold water.

This is all true, as true as I can remember it. The summer of the asphalt, after we drained and scrubbed out the lake, we used to drink cocktails on the small half-moon of a beach my father also built, water birds dipping all around us and my parents, with a shaker of martinis, as content as I have ever seen them. I want to say that this practice continues, that we still drink there in the evening and that my father finds this water warmer than the creek and more secluded as he ages, that he swims there. I want to say that there are whole long days I read there in the sun, while my children play around me and my father looks on, beaming, but my father, a cautious and considered man, always drained the lake before going home to avoid potential trouble, and then one day came back to find it full again, an old towel spread on the beach and beer bottles littered all around.

If you take the idea of a dam and dream it off the tips of your fingers, what must it be like, instead, to dismantle it?

"What's an attractive nuisance?" Joey wanted to know.

"What if something happened?" my mother worried long distance. "Not everyone is careful, like we are."

I wasn't around when my father took a sledgehammer to the bottom of his lake, when he broke the asphalt-covered concrete into plate-sized chunks, when he scattered the sand of his beach, but I have often imagined him red-faced and cursing, the sun a steady bead on his back, my mother pursed-lipped on the shore, the utter isolation of the two of them unmaking their dream. The hole is still a hole, but we no longer speak of it, and unless we go out of our way, we don't have to see it. Except for the children, who sometimes play games there, we almost never do.

My father built a dam once, he had his private dream.

The asphalt made the water in the reservoir, when it was still a reservoir, look black.

The dams we built, and still build every summer on the creek itself, are different. These dams serve our real need for water deep enough to swim in, as well as that of boys to move enormous rocks. We stand in the creek for hours, turning blue-toed and numb, as we arrange and rearrange the rocks to hold back water. We work on these dams all summer, until the pools behind them rise above our chests, and then in the winter they are washed away, and in the summer we begin again.

Between my father's failed dam, and these rudimentary ones, and the great Shasta Dam, and the others, we can imagine an equation of need and desire, but it is still the variable I cannot conceive. My uncle, like Mike, found a job on the dam, and in the course of its construction, saw men crushed by it. L. A. has long since outgrown itself at least in part because water was made plentiful and cheap. If this is about writing, it is about the manner in which writing seeks the variable. And yet the true thing is that, if I had a choice, I would be standing in the creek now, straining to move heavy rocks. I would be doing this in the heat of the day with my sons and my sister. I would not be telling what Patty told me.

Before Ralph left for South America:

In 1935 Congress passed the Rivers and Harbors Act, allocating 12 million dollars to California's Central Valley Project and authorizing work to begin on two new dams—Shasta, on the Sacramento, and Friant, farther south, on the San Joaquin. When the Bureau of Reclamation secured this New Deal funding it ensured the redistribution of water in this state, guaranteed the transformation of California's 700-mile-long dry Central Valley (sometimes known as California's Kansas) from a virtual desert to a lush agricultural basin, and committed itself to supporting the project by constructing not just another great dam, but also a whole community—homes, mess halls, workshops, a recreation center, fire station, hospital and administrative complex—where thousands of men, beaten down by the Depression, would find work and, for the six heady years of the project, a place to bring families, raise children, love wives. By 1938, when construction on Shasta Dam commenced, it had become a magnet for hundreds of unemployed men from all over the West and an emblem of optimistic revival. Boomtowns proliferated among the nearby hills, and men without families camped out as they waited for jobs, just as men from prior generations had camped out looking for gold. A photographic expedition from 1938 shows denuded hillsides, poisoned and defoliated by copper smelting operations, as well as two deserted mining towns, Kennett and Co-ram, whose brick buildings were bulldozed and wood structures burned. This is all part of the official history of the project, but Ralph and I both know it is a lie.

Before he left for South America, Ralph drove me out in his old pickup, first to Toyon, and then to the dam itself, and it was summertime and dusk, just as the deer come out of the folds of the hills to forage for food. There is such a softness to the air that time of year and, even as it cools into evening, a pen-etrating warmth, like a second skin, and Ralph took my hand as we walked through this air out across the dam to the elevator tower at its exact center. These days, there are almost always small gaggles of visitors about, waiting for the next tour, or just lolling on the grass—couples entwined in each other's arms, or mothers reclining as their children run about wildly—but I remem-ber the dam on this evening as completely deserted. It is wide enough at the top for two lanes of road, lined on each side with broad sidewalks, then high concrete walls with steel railings. As a child, I could barely peer over the rail-ings, so Ralph, at some point, must have lifted me up on his shoulders as we strode along on top of the dam his brother had built. Then he stopped and set me down on the railing, facing toward the lake side, just above where debris-riddled water roiled around outflow vents. When I looked down, the constant turbulence made me feel dizzy, so I stared out instead over the water, soft gray at dusk, and with bats swooping down low over it.

"I'd say," Ralph said, "Kennett's just about right there in the middle."

He was almost like a boyfriend to me at that moment, his arm firmly hug-ging my waist. In preparation for expatriation, he had begun to let his beard grow, and though it was summer, he still smelled wood smoky and sweet. I nuzzled my head against his shoulder, and we were quiet for awhile. Then, in a low voice, Ralph told me the story of how, after his experience with the bear, he'd quit working at the dam and gone back to stay in Kennett.

Ralph lived there seven months, in the deserted town, moving at whim from the hospital compound, where his brother, my other, real uncle, was born, to the librarian's cottage, jammed with a grand piano and countless books, to the mine workers' bunkhouses. During this period, my uncle Ralph said, tendrils of translucent green shoots began appearing here and there in the poisoned soil around town, and animals came to live with him—raccoons in the bunkhouses, all kinds of birds in the hospital wards, deer and mice and chipmunks, cougars, and one last pair of tiny golden burros, the final offspring, he felt certain, of a company-owned herd, bred to transport ore in nar-row mine shafts. The cougars moved restlessly from building to building, and though they did not seem dangerous, Ralph was always careful to check for their yellow eyes before taking up residence in some new place. Too large for buildings built to human scale, the bear came and went as it pleased.

Ralph described this time as the happiest and most serene in his life, while not far away, the engineers, and explosives experts, and concrete framers, and men whose job it was to move the railroad tracks from their bed along the river, planned and worked at a furious pace. During the day Ralph could hear the BOOM, BOOM, BOOM of dynamite and dredgers, and with each new set of explosions more animals came to live with him—an eagle, coyotes, skunks, squirrels, some sleek-furred weasels. Nights he would play the grand piano or read the librarian's books, from which, as he read, he would tear the pages out, one by one, and litter them all over the town.

Look, I'm not trying to take anything away from the achievements of the men whose intensity and purpose enabled them, first to conceive of, and then build, such dams. I know where my water and power come from. And I have swum all my life in their blue reservoirs; I have boated, and skied, and camped out on them. It's not for me to say, one way or another, what we should have done or shouldn't, no more than it is for me to judge Ralph. In the days before Kennett went down, Ralph lived among its books and animals not to make any kind of statement about the rightness or wrongness of the future, but because he felt at home there, and because of the bear.

And Ralph was not the only one either, as a few years later, a man going by the name of Harold Williams took up residence at the dam for several months. Like the men who had once poured its concrete, he was broad-shouldered and dark, a taciturn man with such a sadness about him that the National Park Service, unsuccessful in its initial efforts to move him, just let him be. I am told that this man—this "Harold Williams"—bore an uncanny resemblance to Rose's father, Mike, and I also understand that there was a period of time, shortly after their move to Trinity County, during which Rose lived alone in her father's log cabin. But who can say? Eventually, after several months, the man moved of his own accord, and Rose grew up, and Miranda was born, and Ralph wrote to me from the Andes.

Now, though, on that night with Ralph, before he went away and everything changed, as it would, over and over, throughout those years, I sat perched on the steel railing, looking out at the placid, graying surface of the water, below which, as my uncle told it, a whole town lay. All major construction on the dam was completed in seven years, from 1938 to 1944, and when the water started creeping back toward Kennett, my uncle found he could not sleep, but paced the ragged alleys of the town until his own feet bled, and still he could not stop what was coming. His hand on my waist was as big as a paw. The rabbits were the first to leave, he said, the cougars, the last, and when the waters finally came and started lapping at his bloodied feet, he climbed to top of the hospital roof to watch that world end, and there, at long last, he slept.

"It was during this sleep," my uncle told me, "that the bear came for me a second time."

How could I have been wrong?

Now, surely you will ask, as indeed I have asked myself many times: *how could I have been wrong?*

That evening on the coast with my sister when I saw Sky for the first time, there was something about her. I know I have said that before—*there was something, something.* And maybe this is what story is for, for when you catch an image out the corner of your eye and it stays there, but you don't know what it is, not really, can't assemble its different parts in any way that makes sense. Maybe story is just for the assembling of things—history, imagination, fact— without which, however much we may wish that it were otherwise, our lives will dissipate, losing meaning and coherence. Creative writing students will tell you stories are for self-expression, communication, truth, and you will smile and wonder how it is you've forgotten to believe this, thinking, too, about the petroglyph on the far desert wall, and how, despite the life you have spent among words, you can no longer remember, not really, what your children were like when they were small.

Maybe I was wrong about Sky, but I don't think so. Like Ralph, in the months he spent in Kennett, she was both from there and not, torn between staying forever, and always on the verge of taking off. That was in Orick, just another dying town on the northern California coast, where my sister and I somehow ended up on the day a burning forest turned us back from the center of the earth. We were tired, we were cold, and Orick was deserted, its emptiness the hollow legacy of the northern spotted owl and its local logging opposition, long the economic mainstay of the area. In a way, it was already familiar, as in our family we had always known that Kennett had once suffered the same fate, that when the price of copper fell and that of transport rose, the town where our grandparents met and married had declined in the same way, and that when the land itself turned out to be so saturated with heavy metals that nothing would ever grow there again, one by one, the workers left, until only the Indians remained. Our grandparents were among the last white people to leave.

"It was like the end of the world up there," they said.

Orick was not quite the end of the world, but it seemed close enough.

The motel had a phone booth on the edge of the highway, so we stopped, and then stayed, because there were no other vacancies for us.

All the doors were open to the parking lot, and all the doors were green.

And inside, in the back room, Sky was just there, almost as if she'd been waiting for me, her long hair stringy beneath a baseball cap, spots of spaghetti down her sweatshirt. And it was like that, just a furtive shadow at first, and then something—*something*—out the corner of my eye, and then, while my sister was checking us in, I just stood there looking, and maybe, after all, there was nothing, maybe it was just fatigue, or the accumulated effects of our own long day—the river, the fire, the center of the world—maybe I should have turned away, as if, if I had turned away, things might somehow have been different, but I didn't. I looked. I looked because in that exact instant I found myself caught up by the paradox that all things happen as they do because they cannot happen any other way, and that at any given moment, a human action can change everything forever.

Look, I told myself: *No, don't stare.*

My sister nudged me with her elbow.

And I looked, because I did not not look, that's all, and the woman I saw in the back of the motel apartment stood there looking back, as depleted a woman as I have ever seen.

But: *I did not imagine her, she was real.*

The sweatshirt was faded. The baseball cap, like the door, was green.

And I want you to know that it wasn't like in L.A., when you see, by the side of the freeway, some barefoot musician with a shining flute, and it wasn't pity either. In fact, it isn't anything I can really put into words, just one suspended moment among all the other moments, and so I have come to think of it as writing, the same way my son's sealed-off face is writing, and my white-haired lover, and the rivers are writing too.

A long time ago, when Sky first appeared to me in the back room of that motel, I meant for it to be different. I meant to imagine her story unequivocally, to make it altogether mine, and weave a tidy sequence of events, and satisfy our cravings that things should work out one way or another. I meant to answer all such likely questions as where she might have come from, and where she might be going, and what she was doing in my story, any story. Or maybe I just meant to explain to a friend who had said, *she just sounds like a Deadhead, you know,* how she wasn't like that at all, not even stoned, it was her happy-go-lucky motorcycle mechanic motel manager man who was, quite beatifically, loaded.

I meant all that, I really did, but failed to account, in such a narrative, for the ghost of that reservoir that was never built, for the land that would have lain beneath it, for the impulse of the men whose dream it was to build it, for the bears with their soft, friendly eyes. A moment, any moment, however arbitrary, can arrest the course of things and hold them, the way a dam holds water, for an instant, still and shimmering, and then for the rest of your life you will be trying to understand how everything changed in that pause. Sky was like that, and I can't explain it, any more than I can explain the way water rushes over rocks, the way it is always rushing over rocks, always the same, always different, and though I understand that there is some equation between slope and gravity, roughness and water, that can be used to parse the exact movement of rivers, it makes no better sense to me than the logic of the men who build dams.

I'm pretty sure Sky was wearing her man's flannel shirt over her sweatshirt. It was cold, especially after the heat of the day, and she did look sad.

If telling a story is about assembling its parts, just as with a dam, there is a before and an after, a river above and below.

I know that the day had been a long one and that my sister and I were exhausted, but also exhilarated by our strange route away from the forest fire, on roads that were not down on any map that ended here, beside the pewter gray Pacific Ocean. Also, everything seemed sharp and clear. When we'd come over the last wooded crest of the hills and begun our descent toward the coast, we'd found ourselves in a sea of yellow grass so infused with dying light it was as if the earth itself had somehow been transformed into a sun. There was a last burst of warmth, washed clean by the light, and though we knew that fog awaited us below, for this one moment we were overwhelmed with an atavistic memory of California, when it was all light and grass, and I reached across the front seat to touch my sister, who was driving, on her shoulder as we, too, were infused with the light.

"Maybe this isn't the center of the earth," I said, "but it's close enough."

In certain, more deliberate moments I am aware that this whole industry of my imagination is the literal byproduct of chance: I might have had daughters, the fire could have been on the other side of Hoopa, we could have headed east that morning toward the lava beds and desert. Or if Sky were someone else— another sorrowful woman in another dive motel, or possibly a child, or a solitary fisherman returning home beneath a pale, nascent moon—it would be a different story, spinning out. But once Sky fixed herself in my imagination, it was only a matter of tracing her back to her mother, Miranda, who, long before Sky, was also a girl, nine years old and bleeding by the water.

There is no doubt that there was blood; Patty saw it, and it remains one of her most persistent visual memories from the time before she was blind. Also, the boys were drunk, and Miranda, when she cried out, it was—it must have been—from terror. Patty never wavered in her story. It was always all about those boys and sex, and for myself, at the time I conceived it, I was so convinced that Miranda had been raped I didn't stop to consider other possibilities—she might have slipped and fallen, or closer to twelve, it was just her period starting. Even the raw fact of her nakedness: Patty was always so nearsighted. But she saw what she saw, and seduced by the image of the swimming hole, the rocky path down through bear-sized boulders to the water, the sounds of the party below, she made her own assumptions and I made mine.

Plus there is the fact of the sheathed, electric blue penis.

On the other hand, what even happens when a nine-year-old is raped? Surely she must tear, but does she heal?

In some respects, just like the light on the hill above the coast where we emerged, these things are confused and, in their own way, blinding. All we know for certain are Miranda's words: *There's going to be a dam here. Glub, glub. You're drowned.*

～
～
～

Things you can touch:

Besides large things cast in concrete between high canyon walls, this story contains many smaller objects, things you can touch and hold in your hands, what counts, at times, as archaeology: photographs, a split willow Wintu gift Indian basket, my uncle's parrot, a whole oblique assortment of accumulated artifacts that, taken together at once, form the clutter of my desk and life.

At ten, Joey hit an over-the-fence, out-of-the-ballpark home run, and he'd include his game ball if we had ever found it. Sam, his Selmer Mark VI saxophone, his Fender Sunburst electric guitar, his well-worn Birkenstock sandals.

These days, I study toxicology reports from the Iron Mountain Mine, pin old postcards of Kennett next to my uncle's Peruvian sketches, and believe that things you can touch have their own imperative and grace. You cannot really touch a dam, or if you do, the part you will be putting your hand on will represent such an infinitesimal fraction of the whole as to constitute little more than a wish, and this is how it is possible to say that the arc of the dam marks the space between you and your desire.

Without the ball, can we ever really say Joey hit that home run? Can we say that he even played baseball?

This smaller archaeology of things you can touch is what, for most of us, remains. In my family, what remains of Kennett (besides the still defoliated hillsides) are a battered yellow highway sign that once marked point midway between it and Redding, a box of photographs and postcards, and a bag of ancient Indian baskets I discovered in the sagging barn beneath the eucalyptus-covered hills on the most serene curve of the Monterey bay near the slough where blue herons nested. This was where my mother's family came to stay after the Franklin Street world collapsed, and maybe they meant to move as far out of the world as they could get, and maybe they did, but they held on to the baskets, which I would find abandoned half a century later, tied with yellow twisties in a Super Hefty trashbag on the dirt floor of the barn where my aunt stored old things. I don't remember now what I was looking for, or whatever prompted me to untie that bag, but as the baskets tumbled out into the dirt, moldy and in ragged disrepair and lit by sieved light from the rafters above, I had the most acute experience, as if of someone else's memory of a prior California, before dams and when Indians still lived at the center of the earth.

Later, when I asked her, my aunt would give them to me.

"Sure, if you want them," she said. "I've no earthly use for them."

And my parents would pay a small fortune to have them restored.

The archaeologist, however, who could not account for the high saline content or advanced state of rot in a town as hot and dry as Redding, was confounded.

"Science," he said, "could explain this, if I knew what to look for."

But science, I knew, could never explain the movement of families or the fog that rolls in off the Monterey bay every day in the late afternoon, and because I wanted to protect my aunt, I said nothing, just smiled, just looked a bit puzzled, like him. We were sitting in his air-conditioned office, and he was wearing white cotton gloves to examine the baskets.

"This detritus here," he said, peering into one and pronouncing the word *detritus* with a slight sneer, "is a rat's nest. And these are the husks of insects." He touched one, and it crumbled apart, turning into a fine, gray dust. "Redding," he added, "has high pH soils. None of it really adds up."

After that, we sat there for awhile without saying anything, each clearly suspecting the other, neither willing to budge, and in this way, came to an agreement, a contract was drawn up, and the baskets were properly restored. First, they were vacuumed with a high-suction vacuum; then, each underwent a kind of microscopic scrubbing during which it was bombarded with minute particles of glass swirling at high speeds inside a steel chamber, an airbrasive process that went on for many hours, even days, and worked to break down the molecular structure of dirt, cleansing the internal tissues of the fibers themselves: bear grass, woodwardia, willow, maidenhair, conifer root.

"These should be in a climate-controlled environment," the archaeologist reprimanded me when I picked them up, and my father groused a bit that they looked just the same to him.

Now three sit on the shelf above my desk, where I can touch them with my bare hands, and where, once again, they are gathering dust, and what I think is that between them and my uncle's Peruvian sketches on the wall just below lies the entire history of this work.

In my family, the story we tell is that they were gifts, just like the opium pipes also were gifts. But I know for a fact that both were, instead, payments for medical services rendered, many of which failed, by which I mean dead children: payments for dead children. Some of the opium pipes are silver, some, an ornate cloisonne, though it was known to be the case that the Chinese laborers, from whom they were received, were often dead before the family ever even called the doctor. What remains are the baskets, and the pipes, trace remainders of long ago deaths. And then a terrible wailing came from the camps, and then after that, a more terrible silence came down.

In a different sort of narrative, an ordered narrative where what really happened is contained by strong, particular will, we would not have this kind of slippage, one story or icon into another, sight into blindness, fact into imagination, history into self, but this is not that kind of story, and who is there to stop it, who will say *no*? In that different sort of narrative, the iconography would be stable and discrete, a dam would not get mixed up with a basket, and Patty would say things we all understand.

Some of the baskets were for storage, some for transport, a few were crude tourist souvenirs, and one, we suspect, was a young girl's learning piece, uneven and flawed, but urgent. And the willow, split willow Wintu coiled left three stick foundation interlocking split stitch basket must have originally been woven as a gift, for its gracious bowled form is both elegant and useless, its patterns too intricate for everyday use.

. . . *fag and moving end trimmed on the inside, coiled left,* the archaeologist wrote. *Insect damage,* he wrote, *with vestiges of rodent nest attached to the interior base, also affected by a dramatic increase in susceptibility to abrasion due to fungal attack of organic oil resins. . . .*

And how should we calculate the value of such a basket? It is just a basket, like any other basket, but with no other earthly function than to show respect or gratitude, and how had it come into possession of my family? Had my grandfather been honored in some important way, or had there been, instead, some terrible illness and debt? Did it come into my family as remuneration from someone, now bereft, but to whom it had once been a gift, maybe from an ancestor, the last remaining member of that family, a tribal figure in recognition or tribute, or a lover, to whom, in the beginning, it also was a gift, probably to celebrate a wedding or perhaps the birth of a child?

How delicate the handwork of it is, how rich the ancient mud-died fern that traces its elaborate zigzag through and around the redbud, the willow, red alder and conifer root, looping, looping, embracing the circumference, pure, unreadable, willow, split willow. I imagine an Indian woman weaving. She squats in the dust, head, whole body bent over her materials, dark hair glistening. Circa 1890. She works intently, her fingers deft among the pliant twigs. I believe that, though this is a gift for, say, a wedding, she does not anticipate the children the marriage will bring forth; she does not look forward into the next century because it is already over for them and surely she must know this in her heart. I believe that, even so, as she works she must remember, and as she must remember, she must dream. But what must she dream—oh, what?

᷑
᷑
᷑

Ishi, the last wild Indian:

Not far from those hills where the Indian girl wove and some years later, Ishi, the last wild Indian, wandered out of other hills, and some years after that I was born in the middle of what is now the prior century, at the far end of the valley that runs the better part of the length of this long, long state.

In the house my father built above the Sacramento River across from the floodplain that was never overwhelmed, we grew as a family into its separate parts, which were added over time and in response to our growing. The house was gray, with a red door and a valley oak out front that I used to climb or play in the shade of, and that, in early photos, is new and small, but that now, all these years later, has grown huge—taller and wider than I once could have imagined—and spreads a graceful canopy above the house where my parents still live. In the back, down the hill and across the railroad tracks, the river swept slow and strong, and somewhere upstream from there, just beyond the bend in the river, a bank of red clay bluffs rose dramatically out of the water. As a girl, I was strangely mesmerized by them—their stunning height and windswept crest, the way, in certain seasons, whole flocks of birds would erupt from the deep, deep channels of their erosion, and the rich burnt umber they baked each summer—and it would not be until middle age that I would discover they are not natural bluffs at all, but just another remainder, what is left over from the hydraulic mining practices of another century—the bluffs themselves, and the rocky tailings along the river below.

Out the back picture window of my father's house, we could really only see the river during the winter months, when the trees were bare, while through-out the rest of the year, sometimes we could just steal glimpses of pale water, like kisses, through the native cottonwood and oak on the hill below our house, as well as through our own domestic cherry, apple, walnut, and some-times it seemed we could hear it.

In the winter we also had a clear view of the old Dieselhorst bridge, its twin arcs mossy and graceful, and high above that, the black railroad trestle from which, in my twelve-year-old summer, a boy fell to his death. It seemed then as if his screams would go on for hours. I had climbed into the cherry tree—the same cherry tree under which, some twenty years later, I would marry—that smelled so sweet that time of year, and I perched there, transfixed, for a long time. The dying boy's cries rose and fell until the air around me was saturated with them. When it was over, when the thick summer silence descended again, interwoven with the drone of grasshoppers and, in the distance, maybe motor-boats, maybe recreational airplanes, I climbed higher, as high and as fast as I could, and sated myself on cherries so ripe they looked black in the wash of dappled sunlight. Before I came down that day, another train rounded the bend in the trestle and sounded its whistle three short times—*toot, toot, toot*—the way they always did to greet the children who played along the river.

In other summers, still longer ago, my young uncles dived from the bridge while my mother and aunt picnicked on the shore, toes dangling in water still warm enough for swimming. By the time I was a girl, the dam upstream had turned the water dangerously cold. No one swam there anymore. Your fingers ached just dipping them in, and while I want to say that it was not uncommon to lose a fisherman or child to it, I don't really think that ever happened. Still, I grew up with a kind of genetic longing for that other time when swimmers beached themselves like walruses, not on the steaming concrete of the nearby municipal pool, as we did, but down by the shore itself, on its silty banks, rolling, when it got hot enough, into the murky waters of a river you could, if you were brave enough, jump off the bridge into, then drift downstream with the current.

What I'm trying to convey is a sense of a pristine river sweeping wide through a town where summer days rise into the hundreds, and how, in the natural course of events, such a river would become a place of respite, a second skin for swimmers, or for sweaty toddlers, held close in their mothers' arms. This, for example, is the river I will one day dream of swimming home through. This is the river whose sworls I have always imagined, beneath the arch of cottonwoods, pieces of it glimpsed through lush vegetation.

But when a dam is built, the river below becomes a different river than it was before, fed by water taken from deep inside the reservoir, deprived of its original relation to sunlight, depleted of its sediment, starving. And it is cold, colder than you can imagine, too cold for swimming, cold enough, even, maybe to kill you. Maybe this isn't true of every dam, maybe some dams release their waters from the sun-drenched surface of their reservoirs, turning the waters downstream too sleepy and warm for the life they once sustained, but it is true of Shasta, and so we do not swim in the lower Sacramento anymore but walk instead along its new municipal trail and try not to think about how every couple of years a woman is murdered along it, or a child attacked by a cougar.

⌒

⌒

⌒

All things were changed:

Patty did not believe this. Though she knew, in her heart, that all things with the river were irrevocably changed by the dam, she also knew that her father had been part of it, so in her imagination the only reason we no longer swam there was that we had gone soft. Patty claimed that, without any dam, the river would not have provided much in the way of swimming anyway, not the way I imagined it, for it would mostly have been long, shallow riffs, with only occasional rapids and pools. Today, I have such a longing for the way it must have been once, a meandering channel marked by point bars, asymmetrical shoals, ridges, and swales—a beautiful, if unexceptional river. But Patty preferred its engineered state, the riffling sheet of darkly moving water, the rippling undersound of its current. Patty had, she said, the broader view of things. She said that all of California would be a semipopulated desert if it weren't for men like her father. She said the word *desert* with a low, derisive sound in her throat.

Even before Patty was blinded, she was way ahead of her time, and this was a great conflict for her. Patty had such faith, for example, in the fallout shelters deep inside the dam.

"We'll have beds and clean sheets," she said to me once, "and all the electricity we could ever want. When we come out, we'll be pale as moons, but the whole world will be waiting."

We were sitting on the sun-blazed sidewalk out in front of her house, and she looked a little dreamy as both of us contemplated that world, the one that would be waiting. Then I thought about the tunnels my uncle led me through each year when we toured the dam, the caches of food and supplies he'd point out along the way, the secret cubicles, some for ordinary workers, some for those higher up in the ranks. Among the spaces allocated for shelter, there were a few semi-private rooms, but most were long, cramped dormitories, like larger tunnels. I knew, too, that my uncle's refuge was only for him and his wife, that my parents had civil defense deployments in town, and that behind our house, my father was digging what would turn out to be only the first of his holes. To my sister and me, he insisted it was for a cellar, but no one in California has cellars, and it wasn't long before he'd built an underground room there, a terrible cinderblock place that, over the years, oozed mud, stank of rot and pesticides, bred ghastly insects, and once housed a family of bats. And this was for us, in the war.

I know I am not alone in this. We all grew up like that, horrified by the places our parents intended to hide us when the sirens went off. Years later, when my own children were small, I'd hold them in my arms and wait out, first, the L.A. riots, and then the Northridge earthquake, and try to understand what it must have been like for my mother, teaching us to duck and cover and where the food would be when the time came.

With Patty that day, I felt acutely bereft. "My uncle has one too," I insisted.

"It's just for immediate family," she said. "Wives and children, you know."

The concrete of the sidewalk was so hot it was burning my buttocks through the thin fabric of my shorts, burning, burning, all the way to the bone, but the feeling fascinated me and I could not move.

"I'll go swimming in the river if you will," Patty said.

"It's too cold," I said.

"No it's not," she said.

"They take it from the bottom of the lake," I said. "There's never any sunlight there."

"The lake is just a lake," she said. "It's not really what you think."

I was eight years old and I don't know what I thought, but this is what I knew: somewhere at the bottom of the lake lay the town where my grandparents met and married. They lived together in the hospital housing annex, and one of them played the piano, and one of them, the ukelele. Sometimes they worked and sometimes they danced. The grandfathers spent their days removing rock chips from the miners' eyes, and setting bones, and sometimes amputating limbs just above or below a joint. The grandmothers nursed injured workers and feverish Indian children. In the spring, where there would have been wildflowers, there was just soot on the ground, and the poisonous blue flumes of smelting exhaust were toxic enough to kill all the vegetation in a miles-wide swath of devastation that surveyors for the dam later noted, as if what did it matter to flood what we'd already ruined. The Indian children were brought into the clinic only as a last, desperate measure, and when they were buried, the elders wailed inconsolably, and then my grandparents were paid with baskets.

Everything touched by the smelter fumes died—the gardens in Redding, the dogwood and pink-blossomed manzanita, the split-trunked digger pines and sweet ponderosa, the willow, split willow, and maidenhair ferns. Fruit trees as south as Anderson and Cottonwood were stunted, and the smell was so obnoxious people could taste it. By 1919, violent protests had led to an early environmental court case that closed the copper mines, but alternative meth-ods of smelting were quickly developed to revive an industry that would, in a matter of years, be permanently felled by newly adverse economic forces. To-day, mines that have been closed for nearly a century continue to disseminate toxic residues through old tunnel systems, where seeping water becomes in-tensely acidic and dense with heavy metals—cadmium, copper, iron, zinc. And northwest of Redding, not far from where I grew up, Iron Mountain still rises up dead, one whole side of the mountain an eroded, barren slope of dark red clay that looms above us like a monumental inscription on the bare bone of the earth.

There is a photograph. In it, my father's father carefully arranged in a wicker wheelchair, sits with a plaid lap blanket wrapped tight around his legs, his head listing slightly to one side. Bright, but ill-focused, his eyes gaze off beyond the angle of the camera, while on his lap, my laughing, curly haired father reaches out for something, some toy the photographer has offered, some bright dangling bauble. Behind them, my father's mother and his brother stand rigid and apart, each staring grimly from across the cusp of time. In three months my father's father will be dead of influenza, his lungs already ruined by bad air. Everything I know about him, I know from this photograph, from the contents of the trunk he brought out with him from New York, and from my imagination, which is ruthless.

But what I would not have you think is that my father's father was the only living thing the copper smelting fumes cut down. For the animals, too, had all died, the fish in the streams, the birds in the sky, the bears, even Ralph's bear, the last golden bear.

And the basket is just a basket, like any other basket, the whole history of which—whatever cannot be read in its warp and weft—is just gone. Who'd have kept that kind of record anyway? My other grandfather, who survived, used to tell me that you couldn't get the babies past their first year. Typhoid, influenza, measles, poisonous water and air. Grief is not something any person owns, and though I'd like to tell my father this—relieving him, in some way, of his burden—I am certain that whatever words I'd choose would reduce themselves to something hurtful in his ears.

When a basket is woven, each strand of grass, or reed, or wool, or root, must pass repeatedly through human hands, and this, the principle of human touch, is what remains long after the artifact has lost utility or form, something, I think, about life being lived in its physical moment, something, it must be, about grace. Over the course of the first twenty-five years of the white occupation of California, the indigenous population would decline from as many as a million to just thirty thousand, annihilated not only by the inadvertent introduction of disease, but also by the widely celebrated successes of public extermination campaigns in which Indian scalps were bountied at as little as a quarter and as much as five dollars apiece. And sometime between the gilded altars of our missions and these tattered baskets, Ishi, the last wild Indian, walked off the face of this earth where, in the absence of history, it was as if all his people had disappeared without a trace.

Let this be about the trace, then, the ruins of Kennett under Lake Shasta, the baskets woven at the center of the earth, Iron Mountain, Sky. Because maybe the strands that connect us to the places we have wiped clean connect us, also, to what remains of a memory that might constitute a different kind of history, and bind us to the earth, and make possible distinctions between what we know and what we have been told, and let us say no, refuse anymore to be defined by or even a part of a world where all things are made possible by progress. Maybe there is no way to keep our stories separate, any more than we can separate the water in a river from the water before or after it, or the strands of a basket, one from another, without all things—all—unraveling.

Ishi, the last wild Indian, wandered out of nearby hills.

Patty had her own affinity with him. She knew, years and years before I did, that in addition to the town of Kennett, where my grandparents danced to the twangy strains of a battered ukelele and the pervasive grief of a poisoned people, an ancient Indian village also was flooded.

Think of her, then, who weaves the basket as the woman underwater, pensive and earnest as she works. She lives in a tepee in the village beyond Kennett. When she is young, these same hills are covered with buckbrush and manzanita, dogwood, digger pine, sugar pine, yellow pine, ponderosa, fir. The air smells of evergreen, sharp with pitch and of dust, fine as clay, that rises as she walks barefooted through it, then sifts down, covering everything; and it is during this time that her mother teaches her how to weave the baskets, and how everything they need, all the materials—willow, split willow, bear grass, woodwardia, maidenhair fern, pineroot and conifer root, red alder, clay, spring water—lies in abundance just outside their tepee. In the spring, when the roots of trees grow into the streams, the girl and her mother collect them and hang them to dry in their tepee. Between these white strands, the black stems of maidenhair ferns also hang drying, a musty canopy that smells of earth.

All this is when she is a girl. By the time my grandparents have settled in the mountains she must walk miles for pineroot, and the willow, the alder are gone. She herself is one of only a few remaining people who even know how to weave the baskets. Soon, it will all be forgotten, the elaborate warp and woof of plants, the dark designs of the stories they tell. But not yet, not while this Indian woman lives, who, unwilling yet to give in to what cannot be changed, persists in her wandering, sometimes for days, miles and miles throughout the hills, gathering plants and roots and memories, tying them up in huge bundles on her back to carry them home where, as she sings, perhaps, a low song, she will work them finally, weave them finally, trust finally her fingers alone now to remember how it's done, how, weaving itself, the basket weaves her.

If you take the idea of a story:

If you take the idea of a story and spin it off the tips of your fingers, what would it be like, I wonder: the blueprint of a dam? a river? the arc of your young son's first handspring, when he turns into a teen?

Do you even have a son?

Believe me, I am not some wild and scenic rivers nut.

Does a story have a color, hold a shape, move in any particular way? What earthly use are stories anyway?

This is not even much of a story. It is just something that happened, and I wrote it for my lover because one evening above another river and three days into a weeklong yellow raft trip, I perched on ochre bluffs and watched the teal-backed grace of swallows trace patterns in the air between me and the rippling surface of the water far below. It was the time of darkness coming on, and stars first appearing in the vastness of the desert sky, a kind of blossoming of night, and as it closed around me, I knew with stunning certainty that I had finally drifted as far out of the world as I would ever get, to arrive exactly here, and for just this one night, at the perfect and infinitesimal space that separates longing from fate. Around a campfire below, others in my group were sipping whisky, but the configuration of the canyon and wind was such that I could only hear them in sporadic bursts of unintelligible sound, mixed with the thrum of insects, the soft skim of bats through the close night air, the quiet brush of river through its channel. For the longest time I sat on the still warm rock lip of the bluff, watching the water, which is life, below, and I knew too that from that moment on the whole rest of my life would be driven by a deter-mined effort to stay as close as I could to that time and place, that particular center of earth, and any river that flowed to the Pacific. And it was then that I stood, and I planted my feet.

Now, I have no river, and I have no white-haired artist lover, whose ques-tion, nonetheless, still haunts me: *why do you hold so much back?* And as I think about the choices that I've made that have led me to L. A. and a husband who believes that women are not interested in facts, I am convinced that so precise a principle of substitution and replacement has been in play that there was never the possibility even of a trace of a remainder. My lover, who believed I had no will, wanted me to join him back East, just as Ralph once wrote from the Andes: *come here, come here.* It was never about holding anything back, but about the way we walk upon the earth. It is about planting one's feet. I believe this. I believe that if we are mindful, if we listen closely, we will find ourselves connected to the very ground itself, and thus cannot ever be wrenched from it short of cataclysmic events. Those rivers are my compass. Amid all the other paradoxes—the dams and the starving rivers, the lovers, the children who once looped inside our own bodies, language itself—there remains, not as a remainder but as an absolute, the course of the rivers, which like the blood that binds our bodies to our souls, binds me to this center of the earth by which I am defined.

And anyway, I didn't really write it for my lover, I wrote it, as all things, for my sons.

I wrote it because once, long ago, I drifted down a river to a lip of canyon wall where I would hear my lover, for the last time, calling *walk right into it,* and only later would I come to see that I had also drifted to the very edge of language, which, when it finally came to me, was clear and unequivocal, was *no.*

I wrote it for Patty, whom I last saw at that banquet for retired engineers, sometime between when she was seated with her contour map, and later, when she danced with my uncle. Around and around they danced that night, as graceful and light as the deer that used to come down to forage for food at the dam at dusk, but that was later, after we had spoken in the foyer where she sat with her map. Perhaps I should say instead that I spoke to Patty, for of course I was the one to approach her, and I did it deliberately, though with some trepidation. I watched her half the evening before making myself known to her. At the time, I had the strongest feeling about our encounter, as if I had something to tell her, something important. Anyway, that's how it started. Not that there really was anything specific, but that I hoped that there might be some way to assuage her memories and make things up to her, not just for what she'd seen, but also for her blindness. I was drinking vodka and the talk all around us was of the Colorado River, its degradation, limitations, bleak future.

"Give them ten, max fifteen years," I heard one old man say, "they'll be back at the Klamath, but who the hell can afford that now?"

"If they could even get it past the EPA," someone else said.

"That, or Shasta," said another. "Just raise it higher."

"They should have took it when they had the chance," another added.

"There could have been a dam there once," the first man said.

"Glub," someone said, "glub, glub."

"Patty," I said, laying my hand on her shoulder, "it's me."

She turned, but not all the way toward me. She said, "I married the geologist. How about you?"

This was before children, before my own marriage, before even the painter, whose blunt-ended fingers I had yet to imagine, yet to submit to, yet to take in

my mouth, despite the toxic residues of cadmiums and other poisonous metals. I sighed, remembering the geologist as tall and somewhat gaunt, and with a
remoteness about him I knew would suit Patty. This was something we ac-
cepted about her after she had become blind, and I believe that there was
something also between them about rocks.

"I heard," I said. "Congratulations. Are you happy?"

"It takes me back," she said, "your voice. You see," and she held out her
hands to reveal a silver wedding band, set with a small turquoise stone.

I don't know, was I jealous? But suddenly it went out of me, whatever I had to
tell her, and I was instead porous again, like a sieve, wanting her to fill me up, to
tell me things, about her darkness, but also, especially, about her contour map, its
humps and valleys, the places she could put her finger on where there were dams,
and the places where there could have been dams, and the places where there
might still be dams. Patty knew them all, at least in part because, years before,
when her mother left for San Francisco, Patty stuck it out with her grim father.

I couldn't take you with me, her mother would write from a walk-up apartment with white walls. *You'd miss your friends. Your father needs you. Eat well,
and go to bed early. I love you more than all the infinities there are.*

Now Patty said, "What are you up to these days?"

Once, in fourth grade, I made my own contour map of California, the
whole long state, with a scraped out hollow down the middle for the great Central Valley and little bumps for mountains, laced by rivers, in the north, and flat
yellow deserts in the south. Despair welled deep from inside me when my
mother took me out to the garage and left me there alone with a bowl of flour
and water paste that would later dry and crack on my hands and make my skin
itch with a light pink rash. But though the paint ran, smudging my rivers, and
the mountains could not hold their peaks, squashing flat instead, my aqueducts and reservoirs made the whole state green and achieved a perfect balance between agricultural and urban development.

Now, I studied Patty's map, and it was both like mine and not, the state still
long and bent and crisscrossed with a web of waterways, but hers was much
more elegant than mine, and, made by engineers, infinitely more precise.
Patty's hand was resting lightly on the mound of Mount Shasta, where the Sacramento River begins. I knew that though she had missed her mother desperately in those days, she had stepped in without complaint to do the wifely
things, the vacuuming and polishing of windows, the warming up of cans of

soup, the after dinner serving of Nescafe and ice cream. For awhile it was as if Patty's father didn't notice, if it was Patty or her mother, as if they were inter-changeable, and yet Patty kept it up, as if, if she could make her father see her not as a replacement for her mother but as her own separate self, the whole song and dance of his falling apart, her mother's absence, and Patty's own irre-mediable loss, would be compensated somehow, and her happiness fully re-stored. It seemed foolish now to imagine such a thing, that happiness could be restored like that, like a basket, but I knew that had to have been at least part of my own impulse in approaching her, and I thought for an instant how easy it would have been to have turned away instead.

What was I up to? Patty had asked, and what happened was that I was flooded with memories I didn't really want, wanted instead to hold to the present moment, to admire Patty's turquoise ring, to be told that the geologist had found the stone himself, nestled in the rocks beside a river, any river. I wanted the engineers around me to be young, with futures and lives and new dams before them. I wanted to believe in the benevolence of those dams. At the time, I was working in a peach cannery job and headed for graduate school, and I didn't want that either. I wanted that my backpack should be packed and waiting in my car, that I should be headed somewhere with it.

After Patty was blinded things changed again between us. I don't know quite how to explain it. My own mother, as if jumpstarted into action by the sudden need to be useful, to fill in for Patty's mother, started driving me across town to the little frame house Patty still shared with her father but could no longer keep sparkling, and of course it was awkward. We'd couldn't really watch TV, or talk about our clothes, and sometimes, for the longest time, we'd just sit staring at each other, only I knew that she couldn't see me. Torn be-tween fascination and repulsion, I would sometimes imitate her, waving my hands in front of me, groping at the sides of chairs before sitting down. Patty no longer went to school, and she wasn't invited to any more parties, but her clothes were still something to envy, so I wouldn't always tell her when she spilled ketchup on them or if she had missed a whole side in her ironing.

But there were other times, plenty of times when I wasn't like that at all, when we'd sit out on her postage stamp-sized lawn, and I'd tell her about all she was missing, the math teacher who looked like a fish or who liked whom. Once, I even took her with me to a candlelight moratorium vigil, leading her by the elbow across the parking lot to a small clump of silent protesters, and then we just stood there, sometimes singing with the group, but mostly alone with our thoughts, for hours, side by side until midnight, and the whole time I was thinking not about the war the way I should have been, but about how beautiful Patty looked beside me, as if lit from within by the candle she was holding but could not see, and which I kept having to adjust, reaching over and touching her hand to let her know when it was listing, because when I didn't, the wax dripped down and burned her forefinger and thumb, once badly, and still she said nothing, did not cry out or make a mortal sound, though surely the pain must have startled her and been severe.

Meanwhile, Patty's father had become a true fanatic. It was as if he believed, if he could charge the wattage high enough, he could succeed in illuminating even Patty's darkness. I remember the way she'd feel her way around their kitchen while her father ranted on about some new project he'd envisioned, and she'd be smiling. Later, we'd retire to her bedroom, we'd sit on the edge of her bed, and she'd stroke my hand. Once we did something I have come to regret. I don't know what came over me, or her.

You never can count on someone like Patty:

If you take the idea of a story, you never can count on someone like Patty. She is dangerous, erratic. You can't predict her. She is blind. If I called her on the telephone right now, she'd change everything by telling me about some new laser treatment that, little by little, is restoring her sight. She'd say, *his trunks weren't blue, they were cardinal red, itty-bitty Speedos, and thin as worn-out hankies in the butt.* She'd say, *long time, no see.* She'd say, *just joking, of course.*

For this reason, I am not about to call her on the telephone, but that night at the party for retired engineers, having approached her and her map, I felt suddenly a little bit drunk and possessed by the need to know more, perhaps, than I wanted to know but could not stop myself, even so, from wanting.

She said, "My dad tells me you were there when they had that Oroville earthquake."

"Yeah," I said, "I was working at the peach cannery in Gridley."

"Gridley," she said, but she was smiling, "is just downstream from Oroville, where I had my accident."

"Patty," I said.

"Oroville," she said, "is still the largest earth-filled dam in the world, and during that earthquake, it cracked," she said. "Right down the middle."

It was true, the dam had cracked, just as the cannery belts had buckled and swayed. I used to watch them during aftershocks deep at night, and what I'd think about was not the collapse of the building, or the women I worked with who themselves came from countries where whole villages—perhaps their own—are routinely buried in monstrous quakes, or the supervisors who stood at the doors and refused to let the women leave, as if they could not understand their languages or fear. It wasn't even about the kind of people this might make us, but just about the angle of the crack that had opened in the dam, which every aftershock would worsen, and which the engineers were busy studying and worrying. This was something I knew how to imagine from when I was a child—the lengthening and widening of the crack, the sudden collapse of the dam, the terrible roar, the wall of water. Ralph wrote to me from Peru *get out now, the dam is cracked.* He wanted me to join him and the children in Peru. *Come here,* he wrote, *come here.* But my real uncle assured me everything was safe, and though my dreams were of structural failure, I needed the money for graduate school and I stayed.

Now, what I wanted to know, and this was important, took place before any of that. "Patty," I said, "tell me the truth."

She was drunk, I could see. There was a tall glass on the floor, by the inside of the right leg of her chair, and when she leaned over to get it a damp sheen of sweat glistened on the back of her neck. Behind us, aged engineers, white-haired and bespectacled, looped their wives awkwardly around the dance floor. As I watched, Patty took an ice cube from her drink and let it drip into Lake Shasta on the map, but in her drunkenness her hand was unsteady, and before long she was dripping on the mountains, on Shasta's afterbay at Keswick, on Redding itself and the great Central Valley below, all over the map.

Patty said, "Ask me if I'm bitter. I'm not bitter."

I said, "Tell me again."

She turned to me brightly and said, "Let's dance."

Between then and now, a life I could never have predicted for myself has unfolded, replete with both anguish and moments of such unexpected grace that I have to touch myself to be certain I'm not dreaming. Take, for example, the birth of one son, his tiny nails and perfect arch of forehead, and then three years later, a second son is born.

I felt so guilty when I first conceived of Patty's blindness, not just because I did not understand why it had to happen that way, nor even because I took no human action to prevent or change it, but also: what could I possibly know about blindness? It was just a state of being in my mind, a coming down of darkness and closing off of the world, almost serene, almost welcome. And this is not a metaphor either. Imagine yourself imagining darkness: this is the limit even of writing.

Then I married Patty off to her father's protégé, the geologist who, like a son to him, filled in where his daughter was lacking. But I never once anticipated that she would come, in time, to view her blindness as a blessing, or that not long after her father's retirement, her husband would quit his civil service job to go to work as a lobbyist for Greenpeace.

It's like folding clothes: you shake them out, smooth them, and arrange their disparate elements—sleeves, collars, facings—into neat little piles, and then someone gets into them, looking for socks. If there is any one thing we can learn from writing, it would have to be that between what we can know and what we can imagine all things remain in such a precarious balance that however much I might want to convince you that Patty, just like Sam and Joey, is corporeal and hence can be hurt, I must still allow that when I wouldn't dance with her, when she danced instead with my uncle, swaying lightly, I understood two things: 1) it was not and never had been an even exchange, and 2) all along I'd believed it was I who had invented Patty and Miranda, but I never once had wondered where I fitted in.

Why I imagined Patty:
I did not imagine Patty for what happened to her or what she witnessed, or did not, for though her story is contiguous to mine, it never really happened, was instead conceived because I hoped she might know something about the history of the dams in the country I grew up in, what I have come to long for, a certain kind of information about the infrastructure of this state and its complex water system and what drives it, as well as the geology that makes this story possible, and our more recent heritage of loss. Maybe this sounds like

nostalgia but it isn't, for whatever longing I may have for a prior way of being comes not from desire but fact. The better part of California was once an inhospitable valley, subject to eight months of drought every year, washed by a temperate sun, and then there was gold, and then water. Today, people still believe that the impulse to spread our water all around was a generous one, designed to make the garden paradise accessible to all, ensuring our future as a happy and prosperous people, but Ralph says no. Ralph says it was all about power and money, and if you don't believe him, he says to look at the way we treat the gardeners in this state.

And then there is all the rest of it.

In my mind, I admit it is confused. It happened all at once and without my really knowing it, their images converging from two such disparate worlds and then forever linked, but when Patty came upon her, Miranda, nine years old and bleeding, had her foot firmly planted on a rock somewhere just above the center of the earth, which turned, the way it does, and then a quarter century had passed and Patty, now blinded, was elegantly seated beside a contour map of California, waiting to dance with an aged engineer.

And now this moment persists not just because of Patty and her map, not even because of the dams, but because one summer with my sister I swam in five rivers and am haunted by the memory of water, sun, rock among trees.

The Navajo culture believes that the world itself is a reflection of language, which is sacred, and that each morning the people must chant it into being.

Therefore, these are the names of the rivers: the Sacramento, the McCloud, the Salmon, the Mad, the Trinity.

And yes, they're linked here by geography as much as by the rhythm of our trip, or my imagination and capacity for language, but that is how I know them, and knowing them the way I do, I know that what I know will never be enough.

Patty I invent for the Middle Falls of the McCloud River, a glistening cascade over high rock walls down, down into a wide, round pool so deep that the water, beyond its churning edges, is a nearly opaque shade of aquamarine, the color water turns in certain angled light, or under the shadows of rocks and trees. I invent her for the boys who leap from the rocks, clambering higher with each leap, three boys at once, their pale bodies rodlike as they plunge feet-first into the water. I invent her for my own leap from a low rock ledge into that icy fist of green.

The murky eddies of the upper Sacramento. The clear pools of the Salmon, its riffles refracted by sunlight into myriad glittering and luminescent scales. The heat-drenched river bramble thickets of the Mad, swarming with insects, and the small black snake that slithered in between my feet into the water. The long blue limpid ribbons of the dammed Trinity.

I don't know, it is a complicated thing, but when I first imagined Patty something just went off in me, as if in her darkness I would find exactly what I wanted, what I needed, what had driven me for years if I only could have named it. She, too, had visited dam construction sites with her father, and it was easy to believe that he and my uncle had been, for years and years, close drinking partners, both visionary and expansive in their drunkenness. Patty herself was elegant that night in a black velvet gown, and I was convinced that between her and me and that map, a story lay curled like a small animal, but what I hadn't counted on, in the first place, was Miranda, and in the second, was Sky.

Tell me, tell me, tell me what it means to be a woman in this moment.

I never wanted Patty's other memories: what am I to do with an engorged, electric blue crotch?

Miranda, who attached herself to Patty almost at once and as irrevocably as did her blindness, is, I believe, the variable. Thus, the only way to change things is to keep the dam from being built. If Trinity Dam were a phantom, like the Ah Pah, if the river itself had never been threatened, and with it, the pool where Miranda was swimming with those angry boys, I don't believe they would have hurt her, ever. She was just a kid, and they had their whole lives before them. What possible need would there have been for violence if the land they loved and had grown up on, the land that was their only home, the land where they planted their feet, were not destined to be flooded any time now? It is not that I am torn between the concept of a dam and the concept of a river, but forced to choose, there would not be any choice.

~
~
~

July 14, 1991:

On July 14, 1991, a Southern Pacific freight train derailed on the upper Sacramento, maybe forty miles north of the dam, just above the stretch of rapids and slow pools I learned to swim in as a girl, and not far upriver from my father's cabin. In the predawn dusky light, the overloaded train, roaring straight for a bend in the tracks, caught itself on the arc of a sudden curve, howled once, and tipped the contents of a single toxic car down the bank and into the water. As the world watched on TV, the metam sodium—a simple herbicide designed to break down in water into highly poisonous contaminants—worked its slow way down the upper Sacramento toward the lake. That fateful journey took three long days, and then another four went by before Southern Pacific finally came up with a plan to pump air into the contaminated water with long hoses sunk deep in the lake, like boys blowing on straws, in the theory that stirring up the toxic compounds would bring them, in bubbles, to the surface, where they might be rendered harmless by exposure to sunlight. But during those first sad seven days, everything in the path of the herbicide was killed. I understand that the noxious plume itself was the yellow-green color of vomit, that it moved at about one mile per hour, and that it left an natural sheen that lingered for days.

Seven hundred and fifty miles away I watched the news reports in L.A. and thought about that river, the summers I spent there when I was growing up, weeks at a time with my uncle Ralph, thought, too, about my father's cabin, where he built his failed reservoir and where, as they have grown into their own childhoods, my sons have spent their summer days the way I once spent mine. Then, every day was like the one before it, a blissful monotony of near-perfect childhood idleness. In the morning, we'd tramp off to the nearest blackberry brambles, pails slung over our shoulders, and forage deep after the darkest, ripest fruit, despite thorns and bees and what we were convinced must be the ever-present danger of snakes. The berries were dusty and warm, and we'd eat them by the handful, the sticky juices running down our scratched and sweaty arms, and then after lunch, we'd sling inner tubes over our shoulders and trudge two or three miles up the railroad tracks to float back through the rest of the endless day. Between rapids we drifted down calm spots in the river where rainbow-bellied trout traced languid circles among algae-rich boulders beneath us. Birds dived low, snatching insects from the surface of the water. From time to time, river otters, mink, deer would eye us from the shore, where they drank. When our inner tubes lodged in shallow rapids, water would rise up and part around glistening humps of rock on which, exposed suddenly to air, thousands of tiny wormlike larvae arched and wriggled in agitation. Nights, we'd wait by the railroad tracks for trains to come roaring by, much huger in darkness than by day. As we waited, the forest around us rustled where animals moved.

It may be true I don't know facts but what I know is this: a lot of people is a lot of people, grief is grief, and a dead fish is a dead fish.

After the herbicide spill that summer, I stood on a footbridge above a Sacramento River so unnaturally clear I could count pebbles—red, green, gold—in the riverbed below. It was the strangest feeling, for I understood that this glistening transparency resulted from the absence of algae: that water was dead water, with no living thing in it. And it was true. There weren't any trout or suckers or minnows either, no wriggling black larvae, no darting water skippers, slithering snakes, silvery swarms of gnats and mosquitoes, shimmering dragonflies. No hawks, no beavers, no deer, no bears. Gone, too, were the Indian rhubarb, the thick clumps of skunk cabbage that, in normal years, hung like hoods over the banks of the river, the poison oak and blackberry thickets, the grasses. Even the larger willow and mountain alder were yellowed, already losing their leaves. But somehow, in this dead and dying world, some plants had survived, and by then all the animal carcasses had been removed. It could have been twilight—there was that grayness subtly clinging to the world—but it wasn't, it was mid-afternoon, and what I did not expect and could not have been prepared for was that, except for the quiet brush of water in its channel and the occasional rustling of wind, the world around me lay utterly silent— no bird calls, no fish splats, no drone of insect, scurrying of mice.

Then my boys ran up with pockets full of rocks they'd gathered at the railroad tracks and started throwing them—the way they did—over the side of the bridge.

A billion people live in India, give or take some hundred millions, and that, I believe, is close enough.

A cleansing breath:

Sacramento, Trinity, Salmon, McCloud, Mad: these are the names of the rivers I swam in with my sister, a complex web of memory, cusp of desire, what can't be touched.

But if water is part of this story, so also is fire, and this is in part about that, the lure of it, the unspeakable titillation that is the first plume of smoke in the air, the infinitesimal darkening of the white afternoon sky. For of course California is not just the history of its water but also of its fire, by which it is constructed and on which it still depends. Ours is an ecosystem driven by lack, and though only true desert in part, the whole state dries out eight months every year and is prone to periodic severe drought, when, for years and years, it hardly rains at all, and then fires blossom all over.

Fire is not the opposite of water. It is not its corollary. Fire is an element, all its own, and if I tell you that we love it, it is because we do.

California is supposed to burn. I'm just trying to make you understand what happens when the chaparral, evolved to burn out periodically, even, in fact, to replicate by fire, grows instead dense, and denser, approaching a point of critical mass, prior to which a fire can flash through a forest without singeing any trees—it will move that fast, a cleansing burst of flame—but beyond which fire takes a different kind of hold.

Many native plants in California will not germinate until their seeds are burst open by flame. Whole stands of same-aged, same-sized knobcone pines mark where fire once burned through. Fire is our cleansing breath that takes out choking grass and chaparral and lets sun down to ash-rich forest floors and delicate new trees. And the grasses grow back in a season, the scrub brush in two.

I want us to understand this, for it is a principle on which all things depend, how life itself was once in perfect balance at the center of the earth, and that is why we love the fire, which this also is about, the atavistic memory it evokes of a time when a curl of smoke was not a sign of devastation, but a promise of rebirth, the balance of all things renewed and restored.

But if men like Patty's father can dream whole towns and forests underwater, imagine what will happen when they come up with Smokey Bear.

I knew it was up to me to prevent forest fires.

There are things that should never have happened. We introduced eucalyptus from Australia as a windblock. We built our houses farther and farther up into the hills. We stamped fire out.

Eucalyptus is a weed tree, the oils of which explode in fire, tossing flaming branches all around. In the hills, homes capped by exploding eucalyptus burn quickly to the ground, each a terrible, private loss—a sad, sad thing—as elsewhere in our forests the persistent absence of periodic burns ensures that brush roots itself where it does not belong, growing unchecked in weedy clumps around the thick trunks of the forest's old trees, choking out tiny new seedlings, and providing enough tinder that fire, when it comes, lingers long and hot, along the ground, and forms its fatal embers that wait, like tragic secrets, until first the bark catches, just at its papery edges, and then deeper and deeper, as the flames exert their stubborn hold and begin to rise up slowly— this may take a day or two—slowly up the huge tree like a tongue up its trunk, curling and licking and digging itself into the heart of the wood, until at last it reaches air and wind and perfect tinder at the tops of trees, where, whipped by air and wind, it leaps from from crest of tree to crest of tree, joined there by the burning branches of exploding eucalyptus. Then the whole forest ignites, which is not as things are when they are in balance, for in a balanced world, fire passes through, a cleansing breath.

∼

∼

∼

A billion years ago in California:

It has been almost 4 billion years since the first primitive rain fell on this planet, rain that, some 3 billion years later, began to trace its paths through what is known as California. Half a billion years later vascular plants appeared on the terrestrial surface to create modern rivers in which physical and biological processes are inextricably linked, and then, for half a billion years or so, these same rivers worked unencumbered to brade, agrade, erode, and flood, forming the land we plant our feet on—a world carved and held in perfect balance throughout time until the first post-industrial white men arrived here 150 years ago. What is the relation between 150 and 4,000,000,000 years? How can you hold so small a fraction (.00000375, says Sam) in your mind? But in that small fraction of time, we have managed to transform nearly every river in this state until 60 percent of our natural runoff is held in dams, starved, and, with ever more efficiency, moved from one place to another, from where it is in surplus to where it is deficient.

For in addition to our dams, we have smoothed our world out, eliminating roughness so that water flows more quickly where it's going. We have stripped our upper watersheds and lined the lower ones with concrete aqueducts. And we have done this, despite what we know about roughness itself, which holds our rivers in their beds and without which, we are told, the force of gravity would constantly accelerate the passage of the water until, in a sudden flowering, it would just fly apart.

Sometimes, at night, we dream that this happens. We dream that our rivers fly off our earth.

~
~
~

Before the dam was built:

Before the dam was built, the Trinity River dwindled to a trickle every summer, the world turned dry and dusty, and its people were parched. This is how the Bureau of Reclamation was able to convince the local people to acquiesce to the damming of their river. The Bureau of Reclamation promised them a playground, an end to summer drought, water to put down the fire. It promised to transform their land in rich and subtle ways, and the people, sitting on defoliated mining tailings from a hundred years ago, were not about, in those days, to say *no.*

Or maybe they were. Maybe, even then, there was concerned public awareness, maybe even scattered protests to protect the watershed. Maybe people knew exactly what road they were headed down. I was just a girl at the time, ogling with my father. Whatever I remember, I'm sure it is wrong.

Approved in 1955, Trinity Dam was completed in the five years between 1957 and 1962, a zoned earthfill structure that contains about 29 million cubic yards of earth, sand, gravel, and rock. At a height of 537.5 feet, its crest is close to half a mile long and 40 feet wide, with its base nearly seventy times wider than that. Primarily intended to store what is called "surplus water," the plan was to take that very water and divert it to the Sacramento River for use in water-deficient areas of the Central Valley Basin. That much is fact: I have seen the tunnels, and they are huge.

I don't really know what logic the Bureau of Reclamation used. What I do know—because I was there—is that the Trinity River used to dry up every summer into a brackish creek, replete with polliwogs and minnows and skippers darting on the murky surface of the water. I remember the metallic taste of the air, the sheen of dust, the heat, which is exactly what it must have been like for Patty on the afternoon she saw Miranda. Our tongues in our mouths were swollen and dry, and we believed our fathers when they told us that dams would create the best of all possible worlds—swimming in the mountains, farming in the valleys, a happy and prosperous people.

And yet, even then we must have understood that the dam would alter the whole ecology of that water drainage system, affecting everything from salmon, to newts, to birds. Even then we must have known, though we did not fully understand, that the Trinity River, no longer flushed out by winter storms, would be reduced, I am now told, by three-quarters. Even then we must have known that the dam would cut a swath of terrible regret across the country, which we were willing to exchange for what was promised, a twelve-month river with long riffs of green water for rafting, and eddies where children could play. In another generation, people will summer by the lake, and it will be as if it has always been this way, and bears will gather berries at the shore.

One summer, several years after the Southern Pacific pesticide spill into the upper Sacramento River, I came upon a group of state biologists in wetsuits, wading up and down the river in lanes marked out by twine strung between posts. They were counting fish.

"How can you tell?" I asked them, "if a fish crosses into another lane? How do you know you're not just counting the same fish over and over?"

And the answer, of course, was that they couldn't, for that is the nature of counting fish.

Before the introduction of the Shasta Temperature Control Device, the chinook salmon population on the Sacramento had declined from more than 171,000 to 191. But these days, who can say? There's a new fish ladder in town, and I have seen salmon carcasses rotting on the riverbank, but even my uncle, if you were to ask him, would insist that while there is something elegant and principled about this whole exchange, there was never anything wrong with their dream in the first place.

Today, we are attempting to restore the Trinity River to 50 percent of its original flow, even as we entertain the possibility of enlarging Shasta Dam. We think about a monstrous dam like that, and then we think about the 700-square-mile bay delta where the Sacramento and San Joaquin meet to form the largest estuary on the west coast. We think about that estuary, through which 40 percent of our watershed passes and which provides the state's most significant habitat for fish and wildlife, including two-thirds of its salmon population, and we don't know what to think, because we know that the delta is dying and that, with enough water behind a big enough dam, we could make our own floods, we could flush the delta out, we could begin, in time, to heal it. On the one hand, we are on the lookout for dams we can dismantle, and on the other, for rivers we can still tap. Like my uncle, we are six of one, half a dozen of another, and we are not about to change the way we are.

Three rivers systems—the McCloud, the Pit, and the Sacramento—drain into the reservoir behind Shasta Dam, the cornerstone of the Central Valley Project, to which Trinity Dam also belongs and which late-blooming visionary men like Patty's father and my uncle dreamed out the tips of their fingers on blue tissue paper. Below the dam, the Sacramento River turned broad and cold and powerful, but it remains, above, a pine-fringed healthy river, long shallow riffs of rich water interspersed with slower pools.

I am not some wild-and-scenic-rivers nut, but each river you swim in has its own embrace, and sometimes, it is as if my whole life is contained in a vise of longing that is nothing more than the insuperable passage from one such embrace to another. What can I possibly be returning to, when I return to those waters? And if this, after all, sustains me in L.A., where I do not have a river, does it make me some wild-and-scenic-rivers nut, or not?

~

~

~

A different country here:

Once it was a different country here, in California. What kind of knowledge enables us to know this? Where do the boundaries of history, imagination, and memory collide?

Years ago, when we were north for Christmas and the boys were still young, we took a trip through Gold Country and stopped in Coloma to explore the replica of Sutter's sawmill there, to stand at the exact spot where, one January morning in that other time—in 1848—James Marshall, John Sutter's employee, discovered the piece of gold glistening in the sand that would transform the entire history of this state, though both Marshall and Sutter died paupers. Some 150 years later my own sons threw rock after rock in the placid

American River, gray beneath a steel-edged sky, and imagined finding gold themselves, great chunks of it lying on the shore. The thin winter sunlight felt warm through our sweaters. A handful of others out on holiday stood in clumps before bronze historical markers, reading the legends aloud to each other, idly remarking on them. Up near a bend in the river, graceful bare-limbed cottonwoods swept all the way to the water. I remember flocks of birds flying south. Who lived in California in that other time were indigenous peoples, as many as a million in some sixty separate tribes, Mexicans, and a few white people with a vision.

Whereas here at the end of another century, leaflets with swastikas litter the schools of the town I grew up in, and the web of things is such that one hot June afternoon Gary Matson is murdered with his lover. There were four of them, the Matson boys, in Redding, and one of the ones in the middle was my sister's first boyfriend, but Gary was the oldest by several years, and remote in the way those few years in high school make a difference, an athlete, activist, and scholar, someone we looked up to and followed the achievements of after he went away to college, and tried out different paths, and then went back to Redding as an organic horticulturalist. How does a century turn from the point at which we go out into the world with love and optimism, to another at which we are brought to our knees by the murder of one of our own and the man that he loved? If what we suffer from is nostalgia, it must be for a time before leaflets with swastikas littered our schools, but we must also know in our hearts that there was never such a time as that, that it wasn't what we think, and that even if it was, our violence was somehow different then, maybe turned inward or at the ones we loved best. Perhaps all I really wanted with this story was to deliver Sky from one point in history to another, diverting her, like water, to a place beyond violence, where no one was bereft of anything.

My mother's father's father was a Danish sailor, fourteen when he ran away to sea, twenty-four when he married and settled on a fertile hill farm just east of the Monterey Bay—paradise, he called it, on earth—planted apples, bought more land, raised a family, grew prosperous, and sent his sons to Berkeley. There, my mother's father studied medicine and then went farther north to Kennett, where my father's father joined him six months later from New York, his copper-studded wardrobe (my coffee table now) stuffed with useless items from the city. Six months after that my grandmothers arrived, and some time after that, during what I have always imagined as a terrible snowstorm, the uncle was born who dreamed up the dam that turned the town where he was born into a lake.

As I think about this now, I think about the way the whole history, if not of California, then at least of my family, might have been different if Ralph had come first. Ralph, the fearless surveyor, had such a capacity for planting his feet upon the earth. In his green Can't-Bust-'Ems and thick work boots, he'd have scooped Miranda up and carted her off to his bear to have her wounds licked and healed long before Sky was even conceived. Ralph would have somehow found a way both to save the rivers and to responsibly manage their waters, and Ralph would have done this for us all. But Ralph came second, eclipsed in the middle, not even real, and, unchanged by any different human action, things are the way they are and always will be.

The photographs above my desk include an old daguerreotype of my mother's mother's mother, who looks like Harry Reasoner in his dotage; a professional portrait of my enormous, white-haired grandfather, taken when he was mayor of Monterey; and several snapshots of my grandmothers. In the portrait, my grandfather sits at a table in an arched adobe patio, drenched with luminescent sunlight and a working lunch spread out around him—upside-down tins of evaporated milk for the coffee and half a loaf of sliced sourdough bread. In another, my grandmothers are enjoying tea with other nursing students, three of them crowded around a silver chafing dish in what appears to be a dormitory room. Wearing starched white caps, voluminous gowns, and bibbed aprons, they are, nonetheless, dreamy and languorous. My father's mother reclines on a chaise in the back, sad-eyed and somewhat aloof from the others. To her left, by the glare of the window, two of the other students lean drowsily against each other, one looking vaguely away, the other gazing back with heart-wrenching adoration, and at the chafing dish, my mother's mother sits primly stirring something with a long-handled silver spoon, while by her side a fifth dark-haired woman attends with downcast eyes.

Poets dream of being archaeologists, as if their lives were sedimentary, like rocks. Poets don't mind getting down and dirty with the past. But time and again as I have studied this photo, I have been surprised to recognize my own face in the faces of these women, a certain thin-lipped purse of mouth I have never found attractive in myself, a slight leftward tilt of the head, the vague broad-set eyes. They are considerably younger in this moment than I am now myself, and looking at them now, I am struck by how easily a person can move, in language, through the history of a family or a century, woven like a basket in the iconography of who you are. For of course I know too much about what lies ahead, and writing will not change the way things have turned out, not my uncle's suicide, nor my other uncle's dam, nor the homophobic murder of the brother of my sister's first boyfriend. What am I to do with information like this? What earthly good is archaeology for that?

~
  ~
~

Patty and me:

When Patty and I were girls, we did a little spelunking, and once took a boat across Lake Shasta to a limestone outcropping Ralph had pointed out to me before he went away forever. Because it was late in the summer, the water had receded many yards from the treeline, and the shore was angry and red. Patty steered the boat and she went fast, and the whole way over, I kept imagining Ralph's golden bear pacing the streets of the town underwater beneath us.

The caves we were going to were known locally, both for the petroglpyhs at their mouth and, somewhere deep inside, for one enormous room you entered at the top and descended into, some 120 feet, down a ragged rope ladder some-one had left there long before; but access was difficult, and by the time Patty and I had made the steep climb to their entrance, we were hot and sweaty and scratched. Thus, when we entered the cool moist air and started moving on our bellies into the inner darkness of the earth, we experienced, as always, a kind of release from our bodies, and a deep, animal hunger for breathing, as if the air itself had been transformed into something nourishing and loamy. Patty, as in all things, led the way. To me, her knowledge about such things as geology and how to rappel off the slick walls of the cavern, seemed vast.

We found the ladder, on which Patty did some repairs while I watched the calcium carbonate deposits form around me, gigantic stalactites dripping their mineral-rich water to the stalagmites below, and wondered how many eons it would take for the room to fill completely, becoming, where we were, solid rock. The ladder looked terribly frayed to me, but because we were young, we used it anyway. Patty descended smoothly and quickly, as if she re-ally did know what she was doing, but the ladder was difficult for me to manage, and I swung about wildly, finally pausing halfway down to let it still itself while I hung there, in the middle of the earth.

No one knew where we had gone that day.

We explored for hours from the bottom of that cavern, following tunnels filled with miraculous rocks until each one ended or became too narrow for us to proceed. Patty was looking for something, but I didn't know what, and then at last, we found ourselves peering into a tiny white room, filled, like the inside of a geode, with gravity-defying formations—"Popcorn," Patty told me—that grew inexplicably in all directions. The room itself was too small to enter, and so it had remained virginal, glistening and white. We lay there for a long time, looking into it, and then Patty turned off our miner's lamps and we were enveloped by darkness. This, of course, was extremely erotic, but we did not recognize what we were feeling, and the moment passed.

By the time we emerged it was night, and we boated back across the lake beneath a star-splattered, moonless sky.

By the end of that summer, Patty would be blind.

∽

∽

∽

What I want:

Here is what I want: I want that the woman with spaghetti in her hair should not have been the daughter of a woman who herself had been gang raped thirty years before by teenaged boys drunk on beer somewhere in Trinity County when she was nine years old and before the world she was raped in turned to water. I want that she instead grew up in Hoopa, the white adopted daughter of Baptist Indians. It's possible. I want that there never was a fire, that we ended up, my sister and me, guests of the Baptist Indian parents that night in Hoopa instead, honored visitors to a powwow at the center of the earth. Or maybe that she really was a Deadhead, a refugee from Southern California, who went bad in middle school and was sent north for clean living at a residential treatment home, and who looked so completely forlorn at just this particular moment for the simple human reason that, despite the fact she'd lived there six or seven years by then, she had never quite got used to the fog, its bone-penetrating chill, the way it cloaks the world with what never looked like mystery to her, but only dreariness. I want even never to have seen her, to have somehow negotiated the rental of our room in this dank motel on the Northern California coast—the only one with vacancies for a hundred miles, north or south—without catching even this one glimpse of her in the back of the apartment she shared with the beatifically stoned motorcycle mechanic turned entrepreneurial motel manager who rescued my sister and me from the phone booth on the highway where we huddled in a panic, calling AAA motels as far away as Crescent City and Eureka, by inviting us to check out rooms we had failed even to consider for precisely what I came to admire most about them—each green door flung open to the world.

With the exception of four young German tourists, drinking in the parking lot, we were the only other apparent guests, though by morning the place would be full of late-night arrivals, trailing in from fishing trips, beach bonfires, backpacking trips.

The motorcycle mechanic was grinning ear-to-ear, and when we told him we had been headed to Hoopa but ran into the fire instead, he just grinned more broadly, as if, for some reason, ecstatic by our news.

"You must of took one helluva wrong turn," he said. Then he said, "I heard it was arson, them Hells Angels over from Blue Lake. I heard that fire is a doozie."

All of his rooms he had ready so far were clean as a whistle, if somewhat threadbare. Ours had a mural of gulls swooping low over gray ocean waters painted on the wall above the bed. One gull had a fish in its mouth, and this made me think of the spaghetti-splattered girl, whom I would have missed altogether had I let my sister make arrangements for the room, the way my husband always does, but it was cold, and we had been driving those back roads all day, and the motorcycle mechanic motel manager had grease up to his elbows, and his grin, I don't know, it could have gone either way, and there were, as well, the German tourists, so I stuck with her. Up there where we were, in Orick, it is mostly old remnants of a tough logging town, and the northern spotted owl and its fallout.

As it turned out, the mechanic was more stoned than maniacal, and more earnest than dangerous, a happy-go-lucky business entrepreneur with his little piece of heaven an investment in the country and his future. As it also turned out, the motel office was his own apartment, with his woman in the kitchen in the back, the spaghetti in her hair and her history, and the history of her mother as incontrovertible as it was grim. Facts are facts.

She was nine, her mother was.

She was raped.

Some years later, she conceived and bore a daughter. All around the daughter now, open cans of marinara sauce swarmed with shimmering-winged flies.

What you want:

Whereas what you want is story, and I don't know: *what's story?*

Story is its ebbs and flows, its risings and its fallings, its delay. While in the aftermath of what was knotted, these words are more like spinning, more like dreaming, more like digging. Archaeology, not narrative, but there it is.

Only let me tell this my way. I tried so hard to tell it other ways, the way I thought I was supposed to, making things up as I went along, aiming to please with metaphors and plots, imagining that, if I would just try hard enough, I could fit myself into the authorized version of the way things are and how to tell them. And in fact, in those days I could still whip up a mouth-watering meal in no time at all out of what looked like a bare kitchen. I kept my towels folded and charred the wicks of candles, as my mother had taught me and her mother taught her, before putting them out, in testament to our status as a candle-burning family. I knew what my place was—cook, clean, fuck—didn't you?

What kind of woman do you like?

No one likes them angry but if you will trust me I swear to you that it will be all right.

I am the kind of woman women love.

What I mean is *no.* You want *story,* you can have it. I'm giving it back just as fast as I can, because now that I am older I know two important things: how impossible it would have been for anything that I have told you to be different, and language, I know language, how it speaks us.

My husband, who came before as well as after the white-haired artist, believes that history, proper, stops at the Mississippi, and though this is the source of a recurring argument between us, it takes place more in sadness than anger these days.

"I don't want to hear about your past," he used to say.

And this is what would happen: my tongue, inside my mouth, would go all fat and swollen, and a stubborn fish of muteness would come down around my heart. His people came to New York from Eastern Europe at the turn of the last century, passing through Ellis Island with so many countless others, and that, I guess, is history, culture—diaspora—beside which, what is a river, a decimated indigenous people, a monumental dam, a rodent-eaten basket with rot?

When the boys were young we used to lie with them at night, one of us to each of them, and as I'd hum wordless lullabies to mine, his warm head pressed against my chest, across the room my husband, suddenly expansive, would hold forth on basic facts about the world: the longest river, highest mountain, fastest man.

What gives an object, any object, a privileged status in the iconography of culture? What distinguishes a fact from something that happened a long time ago on some childhood playground—a found rock, affection exchanged, the brush of a wind or a secret. Choose a word, any word, choose *mother.* You say this to a woman and it becomes a word so charged and overloaded with meaning that the woman wants to wrap her arms around it, the word itself, murmuring *mama, mama.* You say the same thing to a man and he thinks *mom,* he thinks, *what happened to all my clean socks, mom?* But say, instead, a word like *trail,* like *quest,* like *dam:* a woman's mind goes numb and lonely, maybe she starts talking to trees, while a man strides forth to embrace it as his destiny, the word he has claimed as his own, head up and broad shoulders squared.

For many years I've tried without success to understand exactly why the ideology of quest harbors some objective value in this culture, while that of mothering, like my own past to the man I married, does not. I spread my stories out like remnants of fabric from around the world, and as I finger them, I imagine another woman weaving. How are we separate, I wonder? And how can I possibly explain this to my husband?

Sometimes all I really want is to cup my hands together and hold them out to him, though not in supplication, saying, "Look, this is who I am." Then after a decent pause, I might go on: you think there is a point of origin, a point at which things are transformed, one single point of absolute difference, but our faces, our own faces—*touch mine, here, no here, here*—aren't even our own. Still, one lives—how could one not?—with a continual backward glance, referring again and again to the bits and pieces that constitute a single life, not in search so much of answers as of touchstones.

So you say: *Tell me a story.*

I say: *I was nine then, too, the year Miranda was, twelve when she was twelve, and we came hard into our adolescence during the years of our war. When Clair Engle Lake was beginning to fill behind Trinity Dam, my father took me to watch. I remember tromping in the mud along its shoreline when my nose, as it often did in those days from the heat and dry air and any slight altitude or exertion, started to bleed.*

My father said, *put your head back. Swallow it,* he said.

I never had a daughter, but later, only sons.

Between my husband and my lover there never was so great a difference, and what I could not say to either one of them is *shh, what makes you think I am holding back, and anyway there are no words for it for what I really had to say to you, nor if there were could I have found them, nor could you have held them in your head or heart.* I believe that if either one of them could have held it in his heart, I'd have curled myself without resistance into his embrace, and in this way, too, Sky would have never been conceived.

To Patty, dancing with my uncle at the ball, I would say, something passed between you and Miranda on that day and you should not have turned away. What is the relation between your blindness and the way you turned away that day, the accident at Oroville that turned all of Miranda's fury into your memory and fate?

To Patty's father: you and my uncle and the rest of the men who dreamed dams out the tips of your fingers based on the value, the necessity, and what you perceived to be the inexhaustibility of water: *is it at least possible you might have been wrong?*

To my sons, in their passions and private vulnerabilities, in a voice so sure that it could never be mistaken: *I love you.*

～
　　～
～

To transect the world:

When they first built Shasta Dam, it set all kinds of records—the most concrete, biggest federal project, longest shoreline, some 363 miles spread out in many fingers up the folded mountains, which yield, every summer, a little more each day in a widening swath of clay bank that charts the rhythms of the seasons and the dam, and that in years of extraordinary flood will completely disappear even as water is released over the top of the spillway in a surge of such proportions everyone in town will drive out to marvel at it, and that, more commonly in years of drought, will broaden daily as the water recedes and recedes, drying up whole fingers of the lake and leaving an angry red border around its warm, placid blue waters.

It must be difficult for those who have not been raised to anticipate the appearance of a dam, any dam, to imagine how exactly it is possible to round just another bend in the road, and find yourself suddenly jettisoned from the among the soft, shadowy folds of hills into an altered world, blasted by concrete and filled with strange water. Not all dams are like this—the long descent to Hoover, for example, traces a rocky slash of desert canyon, as if in free fall—but mountain dams are. You twist along on winding roads, maybe following the cut of a river below, maybe just meandering through trees, a dense shadowy forest, and then, with stunning suddenness, the world opens out into light and water, concrete and steel, and your breath leaves your body and you know, in this instant, that whatever else it is about, for the men who dreamed this up, it was more about passion than logic. What I don't know—and at times it seems critical to figure out—is if their passion was for water, or if it was more just for numbers and physics, displacement of elements—power, rage—a whole continuum from imagination to mastery.

The Trinity Dam site consisted of miles and miles of clear-cut forest in a narrow, elliptical basin, and big fields of old mining tailings, grim reminders of a ruined ecosystem. My father, who was neither an engineer nor a surveyor but just my uncle's brother, beamed.

"Just think," he said, "this will all be water one day. Water for play, water for crops. It's a miracle of progress, that's exactly what it is."

Even in my memory, it is not as if I mourned the loss of anything just then. I was nine. It was big and exciting. And anyway, I knew, that part of the country, just like the country behind Shasta Dam, had already been spoiled by its prior generations.

As we stood in the dust of the Trinity Dam site, my small girl's hand in my father's huge one, my nose dripping blood on the very ground that, in year or two, would disappear beneath another lake, a recurring dream came back to me in which, on steep banks above the reservoir at Shasta, I kept trying to grab a yellow construction toy lodged in a clump of manzanita just beyond my reach. Each time I jumped up for it, the bank began to crumble, and I would cry out, *Daddy, I'm falling,* and he would catch me, and, as the earth quieted around us, I would be flooded with relief. This happened many times, until finally he called back, *we are all falling,* and then the bank was sliding away slowly beneath us and, gripped by a panicky terror, all I could think was how deep the water was below, deeper, I knew, than the deep end of the city pool, deeper even, the words formed clearly, as if narrated, in my head, than the tall brick chimney of our house.

I am not sure how far I was at that moment in either time or space from the spot where Miranda met the boys whose rage at what was happening to them expressed itself against her. I don't know what we thought was going to happen to people like them, never mind the trout and the salmon, the black-tailed hawks and the ring-necked ducks, the mosquitoes and frogs and shimmery blue dragonflies.

Maybe we didn't think that way then because we had seen the aqueducts, vast concrete arteries lined up eight together to transect the world. At the time I never doubted them, just as I would never doubt Miranda, who used to play among them. Miranda was so fearless in those days that she would sometimes wander deep into the pipes, following them as far as she could as if, in this way, she might arrive at a place of utter darkness, with only little pinpricks at either end of the world, where she might wait out what was going to happening next.

If it weren't for the Trinity Dam, as well as for Sky, I would have imagined Miranda as much younger than myself, born, perhaps, to the Cuban Missile Crisis, or even later, to the deaths of Bobby Kennedy and Martin Luther King, the fall of Saigon, or the Iran hostage crisis, history in general. Miranda has her own kind of agelessness, perpetually unformed and on the cusp of becoming somehow different—older, more sanguine and finished. And it is so much easier, somehow, to imagine her swaddled tight in yellow bunting, her father a celebrated hostage. Of course, if it weren't for the dam going in, and the creek, and the pool of water where they swam, this could have happened anywhere— San Jose, Los Angeles—and any time, but it didn't, and when Sky looked up that night from her simmering pot of spaghetti it was as if I were looking at someone I had already known once, someone I'd grown up with but who had not aged herself—as if, indeed, I were looking through her to her mother, perpetually nine years old and with the marks of what had happened to her closing over with the toughness of a scar.

〜

〜

〜

The country we drove through:

The country I drove through with my sister on our way to finding Sky—the exact center of the earth, where the Hupa Indians have lived since the beginning of time—would once have been all water if the engineers and other men like Patty's father and their vast will had prevailed. For if they had built the Ah Pah, there would have been no Salmon River—no riffling stretch of green river where we swam, no blue maillot, no limpid light, no rocks, no dogs, no fire. Because I have lived my whole life with the image of Kennett underwater, it is easy for me to imagine the surface of the earth so utterly transformed that this whole trip could never have taken place because where we were was just another mammoth reservoir; but for the engineers, the square-jawed men like my uncle with the parrot, the idea, as they had conceived it, was never about what is wiped clean and away like that, never about loss, never about what happens when men get it in their minds to perfect the hand of nature or God.

Patty's father, as you know, was a mild-mannered drunk. I don't say this to be critical of him, but because it is a fact, and also to explain how it was possible for us to slip away one night, despite how overprotective he had become since the accident, as well as a little bit reclusive.

We were sitting on her bed, drinking tea from the translucent porcelain set her mother left behind to remind us of something we never figured out. It was an evening in early summer, with light lingering late, though I knew this did not matter to Patty. For a long time, we'd been silent, as dusk, and then darkness, came into her room, and though she had what she had in mind, her hand, her whole body was steady. I found myself staring at her fingers, the way they curled around the rim of the cup, serenely embracing its delicate roses. More than anything, I wanted to take those fingers in my own hand, to cradle and comfort those delicate bones, but for some reason I held myself back, hardly even listening to what Patty was saying.

She said, "They could have stopped with Shasta," she said, "one hulking center to their whole water dream, but no. I wonder what happened to that girl."

"What girl?" I said, but my breath caught slightly as she raised her teacup to her lips.

"She was so young and I wrapped her in my towel. She was bleeding, you know."

I didn't want, at that moment, to embrace her. That would come later, and that, too, would pass. Patty had only recently lost her sight. Everything seemed confused, drinking tea on her bed from her mother's cups. Even the weather had been erratic that day, now humid and dark, now blindingly bright. The tea was Earl Grey, which seemed grown-up and sophisticated. Patty was wearing small dark glasses that, at certain angles, would reflect my image back at me. Once she started talking, she couldn't stop, and that was the first time I heard the whole story, everything she remembered—the blistering heat of the day itself, her father's thermos (and Patty knew what that meant), the long drive down the dirt road, the rocks and the boys and the water, and the nine-year-old girl. Patty told it all, and then, like that, she wanted me to take her to the river, and who was I to say no?

"It's a full moon," she said, "I can feel it."

And though she was wrong, though there was barely more than the sliver of an earring of a moon that night, I knew what she meant, there was something.

"Patty," I said, "it's dark. There's a current, rocks. It isn't safe."

That was when Patty laughed, and the laugh was what did it, as if the whole idea of safety, now that she was blind, was irrelevant to her, as if what she couldn't see couldn't hurt her.

By the time we slipped out, it was close to midnight. The air felt sultry. I was nervous, but I didn't know why.

Nothing bad happened that night. Patty wasn't further hurt or damaged. I cut my foot on a old snag, but that was only carelessness on my part.

We drove for an hour or so up into hills, eventually following a dirt road to a Forest Service campground not far above where the river disappears into the head of Lake Shasta. Without a moon, it was difficult to make our way down the bank to the water, but we could hear it. There was a quiet *swuush* of current, no roar, as with rapids, and a mild lapping at the shore.

Patty and I stood there listening for awhile before starting down. That's when I cut my foot. Patty slipped, but only once, and it amused her. There were no other campers around, and no one bothered us. But when Patty took her clothes off and stood there pale and luminous in the summer night, when her foot, long before mine, found its way into the water, when she gasped at its coldness, suddenly, for no apparent reason, I imagined her instead, the tiny cry she made, when the shard of metal pierced her eyeball, and imagining this, imagined as well, as if through her eyes, the blue nylon bulge of the drunken boy's penis. These two things I imagined simultaneously. It was as if a mental image passed directly from her, to me, through the icy water, where I now stood shivering and bereft with a knowledge I would now never lose.

Patty arched her back and dived.

"Patty," I cried out, alarmed, "watch out for rocks."

When she surfaced almost all the way across the river, the rush of tenderness that overcame me was almost more than I could bear, and I knew that what we had just done had been both dangerous and foolish, and that I would pay.

~
~
~

Then:

Then, more than twenty years later and just this last spring, I planted a garden, and all at once Los Angeles became a living thing. This is not something I ever would have anticipated, but as I learned the names of plants, I began to see them everywhere: *acacia, eugenia, jacaranda, olive, star jasmine, happenstance rose, bougainvillea, plumbago.* The earth itself seemed teeming, the air steeped with the exotic exhalations of things growing.

How lush things were here, suddenly, as I imagined my annual summer journey north.

Not long ago I received a postcard from my uncle in the Andes, asking after Patty, "that little girlhood friend of yours, who had the tragic accident." In it, he mentioned that a girl in his town had also recently been blinded, but that in the aftermath of her accident, when she could no longer see the actual world, she had started having visions. At the bottom of his postcard he drew tiny pictures of her visions.

Then he wrote, "Can your Patty see like this?"

Inexplicably, I started weeping. How was it possible I'd never even wondered what Patty might see, if hers was a world of total darkness, or indistinct shapes, or astonishing visions? I wanted to ask her, *Patty, Patty, what do you see?* But I haven't talked to Patty since I first imagined her at that engineer's reunion, hovering over her contour map of California, and what could I possibly say to her now? I'm not even sure where to find her anymore, if she is still in Redding in her father's house, or where she might have gone with her husband, someplace, perhaps, sublimely beautiful and threatened. Also, thinking about Patty always disturbs me, for how can I not feel somehow responsible for her blindness, which I imagined too, like some weird retribution for her having seen Miranda on the day we believed she was raped.

〜
〜
〜

When Patty hit the water:

When Patty hit the water that night she entered it so cleanly there was only the slightest muffled splash, nothing you would even notice if you weren't listening for it, like the muted splat of a precisely arced fish. Watching her, I imagined her skin constricting from the cold, her nipples going hard, like projectiles. I tried to imagine what it must have been like for her to have dived, like that, not toward any surface she could see but only what she heard, maybe, only the quiet ripple of a current, not knowing how far it was between her and the water, how long it would take before she would enter it, and at what angle, or even if it would be deep enough.

Patty swam nearly halfway across the river before surfacing, shaking her head like a dog, while I, with all my senses, waded slowly out into the water, recoiling a bit at each new increment of cold working its way up my calves, my thighs, my crotch. I think I must have been making high-pitched little gasps, like I do. On the other side of the river, the bank rose, clifflike, into mountains, fringed along their peaks with a shadowy lace of trees.

Patty and I swam to that other side, where I helped her climb to a flat slope on a rock. We hunkered there for awhile until we stopped shivering, until in time the moonlight itself seemed to warm us. Patty turned her face toward it, as if she could see, and her skin, like the moon itself, glowed milky, luminescent. This, her luminescence, is the origin of my regret—not the dive itself and the danger it incurred, but its aftermath. And as far as I can tell at this distance, there are several possibilities, none of them inevitable and each vexed.

The first is that we do, after all, make love, one sightless, both naked, skins like damp silk and gritty where dirt sticks to us. I imagine Patty's tongue, how it finds me. I imagine myself seduced by her darkness.

The second is that it is here, not her bedroom, where Patty, absolved by the water and in the sheltering arc of midnight, first tells me about Miranda, her voice so soft, so contained that it would, but for what it relates, be almost obscured by the sound of the river. As she tells me, I do not understand, nor will I know for many years, that Miranda's daughter, Sky, will be waiting for me on the whole other side of my life. I cannot anticipate this preternatural symmetry, nor the pattern of fire and water out of which it will emerge, for I am myself just a girl, naked and fraught with desire. It will be years before I even begin to suspect that not so far downstream from the very spot where we have swum, the glassy blackness of the lake lies like my uncle's handprint on the earth.

As Patty tells it, in her own words, the story goes something like this:

My dad was always dragging me to dam construction sites. You know the way they are about their big machines and the land, when they strip it. Trinity was special. I think he liked the mountains, and maybe how the valley was already wrecked from the mining, and the whole idea they were going to fix it, wipe everything clean. My dad still got ideas like that. Me, I wanted to stay home. It was summer. *Jeopardy* was on. I had this new blue bathing suit that, god, I can still feel, the way it was against my skin and how I thought I looked in it, as if the too-big bra cups really were necessary, or at least and convincing.

We drove around all day, looking at the stumps of trees and these big yellow, dusty CATS. I climbed up in one and pretended to drive it while my dad griped to some man in a hard hat about the hullabaloo some people were making over the river, the salmon, why did we need another dam, all that. But it was just some people. My dad was drinking from his thermos, and he smelled juniper sweet. I'm just trying to make you understand what it was like that day. I knew if he drank too much, if anything happened, that would be the end for us. I was wearing my bathing suit under my shorts and t-shirt. In the newspaper on the seat between us there was an article about John F. Kennedy christening the other dam at Whiskeytown. You remember what things were like in those days, back before the war, back even before the president was killed.

I'm just trying to make you understand.

∼

∼

∼

To understand Patty:

To understand Patty, what you have to understand is that she welcomed darkness, the way I welcomed Sky. Both—darkness, for Patty, Sky for me—represented a kind of rupture between one way of being and another, and sometimes it really is enough merely to embrace the possibility that things are unstable and can change. In darkness, Patty could reconstruct her world as both more compelling and benign than the one she had come to know, and also, I would guess, more private, something all her own and only hers. As for Sky and me, I can't really say. She looked at me a certain way, and after that, the world somehow shifted out of balance.

Between a river, a dam, and a fire, what we must imagine about what drove the men who made the history of this state is their need, or their impulse, or just their sheer desire to control whatever nature put before them, to cultivate the wilderness and make it bloom and bloom and bloom.

Eucalyptus explodes in a fire because of its oil, and then the burning branches fly about, adrift on the furious winds of flame, spreading their terrible cargo of fire. Sometimes I imagine the tall trees exploding. For awhile, I liked to imagine that Patty lost her eyesight to an exploding eucalyptus, not a freak construction accident. In this version the blinding embers flew directly at her corneas but there were no scars, just a milky whiteness where once they had been clear and green.

Hazel, really, with scattered flecks of chestnut. And with a look abut them, too, even before all this happened, of sheer longing.

This story is so much more personal than it is about the end of nature, whatever will remain for my sons. In my garden I planted one tree, an olive tree, silver-green in certain lights, that I imagine will someday arc gracefully above us.

≈

≈

≈

In Patty's words:

OK. So it was later in the day, and hot, and my father, by this time, was drunk. But what I can't remember, did I say my suit was blue? It was green. You can tell it however you want, but it was a tiny bikini.

And you know my dad, he had to keep his oar in. That was just how he was. He knew the ins and outs of every project, from the first surveying crews, the very first trees marked for removal. So with Trinity Dam, even back at the very beginning, my dad used to go out all the time, and one time he found this local swimming hole, just a place on some creek with a little gorge that people dammed up with logs and rocks. It was hot, like I say, and later on, after looking at the dam site for a long time, my dad, he said he wanted to show me this "really special place." We drove for what seemed like miles on a nasty dirt road. Then, even before he pulled over and turned off the engine, I could hear them from the top of the ravine—whooping and hollering.

My father waved me toward the noise and said, "Go. Have fun."

Then he said, "If you see a boy named Alec, tell him to tell his dad if he wants to have the house moved, he has to sign the papers."

His hand waved desultorily through the air, as if separate from himself. I tugged at the bottom of my bikini.

≈

≈

≈

When I think about this story:

When I think about this story—what's made up and what is not, its whole imperative, and what shapes it—I know why this moment by the river persists. I know because when Patty finishes, we will make our way back upstream, struggling through overgrown skunk cabbage and patches of what we hope is not poison oak, to a place where the river is shallow enough for us to wade across. Our bodies will gleam in the moonlight, and I will guide Patty firmly, my hand cupped under her arm, going slowly enough for her to find stable places in the river bottom, places where the rocks will not shift underneath her, or where she will not slip on the algae.

Halfway across the river, I will stop and turn us toward a bend in the river where Mount Shasta seems almost to rise up out of the water. In my imagination, this will have been a wet year, and snow will still blanket the sides of the mountain, its long, graceful, concave slopes. On this night, it will gleam, like our skin, pale and luminescent in the moonlight.

"It's still there," Patty says.

My feet ache from the cold and we are clumsy now, ill-footed on the slick, wet rocks.

"It's all there, Patty," I tell her. "Every bit of it."

"OK," she says at last. "My bathing suit was red, like lava. Lava red."

In a minute we will turn and make our way across the rest of the river. When we come to the railroad tracks on the other side, a freight train will be coming. Patty will hear it before I do, a faint rumble in the distance, and we will wait until its shadow bursts upon us, the roar and its looming darkness like a wind that guts us and hollows our chests. As I count the cars for Patty, she will hold her hand out, as if she can feel the spaces between them. Patty was my girlhood friend—my only girlhood friend—and though I do not know yet that what I have received from her this night—both the memory and the story—will become for me like the spaces between train cars, a rush of empty air at my face, then *swoosh*, the darkness and opacity of yet another car, then the space again, and through it, what is that—the moon?—but then again *swoosh*, and again *swoosh*, and again *swoosh*, and though it has not yet occurred to me that her blinding was no accident but rather a retroactive gesture of my imagination, not punitive so much as benign retribution, I still want more than anything that she can see me. I want this so badly I can taste it. I want her to know by looking in my eyes that I will not betray what she has told me and that, whatever else might happen, I will do what I can to set this story straight, whatever might lie in my power, or that of language, to rescue Miranda and readjust the whole sequence of events so that things turn out all right and balance is restored. I do not yet know about Sky, and we are only girls still, our whole lives before us and, as we imagine them, lush and full of promise.

~
~
~

In Patty's words:

I started down the path toward the ravine. It was steep and dusty, with little clouds of dirt rising up around my ankles—*poof, poof, poof.* When I stopped, I could feel them settle, like powder. I felt excited about meeting this boy, Alec. I thought about his father's house, how naked it would look after they had moved it, perched on four-by-fours with all the other naked houses, huddled on a barren gravel lot. I was going to tell him not to sign. I was going to tell them all not to sign.

~
~
~

A memory of loss:

And it is that, not the boy's engorged penis in his electric blue trunks, not even the blood running like molasses down the inside of Miranda's legs, but Patty's determination to convince them not to sign that returns to me now, sudden and urgent. It is not that I don't care about Miranda. The harm that has come to Miranda is grievous and irreparable, and it is for that, as much as for her daughter, Sky, whose pasty face with all expression gone completely out of it lies, like a moon, at the center of this story, that I am telling it, for once the image of the girl on the rocks lodged itself in my imagination there was nothing but to see it through, not just to its end, but also to its beginning. It is impossible to know at this distance if Miranda was raped, but facts are facts, and one thing we do know is that her home was turned, when she was just a girl, into a lake, and maybe it was only a mountain cabin with windows facing east, and maybe no one else would ever miss it, but it was Miranda's home, where she was born and lived and panned for gold along the curl of a river she loved the way a person learns to love a river that traces every contour of her life, and where she'd move, as she grew, with such alacrity and grace into every language she would ever know, and where later she would walk with the boy who fathered Sky beside another lake carved not by Patty's father or my uncle or the U.S. Congress, or even the men who drove the CATS, but by the eons-old movement of glaciers, and it is for this reason, if not for any other—the reason of the lake that swallowed up the home—that the story of the girl on the rocks persists, for I know, too, as if by some genetic memory or record, what it is to have your home erased by water.

A memory of absence, of loss. Things wrested completely apart.

~
  ~
~

Why do I hold back?

Why do you hold so much back? my white-haired lover asked.

I don't want to hear about your past, my husband said.

Carolyn Kizer describes the aesthetic of the American West as a highly developed sense of irony, tinged with an impulse toward elegy.

In the absence of history, what sustains us—irony, or elegy, I wonder?

A dam, I'd tell my love, *a dam holds back. That is the nature of dams.*

And I would tell my husband: *this is what it sounds like when you take a dam apart.*

OK: it's true, none of this would ever have happened without Shasta Dam. We can even say that it would not have happened without the boom-bust-and-boom times of the early middle of that century, without the flat backs of trains Mike eschewed, without Rose herself, whose childhood dependence sent Mike to Toyon in search of a job, and hence, the shape of this story. If Mike had never gone there for work, if he'd have stayed in Texas instead, he'd never have moved to the Trinities in the first place, never cut the windows facing east, never marooned his daughter, Rose, in such a way that she would conceive Miranda beside the same alpine lake where Miranda would later conceive Sky, and none of them would have ever come to love the curl of a scraggly river among the slag heaps of another century.

One day, before the surveyors arrived with their first secret maps of the future, Miranda was panning for gold from her grandfather's sluice box, her pan a smaller version of his and rusted to the color of earth. It must have been early autumn because her grandfather was away hunting deer, but the pale sunlight still gave off sufficient warmth for Miranda to work into the late afternoon and then through the darkening shadows, longer and colder, unable to stop as she dipped her pan over and over again into the sludge at the bottom of the box, then back into the icy river, and then, slowly, patiently, she swirled it out, the water and sand and tiny black rocks, even the glistening fool's gold, all of it slipping out with the water over the lip of the pan until what remained would be only the heaviest matter of all, gold dust and maybe a nugget or two. Only not on this day, no matter how long she kept at it, when, despite unnatural perseverance, Miranda found nothing, no gold at all, not even enough dust to brush across her eyelids, the way she liked, though it made her grandfather sad and sometimes angry. Miranda believed that the glittering dust on her eyes formed a magic veil through which she could see things the way other people couldn't—mountains, streams and rivers, animals, trees, rocks.

"When I close my eyes, it's all still there," she said, "but shimmering. Also, I can hear things. Just ask me if it's going to rain. Ask me where to put the next sluice box."

Miranda, however, was not a patient child, and would often abandon her panning after one or two tries to wander off and play in the wood, though there were other, stranger times when, for no apparent reason, it would be as if a separate will had lodged inside her body, and she'd be unable to quit. On this day, she continued to work, even as the afternoon dragged on and the light began to dim, and there was something both dogged and inspired about her determination, her working beyond her numb hands and sore shoulders, her chattering teeth. Miranda did not think anything would change by her persistence, it was just that she had a particular feeling and she could not make herself stop.

I want to tell you that a white-tailed deer came down to drink from the sluice box, just as the moon arose from behind the mountains, just as a nugget of gold appeared in Miranda's earth-colored pan. I want to tell you that the tongue of the deer, like the tongue of Ralph's bear, was rough, and that as Miranda watched it lap the water beside the small nugget, it seemed to her to be no color at all. When she reached for the nugget, the deer's tongue rasped at the back of her hand, and a warmth began to spread, down her fingers, up her arm, all throughout her body, even before her hand had closed around her small golden stone.

I want to tell you this because it happened.

I want to tell you that I know it happened because Sky showed me the gold one night beneath the sliver of another moon, along with a clump of stiff hair from the deer's white tail.

Sky said, "They're magic. Touch them."

And I held them in my hands—the gold in one, the deer hair in another— and in that instant what I heard, like someone else's memory of a different place—the quiet brush of water along a sandy shore, the clackety hiss of crickets, the barely heard sough of wind in pine above—turned into something like language.

"My mother understood it all," Sky told me. "My mother could translate the world."

I want to tell you this, but I do not expect you to believe me. Irony and elegy: what is history, truth?

Why does anyone hold so much back?

The feeling that Miranda had about the water, and the sluice box, and that day—what they would yield up if she would stick with them, like a lover, and wouldn't let up, if she held fast to the unfathomable core of their promise— that is how I feel about narrative and truth, held together by the force of a desire, like the roughness of a river that holds it in its bed.

When Miranda's grandfather came back successful that night, the bloodied carcass of a deer slung at the back of his truck, he could not stop her from curling up beside it, though it was rank and stiff, and nuzzling her face into its neck. Miranda's grandfather knew that she knew that this meat would feed them through much of the winter, but what he did not know and would never know was about the nugget of gold and the tough, white hair of the other deer, held fast, one in each of Miranda's clenched fists. Miranda fell asleep beside the carcass of the deer, and then her grandfather carried her in, unable, in that light, to tell if there were tear streaks on her face, and stubbornly incurious about her sleep-clenched fists.

∿
∿
∿

What I imagine:

This is what I imagine if Patty gets to them that day by the ravine. First Alec, then Miranda, then all the other young people on the rocks, begin to think about their houses, scattered as they still are along the slag-heaped river, then they think about them moved and denuded, propped randomly on four-by-fours in sun-scorched gravel lots, their mothers' kitchen cupboards stripped bare inside them, their own rooms empty of their slightest trace. Maybe they don't think about it exactly like this, but what they think is how their lives, all their lives, have been rooted to this place, and now suddenly they have been turned nomadic. They know that everything is changed by this, and that, for the rest of their lives, they will never not be haunted by this splitting off from one way of being to another that will run down through their families, each generation to the next, an inherited memory of loss. They know all this, and they know too that there will never be a way to assuage the image of their homes beneath the lake, and that what their children's children will imagine beneath the glassy surface of the water will persist as a reminder of what was done to them.

What I also imagine is that this is a function of will as much as fate, even language, and that when Patty says, "Don't sign," what opens up inside them is a sense of their own raw human urgency and power. In this version of our history, Patty turns out to be an unreckoned force, and the kids convince their parents, who convince their neighbors, who go on to convince other neighbors, until not one single person in that whole ruined valley will agree to sign over their heritage of rootedness, their memory, and history, where they have planted their feet.

At first, my uncle, Patty's father, and the rest of the men who dream our future out on blue tissue paper are bewildered. What is happening to their master plan? But then things get rough. Though there are not that many of them, the men whose family property lies behind the dam and underneath its projected reservoir have been emboldened by their children's passion and anguish. Maybe one takes a stick of dynamite and blows up a CAT or two. Maybe three or four chain themselves to the concrete footings at the bottom of the dam. No one among them doubts they will prevail, for it is 1962, and we are not yet able to conceive a nation turned against itself, as soon we will be.

In this version of our history, what Patty says to Alec, those plain words not to sign, stalls the entire Central Valley Water Project in its tracks. With work halted on Trinity, the afterbay at Lewiston, seven miles downstream, also shuts down, and Whiskeytown dam on the other side of the mountains never makes it off the drafting tables.

"What is the meaning of this?" my uncle will rail night after night, outraged at first, and disbelieving, but becoming, as the months pass, more and more resigned to what he sees as a wholly irrational turn of events.

Patty's father, too, is deeply troubled but, like my uncle, finds himself completely powerless to intervene.

When we go there with my father to look, it is like a carnival around where the men have chained themselves to the dam, with all the other families camped out in tents, and bright-colored balloons, and mountains of fried chicken, gallons of potato salad, acres of dark, gooey brownies. Because my father is not my uncle and hence not officially connected to the project, we are invited to join them, to hear their side of the story. My father, a reticent man, listens closely all afternoon, as my sister and I play tag, and hide-and-seek, and kick-the-can with the dusty-faced children of the encampment, the half-completed dam just beyond the circle of tents a natural boundary for the excess of our games. Much later, we are invited to eat.

I am not saying this ever could have happened, but in this version of our history, beginning now, in 1962 with the Trinity River Rebellion, California is forced to readjust its water policies, allowing for such things as its natural watersheds and actual rainfall, a painful reassessment that does not happen overnight but that eventually spills over to include state as well as federal water projects. Oroville, hardly even conceived, is abandoned before Patty ever goes there, and so she is never blinded. All up and down the state, farmers recognize the limits of our resources and proceed more modestly, abandoning water intensive crops and methods. Even in L.A. xeriscaping catches on a full quarter century before its real time, and people don't move here in droves. We are a smaller city, living more within our means, and thus we care better for our people.

And while I do not plant my garden there are other plants instead, plants I recognize from the hills around me: manzanita, scrub oak, prickly pear.

∼

∼

∼

In Patty's words:
Then I saw the girl on the rocks just below, completely naked and bruised around her mouth. I think it was a bruise, though it could have been dirt, and

like I say, she was bleeding. Alec was behind her in blue trunks and he had a hard-on, but I didn't know then to call it a hard-on. A boner. They were drinking beer, or maybe it was Coke. Alec, did I say this, was right behind the girl with the bruise, or maybe it was dirt, around her mouth. She was maybe nine or ten, or even older, it was hard to tell, she was so skinny. The party was loud and I wanted to join them, wanted to be part of whatever it was, but it didn't include me. They must have known by then about the dam, but I wasn't thinking about that either. To me, it just sounded like fun, and I was listening to their fun, too young, as yet, to know to call it rage.

My father was above us on the rocks. He was happy. I was happy too, wearing my shimmery new bikini. Sometimes, it gets all mixed up, how I see it in my mind—what happened, the part I made up, or invented, or wished. Sometimes, everything is different, and we stay happy.

OK, then, the girl had this stringy, yellow hair, it looked dirty, and the bruise, which could have been a smudge, though her mouth, I could tell, was all bloody, and the sun hot on my back. It was a rocky trail and I was trying to get down it fast, get to the party, have a drink like my dad, but I kept slipping, and once or twice almost fell. You could see the Trinity Alps rising up behind us, the Red Alps, the White Alps. It was pretty. I was thinking about the dam, too, how great it would be for summer. We were like bottomfish, in our bright-colored suits.

I am pretty sure they were drinking beer.

I am almost certain it was a bruise.

I know she was bleeding down the insides of her legs. But I did not know then to call it rape.

When she saw me, she spat. Then she grinned.

"You know what?" she said. "There's going to be a dam here."

I held out my towel, but she reached her hand high over her head and grinned.

"Glub," she said. "Glub. Stick around, you're drowned."

"Patty?" I heard my father call out above. "You all right, Patty? Be careful."

Then I looked up and saw three boys on the rocks behind the girl and one of them held out his hand. He was wearing electric blue trunks. As the girl turned to let him pull her up she said something, I'm not sure. Then I think she said, "I'm Miranda."

All your life:

All your life you think the world is a certain way. You are, more or less, willing to go along with it. Then, one day, just *poof,* everything changes.

You may think this is a long shot, but imagine, for example, the universe itself and what we know about its basic laws, the principles that govern the big things—like stars and galaxies, and even rivers—are determined by the force of gravity, without which—*poof*—everything would fly apart. But then, on the whole other side of the scale, tiny atoms—the building blocks of everything— are bound together not by physical, but by mechanical laws. And there is also this: while both quantum mechanics and gravity can be scientifically proven, the principles of one contradict those of the other and they cannot hold together, it seems now, by anything more than the force of a desire.

You think things are a certain way—either one way or another—then suddenly you learn that they are both.

Because of course today we also know that the basic building blocks of the universe are not, as we have understood them, particles or forces, but tiny vibrating loops called strings. They are small, these strings, unimaginably small, smaller than a wish, let's say, or, in mathematical terms, one hundred billion billion times smaller than a proton, with vibrations that extend into ten dimensions. I will say that again: *one hundred billion billion times smaller than a proton, and ten: ten.* Ten dimensions, characterized by such mathematical beauty, such sublime symmetry that, taken together at once, they banish the absurdities that arise when quantum mechanics and gravity combine to reveal the hidden mystery that, as physicist Andrew Strominger has revealed to us, such minuscule strings and, say, black holes, are simply different aspects of the same thing: from which we are forced to conclude that whatever it is that holds things together is also what wrests them apart.

You think things are a certain way, then, suddenly, they're both.

Strominger, who claims that aesthetics guides him backward from the problem, always believed himself slower than his fellow students, as if on a different wavelength.

"I don't feel," he says, "like there was some Herculean task, where I worked hard and learned things. It was more like the theory explained itself to us."

How they imagine these strings is with numbers. I want to say they do the math, but it isn't really like that at all. No, the numbers arrange themselves the way numbers will, just as a word will, a story.

"The theory is much cleverer," Strominger says, "than the people trying to discover it. So instead of attacking it, you listen for clues. The people who do the best work are the listeners" (*L.A. Times,* Tuesday, February 4, 1997, A16).

By George, I want to say, I recognize that feeling: you think things are a certain way, then suddenly you're in a different story.

I don't know what it was like that day for Patty. I wasn't there, and our lives have unfolded in such different directions I'm not sure I can even imagine her as she is now. But I also know that Strominger is right and that story is revealed not in telling, but in listening. I know this, and I know that whatever I can do for Miranda, or Sky, or my sister, or Patty, or my children, or even myself, will depend on the quality of my listening. I know this, and yet I am afraid that I have been listening as hard as I can to what Patty said to me since she said it to me now nearly twenty years ago, and for the life of me, I do not know if what she said the girl said was, "It will all be water here. Remember that. Miranda," or if she said instead, "Can you help me?"

∼

∼

∼

Sky was born:

Sky was born.

Sky grew rangy into adolescence and beyond.

Sky, like her mother, started having sex, and at some point became involved with the motorcycle mechanic who took her away from wherever she was to where she ended up, forlorn, on the coast, and we found her.

What on earth can it possibly mean to say such a thing, to say that we found her, found Sky, who was herself an imaginary girl with a sullenness about her few people would have found attractive, never mind compelling. When I was small my uncle Ralph used to wear a wide-brimmed straw hat in the backyard on those rare Sunday afternoons he joined Patty's father and my other, real uncle with the parrot for drinks. Somehow, I came into possession of this hat; somehow, it might be said, I found it. Hats, like rocks or baskets, are things that can be touched, arranged: found.

This particular hat, which I must have found since Ralph does not, properly speaking, exist in the manner that would have enabled him to give it to me, is something like a farmer's hat, tattered at the edges now and with a floppiness it didn't have when Ralph wore it on the porch, slugging beer to their stronger cocktails. Ralph slouched, his legs stretched out lazily before him, with the hat pulled down low so you couldn't see his face or tell what he was thinking. This is still the hat I wear hiking, and I took it on that road trip with my sister, where it sat atop our white pillows in the back seat, my imaginary uncle's found hat.

But Sky—did I say she was imaginary? Sky was as real as me.

Sky was imaginary, and she was real, a both/and kind of girl who was not at all like something you could find just lying around, close your fingers around, claim.

Nevertheless, for the longest time I believed that Sky's life and mine had intersected in that unlikely lobby just so she could bring this story into being. I believed that because, like the hat, there was something definitive about her. There we were in Orick, my sister and I, and though the coast itself was close enough to smell, we were exhausted and wanted only to eat, and then sleep. What I think I mean is that never in a million years would I have imagined that Sky had found me.

And yet I also want to tell you that where we found ourselves, at the Park Motel in Orick, with a group of German tourists drunk in nearby rooms, was part of a particular geography so saturated for me that, despite the lure of dreams, I was restless. I was not restless in the way of wanting to go out and wander. It was, instead, a restlessness inside my own body, as if it were no longer my own.

In my dreams that night, I had grown into a very old woman flying high above Lake Shasta, and the sky was like fog, but transparent. I was old, but not feeble or frail, and though throughout the dream there were minor embarrassments—I was wearing a full skirt and my bloomers showed, I found myself unable to remember small but important details of my life—I was more or less oblivious of them. Perhaps I should have been grateful that my sons, middle-aged now themselves, were there with me, that I could still strap kite wings to my back and fly, that I seemed to have spent a vast number of years in a community of artists by whom I was held in high regard, but instead what remains, even now, of this dream is two things: 1) a kind of physical ecstasy that seemed to come not from the sensation of flight itself, but from the very sight of the lake below, with its ragged shoreline and dusty digger pines, and the ring of mountains in the distance, as clear and brilliant as on any summer day, and I found myself crying for the love of this land, which I knew to be as much a part of who I am as any past experience or even body, and 2) my own acute awareness, which I felt as an intensity of longing almost not to be endured, of a life lived and gone that, though when I reviewed its whole history in my head seemed a long, long time, nonetheless, in the context of this dream, could be felt as hardly more than a breath—*inhale, exhale, shh.*

If it is true:

The first time I went to the ocean near Orick, I was sixteen years old and enrolled in a summer biology class. During the four days of our field trip, one boy would be sent home with appendicitis, another would be busted, and I would learn to pay attention to the world—a single stalk of grass, a glistening agate, moose, fog, first-growth redwoods, a boy in boots. Yet even as I learned to name the plants—*dogwood, five-fingered fern, mugwort*—I was stunned by the failure of language to reflect what I saw or felt, and at dawn I crawled out of my tent to touch the earth.

It was here, among the meadow grass and ferns and coastal shrubs, beneath the arc of redwoods, amid extravagant azaleas, that I began to wander, and for years this wandering was all my life would be. At times, at least until the birth of my sons, the paths I took would seem aimless, at odds with the very desire that drove them, and my restlessness would take me across many states, to mountains and deserts and distant rivers, but I was always aware that, however haphazard my route might seem, it had begun years before on those wet trails above the Pacific where I once and for the first time followed a boy's boots.

"Why do you hold so much back?" my blunt-fingered lover asked.

"Whatever could have happened to make you so afraid?" my husband demanded.

Between them, it has taken me most of my life to understand that this was never about holding back, or fear, or even about the way things were with us, but just the knot of my muteness slowly, slowly untying itself. When I learned the names of plants it was not that the signifier had slipped a little from its signified, undermining the capacity of language to hold anything together, but just that I found myself unable to inhabit the words that were available to me. And then, not all at once but slowly, over time, I began to decipher the single true insight I might, after all, have to offer Sky: that it is not the words themselves, or our ability to use them, but somehow in the spaces between and within them where we can come to know ourselves and be at peace.

On the fourth and final night of that field biology trip, the boy in boots and I took off against the rules. Maybe, I don't know, he touched my shoulder. Maybe he took my hand. Maybe he just looked at me a certain way, and we ducked away from the meadow campground, into the dense shroud of fog and trees. After that it was easy. Once you've slipped away into the fog and trees, no one can find you there, even if they look.

We walked for a long time, that boy and I. We were young and new to the world. Then, deep inside the fog, we came to a high rock with a trail that rose along its back side, twisting through the trees and shrubs and moss that, against all probability, grew there, and though we did not know this as we climbed, already we had begun to leave the earth behind, climbing above it and the tops of its trees, climbing up to and beyond our own beginnings.

Remember, I was sixteen, and a virgin.

We were climbing clear out of the world, and into the stories we would become.

In another part of my life, Ralph will send me a drawing of him on a rock in the Andes, and it will look like me on that other rock, when we'd finally reached the top and I had imagined myself stepping out, arms spread, into the mist. In Ralph's little drawing, you can just make out the spread of my arms, the arc of my back. Once again I imagine myself aloft. Also, I miss Ralph so much.

If it is true that at least one part of the logic of writing is a logic of substitution and replacement, then we may be said to return with it, over and over, to a prior way of being and, through repetition, to set a private iconography of self determined by a host of arbitrary images: the color of one man's hair, a boy's boots, a lake that once was a town, the places where we've planted our feet.

If I found Sky at that exact corner of the earth where I once and for the first time found myself, it cannot be accidental that I return, not just to the place, but the story. I think about that rock, the small tree at the top, the meadow far below, and beyond, the steel gray ocean crashing turbulent against the rocky shoreline, streaked with yellow and green. I think about the mist rising up from that far-below meadow, its delicate insistence as it gathers, and my absolute conviction it will hold me, and if after all this time I no longer regret that I did not embrace the fog that night, it is because this, too, is writing.

We returned, that boy and I:

We returned, that boy and I, on many occasions to the rock above the water on the northern coast of California, where each time the world intoxicated us and we turned a little more into ourselves. If writing is an act of memory and grace, it should give us back at least a trace of what we've lost, but in those days my uncle's dams seemed as natural a part of the landscape as the hills that contained them, and the necessity of Patty had yet to be conceived. Perhaps it doesn't really matter how I reconstruct this sequence of events, for they will inevitably lead to my sister and me shivering in the fog along the coast highway in Orick. It will have to happen that way because, in this particular instance, fate itself had intervened in the form of fire to deliver us back to that coast, where certainly I did not expect to find Sky.

What is the relation between a fire and a dam?

Once, years before, we'd left our tent, the boy and I, to wander out into the night. My hands smelled of wood smoke and salmon as I followed the black shape of his back. And then, because it was so dark, the world seemed suddenly to shift as we stepped off the path and found ourselves stumbling through thick underbrush, grabbing at each other for balance. From time to time, the route ahead would become impassable, and the boy's arm would go around me, and my mind would go blank, as in a swoon. I remember him burying his face in my hair at the top of my head. Then, wholly disoriented and pleasurably giddy, we would take off again, in another direction, until at last we broke out of the trees just at the edge of the lip of a cliff that went down to the sea.

Maybe it was like that for Sky: a way, like any river, to the sea.

The cliff was really a steep, sandy bank, which crumbled away from our feet as we descended, sliding, rolling, laughing. Scattered piles of driftwood below humped in huge mounds, like hills, and then we were among them, shadowed by the moon. As we climbed to the top of one, I imagined running out into the sea, diving under a wave, and then, as I imagined it, we'd build a driftwood fire and warm ourselves with it, and each other.

As the crow flies, we were not that far from where the Ah Pah would have been, but I did not know this then. I knew only to imagine the breathtaking chill of the sea, the fire we'd build, and imagining this, I was pierced by the sharp desire to hold on to something, but the boy had turned away to watch the curl of the waves beneath the moon, and when I turned to look as well, I saw it was an iridescent tide.

～
　～
～

Memories of what never really happened:

OK.

So we were going to take the train to visit my grandmother on a trip we'd been planning for months, and my anticipation of it, like Christmas or the first day of school, was so great that, the night before, I couldn't sleep, tossed instead for much of that oppressive August night, kept awake, too, by the eerie strains of a dance band orchestra that drifted, now and then, from across the river, kicking off blankets and tormenting myself with agitated thoughts about the next day—the train, and my new blue blouse and Mary Janes, and my grand-mother waiting with boxes of chocolate—so beside myself with excitement that, when the dance at last ended and silence came down, I fell into a stupor of sleep and did not even stir when mosquitoes swarmed to feast on my feet, which by morning were so swollen that I had to be carried, shoeless, to our berth. Propped up on a pillow and draped with some light gauze fabric, they looked to me like little animals, unrelated to myself, and my mother, my sister, even the porters, hovered over me so solicitously throughout the trip that I hardly had a chance to mourn my Mary Janes.

This was as content as I ever was as a child, and I have held the memory all my life as among my earliest and clearest—the deep dismay I felt when I awoke to my swollen feet, the unworn shoes, the clackety-clack of the train as the world rolled by outside its windows, the solicitude of uniformed strangers, the soothing sweetness of Coke—but my mother insists this never happened, that we never took the train to Monterey, that I never had a pair of Mary Janes and was not allowed to drink Coke.

Sometimes, now, I think about those shoes, about Miranda, even about the glass door I never walked through—that was Patty. Like myself in my memory of what never happened, she says the glass was so immaculate she never even saw it, but just walked right on through, not even registering at first what had happened—her mother screaming, the blood on her feet—but we were both lucky, with only minor cuts on our inside left ankles, hers scarring in exactly the same place as mine later would from a careless hiking accident (I was wearing sandals), small crescent moons above where the tongues of our shoes sometimes rest.

A naked man once waved his penis at me from the Sacramento riverbank, just beyond where my inner tube had hung up on rocks. Already nearsighted at nine or ten, I wasn't really sure what I had seen, but unlike other images from childhood, which have blurred and receded over time, this one has become ever more acute, so precise, in fact, that it would someday transfigure itself into another moment by another river. For years, I believed the real man was urinating. I thought he was shaking off urine. I thought this long after I knew better.

When Miranda was nine, she was raped, and just over the mountains, in Redding, a young girl was bludgeoned to death on Valentine's Day by the teenaged boy next door, and sometime the next winter a small plane went down in the mountains where the family survived for some time, leaving a record of their last days in the flight log.

In a family, any family, how is it possible ever to be certain? All my life, for example, I believed that my father was my father because he'd been lucky and had a safe deployment in the war, driving a supply truck at the back of the lines, that allowed him to survive, father children, live his life, though in fact the supplies were ammunition. When he finally told me this just a year or two ago, he was ashen and he might have been shaking.

In general, we imagine rivers to be subject to a kind of dynamic equilibrium, largely stable geologic features, with processes like regional incision or subtle shifts in mountain building causing short- and medium-term variation around some slowly changing mean condition, but in fact it is far more common to see dramatic change over short periods, with long periods of stability between, in what geologists refer to as "dynamic metastable equilibrium."

It is the same with families, memory, the history of a person's life, what we believe to be true.

The municipal park in Mount Shasta City, tucked at the foot of the mountain, is the kind of old-fashioned park where whole communities gather—picnickers, and square dance clubs, and children on playground equipment—and it is here that we go to marvel at the source of the Sacramento River, just where it bubbles out of the ground beneath a sign that reads HEADWATERS OF THE SACRAMENTO RIVER. People often meditate or chant here, for it is commonly believed that the mountain is sacred, and there are always other people filling plastic bottles, or reading on benches nearby. We do this ourselves. We fill bottles, too, and take them back to the cabin too, for we believe this is the best water on earth.

But the Sacramento River actually begins in a small lake on nearby Mount Eddy.

∾
∾
∾

All these rocks:

Some years ago I returned late at night to my dormitory room to find a note tacked on my door, scrawled in blue ink on cheap notebook paper: *What are we to do with all these rocks?* I believe it is largely because of this note that I later married its writer.

As I girl, I spent hours rock-walking up and down rivers and creeks, leaping from boulder to boulder, flat slippery riverbed rock to flat slippery riverbed rock, and this was how I learned, in fact, to walk upon the earth. My first bed with a man was a slab of granite, and the boy-in-boots once brought me a gray piece of lava, light as air, from the top of Mount Shasta. You hold small stones, warmed from the sun, in your hand, and what you do not want: you do not want to let them go, not ever.

Imagine the hand of a blind woman.

Imagine a Wintu woman weaving.

For what you also know is that once there was a river, and that where the river was, a Wintu woman wove, and this is what is going to happen: first toxic copper resides and fumes will kill everything around, then, in another thirty years or so, a reservoir will flood its bed, and in another fifty, a load of herbicide, considered harmless by the government and thus shipped without precaution by the railroad, will dump itself upriver and wend it way slowly toward the lake for a week. All this will be true, as it is already true, and who will be the one to weep at the edge of the dead river, washed clean of all life for forty-five miles? Who will gather the silver-belly-up trout that line the sad shores, clotted with withering willow and skunk cabbage? And when the otters die, the deer, the bald eagles, the bear, what will we say? And later, weeks later, when the poisoned water starts to seep into the California water system, if the woman had a child, if the child is the last, will the woman weep, or will she, instead, rejoice?

~
~
~

Tell me a story:

And so you begin: tell me a story. You wait, like a small still animal, all breath. You are not my younger son, who always approached stories with a bull-in-the-china-shop, wide-eyed enthusiasm, nor my older, who mutely absorbed them. Instead, you are attentive, and as the story begins to unfurl off the fold of my tongue, we assess each other, eager and inelegant, a narrator and narratee lying cheek-to-cheek and with a single bated breath.

I begin: *in this respect, what I am telling you is not about story.*

If not story, then what, and if I tell you dams, if I say rocks, you will ask: *what are we to do with all these rocks?*

I am no longer the girl who walked with a boy through the woods in the dark by the sea, and as I have moved from my prior self to this one, the century changed too, all the dams have been built, California has pulled a little bit back from the brink, and suddenly it is thirty years since we invented Earth Day and learned to conceive of the ends of such things as salmon and owls and rivers themselves. In those years, we have reconstructed fire and flood and begun to champion their natural imperative, except that we miscalculated badly, and now too many people live among our hills and in our floodplains, too many people live here at all. Even so, we still want it both ways, and in this new century continue to build homes wherever we want them, negotiate our water rights from somewhere far away, and hold to our expansive vision of the future, for though we have learned to crave the first plume of smoke or darkening of sky that threatens everything around, we don't quite believe—not really—that they can hurt us.

We seem always to be shaking off or anticipating the effects of war.

We spent at least a decade cultivating excess.

We have learned to accept times of such terrible sadness, and know them, in our hearts, to be recursive.

So what we do, we take apart one dam, we dream up another, we try to feel the earth beneath our feet, because time has yet to stun us into acquiescence, because we are still young enough to believe in grace, because there are still decades to come. We do not think to count them—we are not that young, and 80 seems so large and round, in 80 years so much can happen—but they are, nonetheless, the decades of our children, and so we are both vague and somewhat desperate about them. And then one day we find ourselves without a river.

It is not possible always to remember the climate of things that produces one result or another, a country of dams, for example. Recently, I went to visit my real uncle with the parrot, now more than ninety years old. He is sharp as a tack and still handsome, and his eyes gleamed when he told me that, no, he never missed his childhood home, not the hills he roamed about, not the river he swam in.

"That wasn't how we thought back then," he said. "Back then, we had a vision. Back then, that was enough."

The parrot on his shoulder cocked its head at me, and my uncle turned to it, clucking it just beneath its beak.

"What about the casualties?" I asked.

"Casualties?" he said.

"On the dam," I said.

For a moment, my uncle looked confused. Then he laughed. Hardly anyone was even injured, working on the dam, and no one, to his knowledge, was killed.

"But the man who fell off," I said, "the hapless surveyor. Mike's friend."

"Mike?" he said.

"Ralph, then," I said. "Ralph's friend who fell . . . ?"

"Oh, no one fell," my uncle said. "Nothing like that. It was a perfect operation, start to finish." He paused, turned his head again at a somewhat awkward angle toward his parrot and, looking it directly in the eyes, touched it again on its beak. "Who's Ralph?"

Ralph, of course, since imaginary, never ages. As far as I know, he's still living high in the Peruvian Andes, a venerated teacher or healer by now, and as the rest of us grow older, he gets younger and younger. I am old enough now to be his lover, and sometimes when I receive his postcards, I think of following them. It is not that I regret having committed myself, in this way, to these events, but I suspect there must be rivers in the Andes, hundreds of them, white water and tumbling cascades and deep limpid pools, as well as countless smaller streams, artesian springs, all natural lakes. Ralph is lean, brown, and muscular now, but with a studied gentleness about him, and if it weren't for Sam and Joey I'd be willing to do away with this whole story—California and the men who built it, and my white-haired lover, blind Patty, Miranda, all of it, even Sky, all—to start over again, closer to the sun and in another language. I remember the wood smoky smell of Ralph and the taste, a little salty, of his skin when I kissed him, and frankly, it is almost more than I can bear to think that I will not ever curl up to his chest again, never make myself small against him.

Rose's father's rooms:

The rooms Rose's father took in Toyon had twin windows facing east, and yellow pine floors, but the Trinity cabin was just a single room of logs, chinked with clay from the river's rich floodplain. In Toyon, just four blocks away down plank sidewalks, there was a grassy playground and generous community building, but the Trinity cabin was several miles down a dirt road from town, nearly impassable in winter. Rose was ten when her father took her there to live, and seventeen when Miranda was born. When I think about those years and what it must have been like to have been cut off like that, a girl growing hard into herself, I think about one particular kind of darkness closing in, and then how, after a time, Rose's world would have opened up again, turning mountainous and charged with adventure.

I know this because of Miranda, conceived back country on the edge of a green alpine lake, ringed by granite peaks, one hot, late August afternoon, the mossy bed on which Rose lay long since dried out, a brittle carpet that turned to dust beneath her, and the granite it grew on ridged and sharp. The boy with Rose was sweaty from the climb, and wherever she touched him, he stiffened. He was a boy, not unlike others she had known, lanky-limbed and with a single-mindedness of purpose to get out of their town for good, but for this one afternoon it didn't matter that his father owned the hardware store in town or that he himself was good with animals and destined to prosper at ranching. For this one afternoon, even his plans to get a railroad job in Sacramento and travel receded in the wake of Rose's passion, the culmination for the boy of years of lust, during which he'd admired her from across various schoolrooms. It was Rose's sadness that had aroused the boy, and the more he thought about it, the more he thought about wooing her beside an alpine lake, where, after months of chastely hiking back trails, they would lie down together at last and tentatively taste one another.

This, at any rate, was how he planned it, and because I know where it will end—first with Miranda, then Sky—and because we have since been through the sexual revolutions of the latter part of the last century, it is difficult even for me to imagine the tenor of that moment, its innocence and rising heat, and the boy's naïve conviction that, in the aftermath of their coupling, Rose's sadness would lift. Instead, he found himself overwhelmed by crush of Rose's breasts, which, when they came suddenly free of her unbuttoned blouse and the white complexities of her brassiere, were vaster and sweeter than he ever imagined.

Hence, Miranda, once a flaxen-haired, nine-year-old waif, who in time turned buxom and sturdy herself, and one thing led to another and ultimately Sky, conceived, I believe, beside the same lake, on the same rock, also in August but less naïvely.

I was right about San Jose, though. I am virtually certain Sky was born in San Jose, on a dead-end dirt street of aging stucco bungalows, one bedroom in each and with the living room opening out onto a tiny kitchenette. She was born in one of three ways.

~
~
~

Discreetly:

Her mother, barely eighteen and distraught over what she felt certain would be a grievous disappointment not to her mother, whom she believed would understand, but to her grandfather, who had nurtured such high hopes for her, and taught her things about the woods, and let her pan for gold with him, simply disappeared one day, hitchhiking out of the Trinity Mountains with her clothes stuffed into an old army backpack, along with a book on the first nine months of life. Miranda followed Highway 99 all the way down the valley, stopping at every small town along the way in search of a place where she might stay. But it was 1970, and though Miranda wasn't showing yet, not that anyone could really tell in her rolled Can't-Bust-'Ems, to the people in the towns she passed through she looked more like a hippie than what she really was—a back-country girl from the Trinity Alps who bought the only backpack she could afford at the Army Navy surplus store in Redding.

That was such a hot day, I remember, when she bought the backpack, one of those blazing valley days, with heat waves shimmering off asphalt and a smell of something burning into the air. There could have been a fire, there were always fires somewhere, and I wished I were out at the lake, but I needed some gear for a backpack trip with the boy-in-boots, and that was how I ran into Miranda at the Army Navy surplus store in Redding on a day that was blazing and smoky.

One pair of pants, one pair of shorts, two t-shirts, I was sorting out my list in my head: my new red Himalaya backpack with navy zippers and full padded frame, leather hiking boots from Berkeley, a sky-blue, two-and-a-half-pound mail order sleeping bag from REI. We were headed for our own mountain lake.

I noticed Miranda because of her Can't-Bust-'Ems. She was looking at used backpacks, and though tanned, she had a pallor to her like something was wrong.

The guys who worked at the store were ignoring both of us.

"I bet they're stoned," I whispered to her. "You could get that cheap."

She smiled shyly. "I'm pregnant," she whispered back. "Do you know anywhere I could go?"

I shrugged. Really, I felt embarrassed. I was still a virgin: what was I supposed to say?

"Well, there's this place, Agape House," I said.

"Yeah, but that's mostly runaways and drugs." Miranda looked rueful. "I'm not a runaway yet."

She bought the backpack and, as far as I know, continued south. I've thought about that a lot since, how close Patty came that day years before, how close I came in 1970, and how neither one of us, not me and not Patty, did one single thing to help Miranda out.

Up and down the valley, the towns Miranda passed through were so small that she felt people looking at her, and though San Jose was scary, it was big and anonymous, and she found the bungalow without too much trouble. Almost all the way at the dead end of an alley, the place was cheap and private, and most of the neighbors spoke Spanish, so no one bothered her much. She studied her pregnancy book, and successfully delivered Sky by herself at four o'clock on a warm afternoon, and she suckled her, and she named her Sky.

⁓
⁓
⁓

Courageously:

It wasn't San Jose after all, and it wasn't 1970 either, but 1975 and Gridley, in the heart of the Sacramento Valley. I was working at the peach cannery to earn money for graduate school and living in a single apartment at the Markay Motel, now a ministorage, but at the time with low weekly rates and some kitchenettes, and Miranda had a single room next door. It was steamy and hot, and the whole town smelled sweet from the cannery going twenty-four hours a day. When the earthquake hit, I was sleeping off the night shift in the late morning. It slammed, then rolled for a long time, and slowly I became aware, as in a dream, of the other residents yelling in the parking lot, but I was still curled deep into the sweaty drowsiness of summer sleep, and I was naked, and then I heard a different kind of high-pitched moaning from the next room over.

This is how I knew her, knew Sky, years later. I was present at her birth. I boiled the water on my tiny stove as we rode out Miranda's contractions between the aftershocks and tried not to think about the crack in Oroville Dam lengthening and widening above us. It took a long time, Sky's birth, enough for the motel walls to develop long, spidery fissures in the gray plaster walls, and then I wrapped the squalling infant in a worn white towel, wiped Miranda's brow, and handed her the baby for suckling.

And she named her Sky.

∼
  ∼
∼

Miraculously:

OK, the stork came. I mean that. Either place—the Markay Motel, or the green bungalow in San Jose—the stork circled over the roof, and then, just at midnight, brought Sky down, wrapped in pink bunting, blue-eyed and wailing.

Whimpering.

Cooing.

When my second son was born there were complications and it was several hours before I was allowed to hold him. I had a single glimpse, faded, mostly, now from memory, then, pinned first beneath the surgeon's scalpel, and then the stern watch of the recovery room nurse, I waited, my arms empty and aching with longing. But between when the stork dropped Sky off and when Miranda took her in her arms, hardly a second elapsed, not a breath, or a blink, or a heartbeat. This is why, when I saw her years later on the coast, in that other single glimpse, I had such a hard time understanding what had happened. My own sons, once I held them, I held them close for years, and it was never again as if I had not held them in my arms, the memory of the heft of their being both palpable and permanent, etched in my body like a double heart. This is the force of the very same desire that holds things, in their inherent contradictions, together, and maybe, yes, it's a delicate balance, but Sky, when I saw her, had been somehow set adrift, cut off from Miranda and the ties that might have kept her anchored to this earth, and she was spinning out there, enough to make you dizzy, into a dreaded world where everything was wrong.

We were not that far from where I'd once climbed my own rock, high above the sea, and looked out, and believed the mist would hold me. Now, I saw Sky, her dull eyes, lank hair, her unbearable youth and single heart, just as Patty must once have seen Miranda, bleeding.

This is what I thought: if between the one heart and the two, both Patty and

I had failed Miranda, Sky was our late second chance, and whatever else might be required of us would be determined by the cusp of her deliverance.

I don't know how I knew this. I knew it by nothing much more than a quickening of my own pulse, a look of recognition in the glance that passed between us, her forlorn single heart, the shadow of a white sheet against a black sky, in the aftermath of which the story I'd have liked to have told would go something like this:

Sky has aged, though not past recognition, by this point. We look the new millennium dead in the eye and wonder what will happen to those we've left behind, like Patty's father and my uncle, whose dream, after all, was not such a bad or inappropriate dream. It was just the kind of dream men who used to ooze power out the tips of their fingers would dream: a past dream, a long ago dream. The only real tragedy was that, in the endless process of dreaming their dream, these men lost the power of their human touch, and slowly, slowly became obsolete. But not Sky. Sky remains, a haunted shadow of their plans, and though we cannot rescue them from what they've done, Sky has her whole life before her and we owe her that much at least.

⌇

⌇

⌇

However much I might desire:

However much I might desire to be small against Ralph, in the end there is nothing that is not both narrative and language. Even the paradoxical physics by which the universe is held together is both. We are ourselves story, just as we are language. That is the nature of both narrative and love. I have long believed this, and in the wake of Patty's tale, Miranda's fate, Sky's persistence, even the unfolding of my own sons' lives, I am ever more convinced that these two irreconcilable forces cannot be severed from each other, and that in the space between them, which is mute, we come to know ourselves as the force of the very desire that we should speak ourselves into being.

Hence:

The fire that kept us from Hoopa filled that last bowl-shaped valley along the Salmon River with smoke, and shortly after that, I remember saying to my sister, "Why are all the cars here going in the opposite direction?"

"Maybe," she said, "it's a powwow. Maybe they're all drunk. Is it safe?"

Or maybe she noticed the cars; maybe I mentioned the powwow. Someone said it, and then we both felt a little guilty, and then around another bend, the orange roadblock stopped us just at the point where flames were beginning to work down the side of the mountain, not, as I'd always imagined it would be, a hungry wall of fire, but rather red tongues licking, here and there, among the trees, and it was beautiful and mesmerizing. My sister, who was driving, stopped the car.

The man at the roadblock said, "I'm not saying if we're talking minutes or all night, but if the winds shift, we could be in trouble."

My sister's knuckles, on the steering wheel, went white, and the small veins in her temples throbbed. We were seven miles, give or take, from our destination. We had motel reservations. It had been a long day of driving, and turning back was not an option. So we headed west instead, straight over the mountains on bad logging roads toward the familiar arc of coastline and its redwood forest, which, when we dropped down into it through a hill of luminescent golden grasses, caught the light too, each tree as if separately shrouded, the pale milky orbs dimming as we entered them.

Of course we could not know it at the time, but we were headed straight to the place where Sky would catch me looking at her and look back. Maybe that was all it was: Sky looked back. Later, as my sister and I gnawed on popcorn shrimp in a nearby café, I tried to ask if she had seen the girl in the back room at the motel. It seemed such a long way from the light-dappled stretch of the Salmon River where we had swum that day to this greasy-spoon café with a crowd of spotted owl-unemployed loggers howling in the next room over some barroom competition, and what I understood was that it must have seemed there, along the Salmon River, for one brief moment at the center of the earth, as if we would never have to leave.

Now, as the century continued to spin itself out, it was impossible not to reflect on the iconography of time that makes us, holding infants in our arms or swimming green stretches of sun-dappled river, catch our breath and want to hold it, stop time, forever.

In fact we left the Salmon River after what could have been hardly more than an hour. We encountered fire, we turned west again, and not at any point did I tell my sister about Patty or Miranda, whom I had not yet, even then, begun to conceive. My sister would have wanted to know what happened next, and what could I have possibly told her? Suddenly, in that moment, I missed my sons so fiercely, but the only phone in the world, it seemed, was the one at the side of the highway.

"Did you see," I said, "that girl in the back, the one who was making spaghetti."

"Stop doing that," my sister said. "You're always imagining things. She's probably his wife, they've probably got kids."

I said, "Why do you think the doors at the motel were all open like that?"

But what I was thinking was: *if you take the idea of a story, there is always a point from which everything branches, as if the whole world we drove through today began with one hunkered-down girl.*

I was thinking: *wide open to the world.*

When what I really meant to say was that I loved my sister, but this seemed somehow complicated and unrelated to the moment, and so instead I placed my hands upon the table, palms up, to signal I was done, I could not eat another popcorn shrimp, while my sister, a vegetarian for some years now, continued to work at hers.

⁓

⁓

⁓

I could hear singing:

The bed in the motel was scratchy with starch, and when I woke in the middle of the night I could hear singing, interspersed with the flapping of something heavy on the wind. Above me, the fish in the gull's mouth on the mural glowed eerily, dripping bright splats of water toward our pillows. Beside me, my sister slept soundly. The song was high and sweet and sad, and when I parted the curtains, I could see Sky folding laundry on a moonlit table in the motel parking lot, where the German tourists had been drinking earlier. The look on her face was between serene and beatific, the arc her voice was a wing.

When my sons were born and I first held them in my arms, I tried so desperately to hang on to that moment, unaware that time was forever now transfigured from what it was before their births, to what came after, almost like a river gathering momentum in a channel deprived of its roughness, or above and below a dam. I couldn't hold it anymore, I couldn't even mark it, I could just stand by and watch it unfold.

It was like that on my raft trip all those years before, when I had understood, as if for the first time, that however much I might want to slow things down, or stop them, the drifting of the canyon walls on either side of us could never be arrested, no, as I let myself be mesmerized by it, not even slowed. At night, I'd lie beneath the stars, beside the shore, listening to the water, and try to memorize the passage of that day, to play it back before me, instant by instant: the river was wide, then narrow, the red cliffs rose high, then dipped, we entered an ageless wilderness of rock, etched by petroglyphs and wind, that lifted high above us in lateral shifts—burnt sienna, raw umber, dark ocher, night black. It was only a week. I could do that for a week. And my memory lasted a decade. But with children, though you hold them as close as you can, you must give yourself over to the spinning itself, arms spread wide, fingers open, marking time in the raveling present.

Years later, as they continue, intermittently, to fight it out for my affection, I think about the checks and balances of family, what each of us imagines and constructs to keep the others safe, a stubborn alchemy of displacement and love. But that night, watching Sky, far away from all of that, I felt as utterly bereft as I have ever felt, and taking care not to wake my sister, roused myself and went to join the woman outside, who handed me a sheet and went on singing.

The moon kept drifting in and out from behind the clouds, and in the inconstant light, the linens, like the fish inside, glowed. After a long time, she said, "Don't let your shoulders get bunched up and tight. Use your whole body, like dancing."

In her hands, the sheets seemed to lift themselves up, lighter than air, while mine were cumbersome and leaden, and when she was done, hers lay crisp and flat, as if ironed, while the wrinkles in mine persisted. I recognized this as a certain flaw in me, a clumsiness of hand or careless inattention of spirit, but Sky was patient and kind, and every time I'd threaten to dissolve, like a child, in frustration, she'd offer some small word of consolation or advice, and the crisis would pass. Thus, as we worked, a peace descended over me, and the night seemed to stretch before us without end.

Near dawn, when we had finished, all the sheets and pillowcases and towels piled high in luminous mounds around us, Sky stopped singing for an instant and

ls in hers. Looking down, I saw that her skin was rough and cracked,
ch it felt soft and smooth. Though I recognized this as a trick of the
I could not say if it were mine or hers. Then Sky put one finger, light as
s, and turned away, gathering the laundry in her arms.

 later, I dreamed not of the father of my sons, but of my white-
 and the dream itself was almost entirely red, with only a few
hite. In it, he held not his finger, but his cock to my mouth, but
ted wasn't what I thought. Every time I tried to lick him, he'd say,
Shh, shh. In the distance, we could hear the sound of another surf, and then,
all at once, everything was quiet and grim.

〜

〜

〜

Where she might call it home:

As an adolescent, Sky considered her lank hair a personal strike against her.
Each morning, doggedly, she'd blow it dry, her whole upside-down head
throbbing from the rush of blood, teasing and brushing and praying that this
time, against all odds, it would not go limp by ten, maybe even hold enough
body all the way to lunchtime for her to toss it more effectively behind her
shoulders in a gesture she believed looked alluring to boys. Permed, Sky's hair
just got kinky. Once or twice she tried her mother's brush rollers, but this gave
her terrible split ends.

Then, like that, one day Sky shaved her head, and was amazed at the light-
ness of her head, which created such a tremendous feeling of individual freedom in her that she wore her hair shaved for two years. By the time she let it
grow again, she'd already dropped out of high school, and between dope and
beer she couldn't choose.

If you think I'm looking down at Sky nothing could be further from the
truth. Sky is like a petroglyph herself, unexpected on some far desert wall, and
with an imperative about her, even hunkered down over spaghetti in what seems
like advanced depression, but especially folding laundry in the night. In fact, Sky
and I are very much alike. Sky followed her grinning motorcycle mechanic as far
north as she could because Sky, more than anything, wanted to find some place
in the world where she might call it home, and if there is any other reason I keep

returning to those rivers, I couldn't possibly imagine what it is.

If you take the idea of this story, what spins itself out can be unspun.

At least this is what I will have told my sister when I convince her we cannot leave the girl in that place.

"Did you ask her what she wants?" my sister said.

"Did you see the tattoo on her scalp?" I said.

"You don't know a single thing about her," my sister said. "What makes you think she'll even want to come?"

"It's red," I said, "like an animal flying."

"I told you," she said, "you always do this."

"You should see her fold a sheet," I said.

"You just make things up as you go along."

"It's spectacular," I said.

"What makes you think," she said, "this any different from picking up a random hitchhiker? It's dangerous," she said. "You should be careful."

"Oh," I said. "Please. Just trust me."

And to my surprise, they both did, my sister and Sky, who came along with us even though she was different by day, dejected, and with that dullness about her. I wanted everyone to know this was as much about Miranda as it was about her daughter, but I was, by that point, acting on instinct, and it was a long way home. Beyond that, I had no firm idea in my head, no clear way out of the plot I had constructed, and as the fog began to lift on our way south, I mostly regretted that I had involved my sister in what, strictly speaking, was not really her story.

Or was it?

I was torn, on the one hand, between being worried that I might indeed have placed us both at risk, and on the other, that this whole episode would quickly be transformed into another one of my quirks: *do you know what Kate did this time?* And I frankly, I could see their point. It is one thing to invent a forlorn, single-hearted character, and quite another to attempt to rescue her.

We were on our way to the Mad River, where, once again, we would swim. Sky sat hunkered down in the back seat, where, though still pale, her color was starting to come back. What did we really know about her? I didn't even know when my idea to take her with us had begun to form, nor what I planned to do with her now, short of delivering her back to the dammed Trinity.

In that instant, a single-mindedness of purpose overtook me to go and find Miranda, for I knew before I had put it into words that if I could reunite them, mother and daughter, it would somehow restore their double heart and make them whole again, and that perhaps this would just be a beginning, that we could go on from there to look for Patty, maybe even Ralph, all the way to the Peruvian Andes where I have heard they build houses on stilts in lakes, houses that rise above the surface of the water and hover there, like ungainly birds, shelter and home, and then maybe we could live there, all of us together, including Sam and Joey and my sister, all the real people as well as the imaginary ones, in houses on stilts above natural lakes near the rivers that flow in and out of them.

It was my idea but my sister went along with it. We were driving hard now, the windows wide open, and as taken as we were with our own adventure, it failed even to occur to us that Sky might have her own ideas about it.

All my life, it seems, I've been telling family stories. I have done this without much doubt or remorse because stories spin off of my tongue like paintings or dams spin off the tips of other people's fingers. In practice, it's fairly easy to weave such elaborate circles around people you love that by the time you're done they're dizzy and confused about their own identity and history. But telling a story, any story, is not at all the same as building the infrastructure of a culture, for if you think about it, that is clearly different, such things as goods and services, how people have come to be moved, and water. Because despite how fervently we may argue about language or story, geography is palpable, and beneath the hand of a blind woman, any blind woman, the humps and curves of a state contour map are what they are. Though many years later it may all seem natural, though we may forget that the landscape we have come to love is, at least in part, invented, we cannot change the fact that the bluffs across the river were scoured out by mining a hundred years ago, or that the rapids that take us up are regulated upstream by someone else's dream of one dam or another.

What I am trying to suggest is that if you take my sister by one hand and Sky by the other, how will you know the difference?

A family, terrain-like, becomes combustible under certain specific conditions: tinder dry brush, thick from the past season's rains, and hot summer winds, as if nature were both intentional and cruel, and this, both our love of and our vulnerability to fire, is predestined.

In the waters of the Salmon River, my sister looked lambent and as beautiful as I have ever seen her, and I wonder, if we swam like that when we were forty, what's to stop us when we're sixty? And while at one time the engineers did have their plans for that river, which would have been subsumed by the vastness of the Ah Pah, it didn't happen, the project was never even started, my sister and I, before the fire stopped us, found ourselves at that most serene stretch of that still-wild river, and we swam there at the center of the earth, and that could have been that.

But do you know the way a forest fire can cut off a mountain road? The flames, as if with a life of their own, leap up all around, licking at trees, driven higher, faster, forward by their need for oxygen. With the right wind they can move twenty, maybe thirty miles an hour. In certain kinds of winds, there is no escaping them.

With my sister and me that afternoon, there was no particular wind, just a stubborn clump of fire and our maps. We could have turned back, surely, driven through the night, taken on that twisted one-lane forest river canyon road through midnight blackness, arrived at the cabin before dawn, chronicled our adventure for my sons, and gone blissfully to sleep.

But we didn't. We headed farther west, toward Sky and the rest of this story.

~
~
~

With Sky it was already written:

With Sky and my sister and me it was already written that when we'd turn back east into the mountains toward her mother and the Trinities down another winding road, dappled with sunlight, and hot, hot, I would be driving, and Sky would be growing lighter somehow, as she had been in the night with her translucent sheets, her face both expectant and sweet. I did not know a single thing about her. I couldn't say if she had ever been to this part of the country, and though I had this feeling she was born in San Jose, it was just a feeling I could never prove, no more than I could say for certain why I had decided to take her back with us along the Trinity where I think what I also had in mind was to release her, like a fish, into its water.

In my head now, what I see if I close my eyes is not only Patty's map, but my children, much larger than scale, leaping lake-to-lake, throwing stones from one tiny reservoir to another, gleeful and boyish. I see my sister sunning herself on the banks of all five rivers. I see Sky where I have left her in the blue-green Trinity, loose and luminescent, and swimming upriver as hard as she can, toward the spot where her mother was either raped or not. Ahead of her swimming, I see the dam: what will happen when Sky meets the dam?

As a girl, looking out on the placid waters of Lake Shasta, I would sometimes imagine myself diving down, down to the streets of my grandparents' town, where I would wander happily, discovering such treasures as an ancient teacup, a pair of wedding shoes, a ukelele, pages from books. I don't really know what I expected from Sky, but perhaps what I wanted, letting her loose, was to see her dive down too. Probably, too, I wanted to divest myself of Patty's memories, as well as of my own responsibilities for them.

Sky was born and she grew into a woman, spinning, like this story, ever closer to the end of the last century, when gunmen mowed down Jewish children in L.A., and gay men in Redding, and, somewhere on the far other side of the country, the Bureau of Reclamation dismantled its first dam. Closer to home, Clear Creek Dam came down next, and between this darkening and lightening, I wrote to Ralph because I wanted someone to explain to me how it is possible that, on the one hand, we can rebuild the underwater structure of a dam to save the native salmon population, and on the other, bury the brothers of our childhood sweethearts because the concern we extend to the animal world remains foreign and elusive to our own.

If we can take apart a dam, I wrote, *can we bring Gary Matson back to life?*

And Ralph wrote back: *Don't let anyone tell you stories are about language—stories are about love, for love is everything, and so are stories.*

When I received his letter I cried for a long time because I knew it was the last time I would hear from him, and also because he was right.

Now as this story spirals out in the hard fist of time, I remember, too, the arc of Patty's back above the darkened surface of the Sacramento, its curve as she entered the water. There was never any hesitation in her movement, only grace, and something like conviction. If I had known then what I know now, I would never have gone there with her, but in my eagerness to compensate her for her blindness, I did what I did. Later, even with that barest slip of moon, she looked frankly beatific, and it was then that I knew I would pay.

∼
∼
∼

About the world:

I confess I am confused about the world, and in error about many facts.

On the long drive home with my sister that day, we did see yellow rafts adrift on the Trinity River, and though this memory persists, like a troubling afterimage, I am fully aware that the annual flow of the river has been reduced by three-quarters since the dam was finished more than thirty years ago, water we are now giving back. This is still the logic of substitution and replacement—reduction and enhancement—that, like a trompe l'oeil, enables us to persist in the inherent contradictions of our father's dreams. If the summer flow is more constant, it fills a narrower channel, which no winter storms ever fully flush out and, as a consequence, is slowly filling in. That water comes to us, in Southern California. That is where it goes. It goes south.

Also, my older son corrects me, strings vibrate in eleven, not ten, dimensions. The fourth dimension is time. Beyond that, what can any of us imagine?

Even so, the principle remains the same: a lot of people is a lot of people, misery is misery, and a dead fish is a dead fish. We know this, but we know too that knowing this is not enough. Sky, a stringy-haired, sullen-eyed girl, her mother, Miranda, a waif, my sister and me, even blind Patty, if what we're longing for is not redemption, I don't know what to call it, a lifting up out of ourselves, out of story, even language. Paradoxically, it sometimes seems to me that this is never anything that we can will.

Near my father's cabin, I sometimes walk down the creek to where it joins the river, and choose a rock, any rock, that rises up out of the water, and sit there for awhile—sometimes hours—in the wash of sun and water at the very center of the roiling juncture where rapids back up from the river into the creek, and creek edges out, a churning curl, into the river, and it is there, just there, where it is neither creek, nor river, but both, in that very place and moment where the waters converge and will always be converging, that I am as close as I ever get to the place beyond language where writing begins.

For a billion years, or so, these rivers have done their work unimpeded. Now, suddenly, they are up to us.

And yet I do not say so without ambivalence. All up and down the Sacramento, fish ladders are being built around diversions, and the new outflow system at the dam is fully operational, and no one knows if any of it will work, and some salmon runs are in trouble and some are clearly thriving, and as we think about what it may mean to attempt to restore a river to what it was in what is now a prior century, we are unable fully to admit our longing for a world that once seemed to exist in fewer and smaller dimensions.

~
~
~

There might have been a dam:

On bright days, along curved mountain roads, light plays tricks on you, momentarily blinding as the car passes in and out sunlight and the dappled shade of trees. Maybe you see things that are not there, maybe you even hear them. Sometimes the blindness is fiery and red, and there is nothing that can penetrate or part it.

As I said, I was driving. Sky was in the backseat, and we were delivering her somewhere. I was thinking about the river and Miranda, how maybe we would find her sunning herself on a lip of gray rock. She'd be my age, but look older, and her skin would be brown as a nut. Also, she'd recognize us at once, opening her arms to embrace us and take back her daughter, Sky, folding Sky's heart up into her own in a gesture as inevitable as it would be primal. I was driving through dappled shade beneath a clump of trees and thinking about this embrace, after which, I imagined, I would finally call Patty on the telephone. I wasn't quite sure how I thought this would happen, but I knew that in the exact instant our call connected, Patty's sight would be restored to her as suddenly as Sky's heart had been to Miranda, and then she would drive out to join us, bringing Sam and Joey with her.

From the sleepless night before folding luminous laundry lighter than ourselves, to this dogged drive back toward the center of the earth where this story began with some engineers' idea of yet another dam, it was all becoming clear. I turned momentarily toward Sky, who seemed to be humming, and when I turned back, a sparking arc of orange flame leapt across the steamy asphalt far ahead of us, where shade exchanged itself for blinding light, and though I slowed the car as I approached the cusp between one form of light and another, the arc of flame continued to leap. As the car slowed, I was studying the arcing intently, as if it were a sign of something both divine and powerful.

Beside me, my sister exclaimed, "Just drive over it. Just drive over it."

In the back seat Sky's voice rose up with the same song from the night before, only now, I swear, she was grinning.

The car rolled to a stop as if without me.

"Just drive over it," my sister cried again.

"I can't," I said, the words forming as if from some separate consciousness inside me. "It's a downed power line. Isn't that something."

A gust of wind blew over us, and the line arced higher. Looking off into the forest, I couldn't tell how far the line was down, but the grass on either side of the road looked dry and the brush was low and close.

"Is it dangerous?" my sister said, as Sky laughed and got out of the car.

"I don't really know," I said, "but look how beautiful it is!"

"We should put the flares out," my sister said. "Pull over."

"Sky," I called, getting out after her, "don't go too close."

Then the wind died down completely, and in the sudden stillness, we could hear the power line sputtering, an occasional crackle, and Sky's comment, barely more than a whisper.

"What makes you think you have the right?" she said.

Maybe if I'd seen her move toward the line I've have found some way to stop her. But she was smiling in a way I'd never seen before, and something went off instead in me.

"You were wrong about my mother," she said. "And you were wrong about me."

As she bent to take hold of the line, a palm-sized tiger swallowtail circled her head, its translucent wings flapping the superheated air. She paused a moment, as if considering her options, straightened and turned back toward me. Once again, we were looking at each other, but nothing recognizable in her remained, not even the arc of her hand as she brushed at the butterfly, waving at me. Watching her, listening, I knew she was right. It was the strangest thing. The girl whose whole history had opened out to me as in a dream had turned suddenly opaque, unreadable, like the power line itself, and what I felt was neither curiosity nor grief, but something plainer, like regret: where, in the whole scope of this story, had I fitted in, and my sister, my sons?

At that exact moment, my sister turned from the back of the car, where she was still looking for emergency flares, and seeing Sky lean toward the power line—all this took place in an instant—opened her mouth to scream "No!", her own face white and filled with terror as she lunged toward Sky.

"The world is a happy place, believe me," Sky said.

And then, before either my sister or I could stop her, she bent and took hold of the power line, and she broke it apart, and she stood there, one sparking end in each fist. I want you to believe this because it is as true as anything I could narrate or imagine, literal, actual fact: Sky broke apart the power line and stood there, facing us, with one end in each fist, and what I want to tell you is the grass and trees and sky at the center of the earth erupted into flames. I want to tell you that Sky stood there at the center, flame herself, and it was she who was consuming everything around, not the fire that erupted, and there was nothing we could do to stop her, and it was, there isn't any other word for it, so beautiful, a beautiful thing. I want to tell you that, or I want, instead, to tell you that Sky shook her broken power line at us and laughed. Just that, she laughed. I want to tell you that Sky opened her palms to us, revealing a nugget of gold and something like hair. I even want to tell you that none of this happened because years before, the Ah Pah had, in fact, been built, the dam that was the crowning glory of the engineers, and so we could not be where we were because it would have been all water there: hence, no power line, no possibility of fire.

If I could convince you of any one of the above, I don't know, I really would call Patty, go visit my sister, hug my boys. But how in the world could I ever convince you if I can't convince myself of any other fact than the downed power line, than the flames that licked around it, than Sky, who turned away from my sister and from me and went instead to embrace, not a river, but the line that delivered power from the dam that held the river back. And then nothing happened. Sky stood there with the power line, which I knew, by its sparking, to be charged, and while I even want to tell you she contained it, I can't even lie about that. She just stood there in—what, defiance? steadfastness? grace? And maybe somehow she defused it, and then maybe she walked away, maybe in one direction or another, maybe laughing.

Maybe she said, "You were wrong."

Maybe, "Glub," she said. "Glub."

As many times as I've imagined the whole world erupting into flames, and Sky at the center of it, calm and in control, not ascending so much as laying her own claim to where and what she was, and with a queer serenity about her, I know it isn't anything I can truly know.

"Just drive over it," my sister said. "Get the flares," she said.

On the other side of the power line a logging truck rolled to a stop. The trucker got out. He scratched his head, fired up his CB radio, yelled at us to be careful. And maybe Sky leapt over the line and got into his truck, and maybe he knew where they would find Miranda—truckers know all kinds of things like that. But as probable as all this may sound, what I'm trying to tell you is that none of it happened the way I thought it would, none of it worked out, not like I thought. And it's not because there wasn't a downed power line either, nor even that there weren't once plans to dam this whole part of the country. It's because there wasn't Sky, because Sky is made up like the rest, and if there wasn't Sky there can't really be a way for me to tell you what happened to her, no more than we can know what happened to Miranda.

In the end, it is really only my sister and me, and the world we drove through on roads we just discovered on a map. If Sky came along for the ride, it has to be because she wanted to find out what happens. All I can tell you is that when the power line arced it was a beautiful thing, and it was a beautiful thing because we knew at once what we were looking at—we could name it with exactitude, excitement, fear—but we never could have imagined it, not in a million years.

In the very space between light and shadow, the power line arced, a beautiful thing.

From the back seat, Sky touched my shoulder.

"Just drive over it," my sister said.

"I can't," I said.

The power line was already down. The fire was already starting. Sky was already starting toward it. But there will never be a way that we can know what is going to happen next.